**Holly Kerr**

**Three Birds Press**

Copyright © 2019 by Three Birds Press

All rights reserved.

No portion of this book may be reproduced in any form without written permission from the publisher or author, except as permitted by U.S. copyright law.

www.threebirdspress.ca

www.hollykerr.ca

Beautifully Baked

## *Chapter One*

♥

## M.K.

EVEN THOUGH I'M NOT much for marriage, I like weddings.

They're sweet, pretty, and usually, they involve good food. Even though I'm not one to get weepy at declarations of love, it's nice to see people willing to stand up and tell the world how much they care about each other. It's...hopeful. The flowers are beautiful, men in tuxedoes are always nice to look at, and did I mention the food?

I like food even more than I like weddings.

The meal itself is nice, with the chicken or fish choice and seasonal vegetables arranged just so on the plate. The wedding cake is always a treat, a tower of artful confection that has taken someone days to bake and decorate. But it's those weddings with a sweet table that I get excited about.

Finger pastries. Tiny cubes of cheesecake. Petit fours and macarons, pastries, cakes and fruit-filled delicacies. I love it all.

I love to bake it all.

But this wedding isn't going to have a sweet table. I don't think there'll be a table at all. Or a meal. Maybe not any flowers unless Thomas steps up, and definitely not any cute groomsmen.

Flora decided to elope to Las Vegas instead of the big wedding her brothers wanted. Actually, Flora's brothers don't want her to marry Thomas at all, made clear by them forcing her out of the family business. Up until three days ago, I—Flora's best friend—had no idea *Flora* wanted to marry Thomas. They'd been together nearly eight years, happy with their weekly Friday night date and occasional sleepover.

I hesitate to use the word happy. *Content* may be better. *At ease* with how their relationship worked.

I really don't think the relationship works at all, but I'm not saying anything. Long ago, Flora and I made a promise not to badmouth boyfriends, and I've stuck with it even though sometimes it feels that blood is running down my chin from how much I've bitten my tongue.

I glance in the mirror in the hotel room and pull my dark hair into place over my scar. Ray's been begging me to try a pixie cut for years, but the gentle graduating bob works for the structure of my face. And there's no point changing something that works for you.

"You look beautiful." Flora smiles at my reflection and steps out of her shoes, leaving her only a few inches taller than me. "You always do."

I smile but can't quite meet her gaze in the mirror. "I'm supposed to be telling you that."

As much as it's the truth, the sight of Flora in her wedding dress produces an oily puddle of disappointment that sits heavy in the depths of my stomach.

She does look beautiful, but she doesn't look like Flora. Thanks to Pinterest and Youtube videos, Ruthie and I managed to wrangle Flora's mass of hair into an innocently elegant updo. It's been a long time since the days of me practicing my French braid technique on her, and since Flora's usual style is a straight-back ponytail to keep it out of her face when she kneels over her plants, I forgot she has so much hair. With a
critical smile, I tuck a wayward strand back into place, wondering if she needs another spray. There'll be a protest about that—Flora hates most hair products because she claims the chemicals and fragrances suffocate her plants. I had made a special stop at the health food store to find her the most non-toxic, less hazardous spray before we left for Las Vegas.

Flora tugs at the sleeve of her dress. "Is it okay?"

The dress is pretty, but again, it's not Flora's style. Cream coloured with a lace overlay and a mid-calf hemline, the dress is too conservative, too ladylike, too restrictive—not Flora at all.

Just like this wedding.

"You look beautiful," I say dutifully. "The perfect bride."

Flora's wide mouth creases into a grimace. "I'm trying," she mutters.

And that's why I don't say anything about the dress or even the shoes because I know how hard she's trying.

But she shouldn't be getting married.

When we were seventeen, Flora and I made a pact that we would remain unmarried for our entire life, save when we were old, about forty, and needed someone to look after us. We would be strong, independent women. We'd travel, focusing on our careers, and especially our friendship. We would laugh in the face of commitment, and if we did find love, he'd have to be pretty amazing to make us believe in a future together.

It was an easy thing to promise since, at the time, I had still been recovering from the bicycle accident that left the scar running down my face, and Flora had been badly dumped by Scottie Davis.

Things shifted over the years as things do. Ben convinced me that marriage wasn't all so bad, enough that I accepted his ring.

Unfortunately, he also convinced me he believed in monogamy. Since then, I've jumped back on the anti-marriage train.

But Flora never left. It might have been because of Thomas and the way their relationship only moved in fits and starts, rather than the gradual onwards and upwards of planning a life together.

But I'm still in shock that somehow between margaritas with me on Monday night and today (Friday), Thomas somehow convinced Flora to change her mind.

And now we are here in Las Vegas.

"Where's Ruthie?" Flora asks, stepping back into the nude heels that go so well with the dress but turn her into a knock-kneed little girl playing dress-up.

"She went down to the front desk to see if Thomas had the flowers sent over." Guilt hangs over me about the lack of flowers, like I'm the one who forgot them. But it's the maid of honour's duty to ensure everything runs smoothly and Flora always says I am the queen of organization. You make a plan and stick to it and things always run perfectly.

There is no plan in place for this wedding.

Yet another reason that the little voice inside me is screaming to *delay. Stop. Get Flora out of this mess.*

I'm doing my best to ignore the little voice but it's becoming more and more difficult.

"He'll bring them to the chapel," Flora says with her usual confidence. Nothing ever seems to faze her, except Thomas.

Shouldn't that tell her something?

Flora checks her hair one last time. "We should go." She gives a sigh that sounds a lot like resignation. I doubt she even realizes she made the noise.

"I'll text Ruthie." I pick up my cell to summon Ruthie, only to be rewarded by the sound of "Trouble," by Pink, blaring out of a cell phone somewhere in the ball of sheets on the bed. "She needs to keep her phone on her, today of all days."

"Everything'll be fine," Flora says as she stares at her reflection in the mirror. My heart breaks a little at the wistful expression on her face.

"Of course it will. But...this is what you want?" I take a deep breath, fighting to come up with the right words. "Such a small wedding? None of your family?"

"You're here." Flora's smile doesn't meet her eyes. "And Ruthie, unless she's found a better option."

"Ruthie wouldn't miss it. Do your brothers even know you're here?" I ask in a gentle voice.

Flora shakes her head, her expression, for once, unreadable. The words bubble up, begging to burst free. If I'm going to say anything, now is the time, because once Flora takes a step down that aisle, everything is over. Everything will change.

"Everything'll be fine," Flora repeats, and the bubble breaks.

Weddings shouldn't be *fine*. But this is Flora, and Flora makes everything all right. She's fun and positive, cheerful and funny.

There must be more to Thomas than I can see because how could Flora love someone who's so wrong for her?

And so I follow her out the door of the hotel room and into the elevator, keeping up a stream of inane chatter to mask my hesitation. We catch Ruthie at the front desk, flowerless, her long braids sliding flirtatiously through her fingers as she smiles at the assistant manager behind the desk. We find a taxi outside to take us the few blocks to the chapel off the Strip.

Everything will be fine, but it isn't how it should be. This can't be her happily ever after.

As we pull up to the little chapel, I smooth my hair as my emotions spin like a tumble dryer.

"We doing this?" Ruthie calls from the front seat.

"Why shouldn't we?" Flora asks in return.

*So many reasons!* But I smile and open the door, reaching out a hand to help Flora steady herself in the heels. She takes a deep breath as she glances at the tiny chapel.

"It looks nice," I assure her. "No Elvis, just like you requested."

Flora grips my fingers with an icy-cold hand. "Thanks, M.K. For everything."

"I haven't done much of anything. You planned this whole thing."

"But knowing you've got my back made it easier."

"I've always got your back."

She squeezes my hand. "This'll happen for you, too, you know."

I really hope not. "I know you don't want to be late for your wedding, so let's get in there." I give her a tight smile and lead her inside. Ruthie brings up the rear.

The lobby of the chapel smells of cheap beer, bad perfume, and fear. It's not appealing, and neither are most of those unfortunate souls waiting to be married. I avert my gaze from the leering smile of a balding man wearing a cliché of a cheap tuxedo—powder blue and ruffled with the cummerbund almost disappearing under his stomach.

I peek back for another look. "How you doin'?" he says, catching my eye and sounding like an obnoxious version of Joey Tribbiani.

Flora turns to him just as Ruthie opens her mouth to respond, so I give Ruthie a shove so she won't cause a scene. "Let's see if Thomas dropped off flowers for you."

"I wonder what they are." Flora is giddy at the thought, as excited as some women are with jewelry or a new bag. Flora loves her flowers. "A bouquet of tulips would be simple or even roses, even though roses are kind of unoriginal."

"We're talking about Thomas here, not you, Fleur, the flower queen. I still think that's what you should have named your store." Ruthie grins down at her aunt.

Flora's family dynamics are complicated.

"M.K., where are they supposed to be?" Flora asks, her gaze searching for someone holding her perfect bouquet. The chapel lady hurries over, hands fluttering as she instructs us on our positions and timing. Flora keeps looking and asking.

There are no flowers waiting for her.

In the flurry of confusion of Flora insisting there must be flowers, and the Chapel Lady trying to convince her she doesn't need them, my heart sinks for my friend. This is not her perfect day; this can't be her happily ever after.

Ruthie mutters under her breath, most likely voodoo curses against Thomas.

I give her a sharp elbow to stop. "He forgot them," I say to Flora, the tension making my voice snap. "Or else he didn't think you needed them."

"He forgot," Flora echoes, gazing into the dimly lit chapel where Thomas is already standing at the end of the aisle.

"I'm sure he'll make it up to you."

"Can he, though?"

"Flora, I know it's important to you, but flowers—" At the sight of her stricken face, I trail off with a humourless chuckle. "Are really important to you. He should have remembered."

She nods.

"Here." A quick grab pulls off a leaf of a nearby plant. I'm sure Flora knows what the Latin name is, but all I know is that it's green and alive and might help her get through this. As she looks at it, I know I should be trying to get her out of this instead.

I didn't need to do anything since Flora handles that herself.

# Clay

DEAN IS MAKING A huge mistake. It's not that I'm against the institution of marriage. I'm really not. Marriage can be amazing. My parents are still happily married, and both of my brothers have found the women of their dreams to spend the rest of their lives with.

Neither of my sisters-in-law are anything like Evelyn.

I barely know her, so I shouldn't comment on her personality, but what little I know of her, I can tell she's not going to make Dean happy.

Like now. Dean's waiting for his bride-to-be outside a chapel in Las Vegas. The man should be over the moon with excitement, not standing ramrod straight, as emotion-less as a tree.

Not that Dean shows much emotion on a good day.

This should be a good day. This should be his best day ever.

It would be my best day. Not that I've thought about marriage much or made an effort to find someone I'd like to settle down with.

Why bother searching when women keep falling into my lap so easily?

I smile at one dark-haired beauty as she walks by. She looks at Dean first, then me, which is the norm. Dean, with his height and his hair, is like a colourful fishing lure, there to attract.

Not that he wants to attract. He doesn't even notice he does. Me, I think I have some radar built in that tells me when there's a woman within twenty feet. And it doesn't matter if they're giving me an admiring glance or not—once I smile at them, I always get one in return.

Sometimes it gets tiring.

Not that I'm saying I'm irresistible to women because I'm not. But I've never had a problem meeting them, even in the least opportune moments. But the lure works for me because Dean stands out. He catches the eye. And then they turn to me, and I reel them in.

As I meet the interested gaze of the dark-haired beauty, I think about reeling her in but turn away at the last moment. This isn't the time. This is Dean's wedding.

There will be time enough later. When Dean is with Evelyn.

When I'll lose my wingman, my personal lure, forever.

Dark-haired beauty is replaced by an older redhead and I widen my smile. Even with the harried man at her side staring at the phone like it's a lifeline, she does a double-take.

I wink, and the smile lights up her face.

All women want to be told they're attractive, either with words or actions or even a carefully raised eyebrow. I'm good at that. I'm also good at finding something beautiful in everyone female I meet, whether it's inside or out.

I glance at my watch. Does Dean realize Evelyn is late? Is he worried? Is he annoyed? Is this what life is going to be like for him—waiting for Evelyn?

I hate to be kept waiting.

I wonder if Dean realizes that this will probably be the last time we'll hang out like this. Flying into Vegas this morning, spending a couple of hours hitting the tables, wandering the streets before stopping for a couple of beers. Dean's just so easy to get along with.

I'm going to miss him.

I'm going to miss him because Evelyn is a bitch and has this weird hate on anything baseball-related. Which makes it all the more ironic that she's with Dean because everything about him is baseball-related. I love the sport as well, but I have other interests. Dean lives and breathes ball. And since I'm part of Dean's baseball world, she's going to try and cut me out.

I hope Dean sees what she's like. I wish he'd listen to me if I could come up with the right words to convince him. But how can you tell your buddy he shouldn't marry the woman he's in love with? And how can you say any of this only moments before he's supposed to go through with it?

I miss the first chime of my cell because I'm watching Dean and wondering what he's thinking. He doesn't notice any of the tourists milling about or the admiring glances of the females who pass by.

He never notices.

My phone chimes again, and I pull it out of my pocket.

Evelyn.

Unfortunately, I've never been able to find anything beautiful about her. And now I never will.

I glance at the text and then read it again because I can't believe what I'm seeing. I take a few steps away from the door.

That's when I hear the shout: "Flora!"

"Jesus!" Dean stumbles forward a step and turns, catching a blonde in a white dress before she falls. Two women appear in the doorway; one tall and solid with long braids, the other small and slight with swinging, dark hair.

I do a double-take on the small and slight one.

"Flora, come on! How could you not see him?" The tall and braided blonde laughs as she pulls the blonde away from Dean. From the expression on his face, he doesn't want to let her go.

I don't even notice her because it's the dark haired one that has my attention. Her blue dress highlights her delicate build and suddenly I'm hit with the urge to gather her close for protection, like she's breakable.

I don't realize I'm smiling until she looks up and meets my gaze.

I've never had so much electricity within a single glance.

It's like there's a lightning storm without the thunder. I'm instantly struck with the need to find out what brought out the relief in her eyes, to give her my jacket in case she's cold in her sleeveless dress and to see if her waist is really as tiny as it seems.

I'm stunned, to say the least. I can't even give her The Smile, just some half-assed grin that makes me look like a moron.

"Get out of my way" the blonde cries. "I need to get out of here." And then she hikes her dress up above her knees and runs down the street.

And with an apologetic glance, my dark-haired girl is gone, rushing after the blonde.

She's just gone.

"What the hell?" I shake my head in wonder and disappointment as I lose sight of the blue dress in the crowd. "What was that?" I ask Dean, who looks as stunned as I feel.

"I was standing there and she runs into me. Literally runs into me."

"Was she cute?" It's my go-to response for every female situation.

"Can't say I noticed," Dean says with a roll of his eye.

"Deano, you've *always* got to notice."

"In case you missed it, I am waiting to get married." He waves at the doorway of the chapel. "Waiting. To get married."

"Yeah. About that." I wish he'd said the girl was cute because it might make this part a little easier. I hand him my phone, watching his expression change from worry to resignation. "Bro, it says she's not coming," I say helpfully.

Dean hands the phone back to me. "I got that, thanks."

"That's all you're going to say?"

"What do you think I should say? She's not coming."

An uncomfortable silence falls between us, broken by the chatter and fits of laughter of those on the sidewalk. I watch as Dean stares off into the distance, wondering what to say to him. I've known Dean since he moved to Toronto two years ago, meeting him at the Baseball Zone, a training facility I hang out at when I feel the need to smash a bunch of balls into oblivion. We hit it off right away, but it took a bit to convince him to join the team. Once I found out about the injury and the aborted MLB career, it made sense, but a guy with Dean's natural ability needs to be on the field.

Plus the team has done so much better since he joined.

I'm not ashamed to say he's become one of my best friends, but we're both guys' guys—not much discussion about emotions or deep thoughts. I can go head to head about the Jays' rebuilding but not about how he feels about Evelyn.

I assume he loves her, so I assume he's upset that she just ditched him at the altar.

Who does that? It's like something out of a movie.

"Maybe we should get out of here, head back to the hotel?" I finally suggest. Dean continues to stand in the doorway, not noticing the couple who is trying to slip past his six-foot-five frame. "Deano? Wanna get out of here?"

Dean finally turns and runs his hand through his hair. "I guess."

We walk back to the hotel in silence, me following Dean as he cuts around clusters of tourists on the sidewalk. I'm not a short guy by any means, but being around Dean always makes me the smallest. He's like the quarterback, weaving his way through the defensive line, all ready to throw a tackle on him. In this case the defense is the interested glances of the women he passes.

How can he not notice? Dean's a smart guy, but he's clueless when it comes to women. Like Evelyn.

What am I supposed to say about her?

I've only met Evelyn a few times, but none of them went well. And it wasn't just because she didn't fall for the charm, as Trev calls it. He was there the last time when Dean brought her out for a drink, and Trev noticed as well as I did how Evelyn didn't even make an effort.

And how Dean spent the entire night fawning over her.

I'm all for making a woman happy, but not if it's going to force me into becoming some p-whipped wuss.

I like Dean a lot, but not when he's with Evelyn.

I think back to the message Evelyn left me:

I'm not coming.

Maybe that's not a bad thing.

## Chapter Two

♥

## M.K

RUTHIE AND I CATCH up to Flora, who is surprisingly fast in those shoes. I hail a cab, and Ruthie practically tackles Flora to get her inside. Once we're bundled into it, no one says a word for a minute.

"Aren't you forgetting someone?" the driver asks.

With his singsong accent, it takes me a moment to understand what he's asking. "Pardon me?"

"Didn't I just drop you off?"

That's when I realize he's the same man who drove us to the chapel. I have no idea how to respond, and Ruthie only laughs. I'm sure this is just another adventure to her. Ruthie is always looking for excitement, always dragging Flora and me along. But this isn't an adventure. This is Flora walking out of her wedding to Thomas.

"Couldn't do it," Flora says from where she's crammed in the backseat between us. She has the deer-caught-in-the-headlights look about her. Stunned. Shocked.

I'm shocked. Flora is known to be impulsive at times, but I never expected that.

"No kidding." Ruthie laughs harder.

"It's not funny," I snap at her, which only makes Ruthie laugh more.

Flora takes a shaking breath. "I don't know if I should laugh with you or start crying."

"No man is worth you crying over him," the driver says as he slowly makes his way back to the hotel.

"He's right." Ruthie tries to give him a high five through the seats, but luckily he keeps both hands on the wheel.

Flora elbows me and I glance down at the hand she presents to me. The leaf I gave her is wrinkled and wilted with green bits trapped under her nails. "Thanks. I guess I don't need this anymore."

"Is this because he forgot the flowers?" I ask gently.

That's when I notice her eyes are dancing, even though her face is tight and pale with guilt, much like she looked when she got caught trying to sneak into the boys' bathroom in grade two. A strange noise escapes; part giggle, part sob. "I just walked out on my wedding."

"You did."

"Technically, you ran out," Ruthie says.

Another giggle/sob bursts out of Flora. Her eyes are still dancing but I think it's beginning to hit her now. "What do we do now?" she whispers.

"That's my line," I say, squeezing her hand. "And I'm not really sure, but we'll figure it out."

"Time for a drink," Ruthie announces.

"Did you see that guy I ran into?" Flora demands.

"I don't know how you missed him." Ruthie laughs. "He's standing there, looking so big and buff, and you ram straight into him. If that's a new way to pick up guys, I'm not sure it's working."

"Like she's in the mood to pick up," I scoff. Then I pause as I remember the other man. Shorter, with perfectly styled dirty-blond hair, and dancing green eyes. Clean-shaven, which is good; looking very attractive in his fitted, gray suit, which is even better. I like well-dressed men. And the smile.

I like men who smile. At least ones who smile like that.

"Did you see his friend?" I ask carefully. I glance over my shoulder, out the back window, but of course I can't see them.

I'll never see him again.

# Clay

WE BUMP INTO THEM at the hotel bar. One minute, Dean is pushing his way through the throng of people and then suddenly he's got his hands on a guy who looks like he's about to hit a woman.

The woman turns out to be the one who ran into him at the chapel.

Of course I don't recognize her, but as soon as I lay eyes on the dark-haired one in the blue dress, my eyes light up with recognition. "Hello, there."

"Hi," she says, looking flustered.

"We're looking for a table." I whip out my best smile, full on and focused. "Care to join us?"

Thanks to Dean's height, it's relatively easy to find a couple about to leave and snag their table. I can't stop looking at the brunette. Petite and delicate, her features are like a doll, with a waist tiny enough to span with my hands.

Dean looks like a giant beside her, but he can't take his eyes off the blonde. I can't stop smiling.

"I'm Clay," I say after we are seated. "Maybe I should have started with that."

"We would have lost the table." She looks hesitant, her smile uncertain. "I'm—" A cheer erupts at the same time as she says her name.

"Emmy?" I ask with a frown.

"M.K." It's too loud for a proper conversation. "My initials. M," she enunciates. "And K."

"Emkay," I repeat.

"And you're Clay."

"Clay," I say. This is a stupid conversation, just repeating each other's names, but I can't seem to get past her eyes—almost black—or her smile, which turns her from pretty to downright stunning. She tucks her chin-length hair behind her ear and I catch sight of a wicked-looking scar that runs the side of her face.

I want to know how she got it.

I lean closer to her. "How's your night been?"

I love the way she rolls her eyes and smiles at the same time. "Unbelievable. Flora should be getting married but isn't. She left him at the altar. I guess, technically, he left her, but she said it first."

The bar is so loud that I only hear every third word, but I get the gist of what she's saying. Runaway bride. Got it.

"The same with him." I gesture with my chin to Dean. "She never showed. Sent him a text."

"His girlfriend."

"Not anymore."

"Do you have a girlfriend?" She seems surprised when the words pop out of her mouth, like it's not in her nature to be so direct.

I'm completely charmed by it, by everything about her. There's something about this girl that makes me want to find out more. Find out everything—her history, her secrets, her hopes and dreams.

I lean close enough to bump her shoulder, inhaling her perfume. "Not yet," I say with an encouraging smile. "Got anyone in mind?"

She doesn't respond, but her smile says enough.

Of course, I'm too busy wanting to know more to ask her anything relevant. Anything that would help me find her later.

I let her leave, convinced we'll see each other later. So convinced that I don't even ask her last name. Or a number, which is unheard of for me.

I only watch the sway of her hips as she walks away with her friends, admiring the way she looks in that dress, without realizing I've lost her.

## Chapter Three

♥

## M.K.

*T*WO WEEKS LATER...

I place each macaron on the tray, leaving the exact space between each of them. A row of strawberry-balsamic, one of black sesame, the meringue cookie looking more gray than black, a line of hazelnut, and vanilla with flecks of bean dotting the filling. Another tray carries salted caramel, Earl Grey tea, mango, and chocolate.

My back winces as I straighten up, and I let my hips sway to the classic Whitesnake song on the radio to stretch. I adjust a mango macaron before carrying the tray out of the kitchen to set inside the L-shaped glass counter closest to the cash. Macarons finished.

I take a moment to survey my domain. The love of my life. My patisserie, Pain au Chocolat.

The lights are still out, the closed sign hanging on the door because I won't open for another hour. I like being here when it's quiet and still, the '80s rock drifting in from the kitchen the only sound.

Pain au Chocolat is an old pub/failed smoothie bar/grilled-cheese restaurant and as I like to think, the most successful of the previous establishments. There isn't a lot of space for lingering customers—three tiny round tables placed just so, three square tables at the bench beside the counter—but I've made the most of what I have, and the chairs are definitely more comfortable than Starbucks. Each table has a slim glass flower vase. Flora provides flowers for the tables in exchange for coffee and I've had countless customers take their coffee and scones and head down the strip to her shop. I notice a limp stem of one of the gerbera daisies and make a mental note to replace it.

Flora helped me paint the walls a clean eggshell white with blue and yellow accents, and I picked out every framed print of the French countryside. It's a neighbourhood spot, with regular customers that I am forever grateful for.

I sweep a glance at the counter—the white cups and mugs are simple but thick enough not to worry about constant breakages, unlike the delicate cups I used back when I first opened.

That first year was a never-ending drain of my savings. The second year was a bit better but still a loss, but I broke even halfway through the third year. I've never looked back since, with Pain being named one of the city's best patisseries for the past two years, with "...gorgeously buttery croissants and sweetly eclectic macarons taking centre stage, along with the namesake, pain au chocolat. Best I've tasted."

I had the review framed. It hangs on the wall beside the cash register.

The coffeemakers behind the cash register gleam in the dim light from the streetlight outside. The coffee is the last thing I do before

I open, but I'm tempted this morning. Flora and I went out last night, and I got home later than expected. One of the first things I learned was that I need an early bedtime for the even earlier mornings.

I don't remember the last time I slept in past six a.m. Even the weekend in Las Vegas saw me up with the sun, wandering the hotel for a decent coffee and croissant.

The buzz of the timers sends me hurrying back into the kitchen to swap the oatmeal chocolate chip muffins in the oven, which are always a favourite with the regulars, with the cranberry pistachio, the chunks of white chocolate oozing at the top.

Even at the early hour, the kitchen is immaculate—everything in its place and a place for everything—but the classic rock and heavy metal music I prefer seems a little out of place in the pristine environment.

But since I'm by myself this morning, I'm going to listen to what I want.

Pain has been mine for five years now, but there had been eight exhausting months after I first bought the patisserie when I couldn't afford to pay anyone to help. I had done everything myself, and I look back fondly at that time, much like the mother of a newborn would, forgetting about the sleep deprivation and exhaustion and only enjoying the memories of the time spent with the baby. This patisserie is my baby.

As I pull out the last empty muffin tray and fill it with the banana nut batter, I glance at the corkboard above the counter.

It's covered with recipes, and lists and staffing schedules, all neatly laminated to keep safe from flyaway bits of batter or dough.

I wipe a gob of muffin batter on my still-cleanish white apron as I glare at the schedule.

I shouldn't even be making the muffins because the schedule above me clearly shows that Rhoda's shift began at five thirty, and it's now five fifty, and she's nowhere in sight. This is the third time Rhoda has been late and unless she has a darn good reason, it's going to be her last.

I heave a sigh of frustration. There's no sense getting upset about it now because I still have the pastries and breakfast bars to set out and make the breakfast sandwiches. I've always disliked that the most: taking the time to make the perfect egg sandwich only to have it sit uneaten for the entire day, watching the cheese become hard and rubbery, the egg cold and uneatable. I'm sure I'm the only person to have sympathy for leftovers.

I make a mental note to call Adam to beg him to come in early.

Whitesnake ends and Poison begins, the classic ballad, "Every Rose Has It's Thorn." I rush across the kitchen to change the song. Ever since Flora's non-wedding, I don't listen to ballads, especially ones about flowers. In the two weeks since we got back from Las Vegas, I feel like Flora and I have talked about nothing but that weekend, especially how she left Thomas at the altar. But last night's revelation about her and Dean's hookup brought my own memories about Clay to the forefront, and I'd prefer not to be reminded of them today.

Not that I have any real memories about Clay.

Clay, who I locked eyes with at the chapel.

Clay, who I spent an hour getting to know in the hotel bar, and afterwards spent the rest of the night smiling whenever I thought of him.

Clay, who I'll never see again.

It drives me crazy that I spent all that time talking with Clay that night, but neither of us once gave personal information. I know his name is Clay; he has two brothers, likes baseball, and has a smile that makes him look a bit like Tom Cruise. The younger Tom Cruise, although the man has aged incredibly well. Will Clay look as good when he's in his fifties?

I'll never find out because I'll never see him again.

I push away any thoughts of Clay because there's no use mooning over a man I'll never see again.

There's no use mooning over men, period.

Motley Crue replaces Poison, and the wild drumbeats of the music quickens my pace as I scoop the muffin batter. My everpresent regret, as well as my current irritation with Rhoda lift slightly as I sing along to the music.

Adam arrives within a half hour, and with his help, I'm able to get everything ready to open. But I don't have time to change into my dress or even swap my apron for a clean one. I pull my hair down along my cheek, feeling self-conscious about the scar without the usual foundation masking it. I didn't even have time for a slick of my usual lipstick.

Adam switches the music from hard rock to his favourite easy-listening playlist, the one with the French songs thrown in, as I unlock the door with my usual sense of pride.

"Good morning." I hold the door for Mr. Cullen as he pushes in his walker.

"Coffee ready?" he barks.

Thanks to Adam, it is. "Of course," I say with a smile. "And I have some lemon-poppyseed muffins that I think you'll really like."

I don't understand his harrumph as he wheels by me.

The next few hours have a steady trickle of customers, mostly those stopping by on their way to work for a coffee fix. I pride myself on the coffee, using only the best beans I can afford and hiring young and imaginative baristas. I poached Adam from a Second Cup on Yonge Street because he made the best flat white I've ever tasted.

Just before eight thirty as I'm refolding the newspaper from Mr. Cullen's table, I glance up to see Imogene come in. She manages Fleur for Flora and is roundly pregnant. I'm wary around women who procreate so easily and so happily. I'm a little afraid it'll rub off on me.

"You're in early." I smile.

"I'm sick of trying to light a fire under Flora," Imogene grumbles, resting a hand on her protruding belly. "This baby is coming whether she likes it or not, and she needs help when I go. I'm finding my replacement today."

"Do you want to find someone for me, too?" I ask wistfully. Despite her small stature, Imogene is a force to be reckoned with when it comes to getting things done. It's a toss-up between her and I who is better organized, and between the two of us, Flora's life has never run so smoothly. "Rhoda missed her shift again. She said something about taking a dog to the emergency room, which I can understand *if* she had a dog."

"As long as you're not getting rid of Adam." Dimples crease her cheeks as Imogene waves to Adam behind the counter.

"Decaf coming up because you're looking *extremely* pregnant today," he calls.

"Make sure you make Flora's extra caffeinated." Imogene glances critically at me. "This is the first time I've seen you not looking impeccable."

I smooth my apron. "I'm not impeccable."

"You're the most well-put together twenty-nine-year-old I've ever met. You wear dresses and fancy shoes with perfect make-up and hair on a daily basis. If I wasn't so exhausted thinking about the trouble it'd be matching everything, I'd be very jealous of you."

"I like to look nice," I murmur with an inward cringe. Thanks to Rhoda, my dress is still hanging in my office off the kitchen. "This morning though..." I stick out my sneaker-clad foot. "Too busy to even change my shoes."

"I thought it might be because you and Flora went out last night."

"We did, but I can't blame that. And there was no Ruthie." I slip past Imogene to head back to the counter.

"Ah. No jail time then."

I mock shudder. "Once was enough."

Adam claps his hands from beside me. "I love that story! Fighting during a Power of the Tower performance—only Flora!"

"I don't think I'll be going back to Las Vegas anytime soon," I say ruefully.

"No elopements in your future then?" Imogene asks. I roll my eyes at her and don't bother to answer.

Flora likes to live her life with no regrets, but I have a feeling that deep down, she's regretting the spontaneous trip to Las Vegas to marry Thomas. Even though I now know her exact thought process that led to her sprint out of the chapel (and into Dean), I still don't quite understand what brought it about. After an eight-year relationship that, in my mind, wasn't that healthy, why would Thomas finally propose? Or finally relent to Flora's suggestion that they take things to the next level. They had only moved in together a few weeks before—hadn't that been enough?

Whatever the reason, I'm very happy Flora didn't go through with it.

I'm not very happy that I didn't even bother to get more information from Clay, however. I push my regret down deep as I send Imogene back to Fleur with a clearly labeled coffee for Flora.

Things get busier as the morning progresses, with tables filling up with yoga-pants-clad women pushing strollers, a noisy book club having their monthly meeting on the bench by the window, and the older couple who comes in every day, sits at the same table with their same coffee order, and never talks to each other.

Adam and I always have endless discussions about the couple after they leave.

"Mmm," Adam says later, bumping his way out the kitchen door while holding a tray of almond croissants that are one of my best sellers. "Mr. Sexy Pants."

I glance up in time to meet Paulo's smiling gaze, as admiring as always. He works at the fitness centre at the end of the strip mall, and is one of my most faithful customers. Even though there's nothing like the sight of a good-looking man to put you in a better mood, Paulo is the last one I want to see right now. I'm still wearing my kitchen pants—black and baggy and full of stains, and no one needs to see me like that.

"Ah, my baking *bonita,*" Paulo says as he reaches the counter, his accent making the words sound like a croon rather than a simple greeting. "You look so *rumpled* and *flustered* this morning. *I love it.*"

I don't like being rumpled and flustered, even when it sounds so sexy coming from Paulo. I think longingly of my neat and clean dress still hanging in the office; a summery pale yellow with sprigs of lavender sprinkled along the hem. At least I finally managed to grab a clean apron.

"It's been a busy morning," I say with a tight-lipped smile.

"I'm sure you had a busy night, too."

I'm fairly certain Monday night with drinks doesn't constitute busy for Paulo but I don't need him to know my love life amounts to a big fat zero. "What can I get you this morning, Paulo?" My finger hovers over the button for his usual mocha caramel latte with the extra shot of espresso that he orders every day.

"Ah, today I feel like a little variety," he says with a wink of his chocolate-brown eyes with the lashes to die for. "Surprise me."

I don't do surprises, with lattes or anything else. "I'll get Adam to make you something yummy," I promise, cringing at my use of yummy. Even though it's been ages since I've had a second date with anyone, I do know how to talk to men.

"I like yummy," he says with another wink.

"Adam," I call. "Can you make Paulo something special this morning?"

"I'd like nothing better." Adam gives Paulo his own seductive wink, and I'm startled to see how Paulo's face lights up.

The man likes to flirt. It must not matter with whom.

Paulo moves aside to chat with Adam, and Mrs. Gretchen takes his place. She's an older lady who is as feisty as my chocolate chili chai tea. To prove it, she gives Paulo a long and lingering glance before ordering a flat white and a cranberry scone.

"How are you this morning, Mrs. Gretchen?"

"I'm better with the eye candy you have in here." Mrs. Gretchen's wink is nothing like Paulo's or even Adam's, but seeing it makes me feel better than either of them could.

"He's..."

"Yes, I know exactly what he is." Mrs. Gretchen gives a vehement nod of her snowy, white head. "He'll break your heart as quick as he'll order a second coffee, so you stay clear."

"I have no intention of getting any closer," I say ruefully. "Even if he was interested."

"What garbage is that? You're a looker, with a nice little place of your own here. Any decent man would be lining up at the chance."

My smile widens. "Yes, they would. Thanks, Mrs. Gretchen. That's exactly what I needed to hear today."

"You should meet my neighbour," she says decisively. "Big, strapping boy. Sweet as a muffin."

"I think I'm fine flying solo right now," I assure her, handing her the warmed-up scone on a plate.

"You always find your match when you're least expecting it," Mrs. Gretchen says, dropping a quarter in the tip cup. "Like when I was in France during the war. The last thing I wanted was to have the handsome Frenchman catch my eye, but that's exactly what he did."

"Have a great day, Mrs. Gretchen." I smile widely at her. She drops comments like some people drop names, always enough to intrigue me about her past.

"Bye, Mrs. Gretchen." Adam waves from behind the foamer. "She's the coolest lady," he says to Paulo.

"As is your boss," Paulo says sotto voce. "Tell her if she wants a busy night to call me."

"I'm standing right here."

"Of course you are." Paulo grins, and my stomach gives a little flip.

*No.* Just no. It doesn't matter if my last relationship was two years ago, or twenty years ago. Paulo is not a good idea.

Unfortunately, Adam doesn't agree. "He's so pretty," he says, leaning his chin on his fist as we watch Paulo walk out, the tightness of his pants making it a welcome sight. "I really wish you'd give him a try. He just teases me, but I think you'd have a good shot."

"He's not my type." I adjust the porcelain cups on top of the coffeemaker.

"Tall, dark, and Brazilian? Boss Lady, he's everyone's type."

I make a face. "You sound like my mother."

"How is Mama Donnelly?" Adam turns his interest to my family. As soon as he found out my family owns a winery in Niagara-on-the-Lake, he was hooked, asking me questions about wine, grapes, and living with three sisters.

"She'd hate to be called that," I chide him. "She only kept the name because of the winery."

After my father left, my mother, rather than accept the terms of the divorce, fought with everything she had—not for the marriage, but for the control of the winery. Even though Four Leaf Clover Wines had been in my father's family for two generations, my mother is now president and CEO, retaining a 51 percent share.

"You can leave this family," my mother had shouted at my father. "But that winery is your daughters' legacy and I'm not having you screw it up like you screwed up our marriage. I'm taking over. You can do what you want."

My father, being a weak sort of man, did just that. I haven't spoken to him in three years.

My mother, on the other hand, rules the winery, our family, as well as most of the village of Niagara-on-the-Lake with an iron fist clad in a silk glove. She's made a success out of Four Leaf Clover but hasn't forgiven me for choosing to follow Flora to Toronto and open Pain, rather than take my place at her side, like my sisters have done.

I haven't forgiven her for a lot of things either, so that makes us even. And it hasn't stopped her from doing her best to make a match for me. Mrs. Bennett of *Pride and Prejudice* has nothing on Margaret Donnelly.

"Is she still trying to set you up?" Adam asks, leaning against the counter. I point to the nearly empty banana-nut muffin basket; Adam is a good worker but sometimes forgets to actually work, preferring to gossip and chat. Being more of a quiet sort, I don't mind his talkative nature, and the customers love him.

"When I went home last month, she'd invited one of my brother-in-law's work colleagues for dinner," I say when Adam returns from the kitchen with a full basket.

"Was he cute? Did he ask you out?"

"Yes, but there's no way I'd say yes."

"Because it was a Mama Donnelly setup?" Adam asks sympathetically.

"That, and the fact that he refused to eat any vegetable unless it was proven to be hydroponically grown. He said at least four times that widespread farming 'raped' the land." I use my fingers as quotations. "He couldn't be a party to that."

"That's one I haven't heard before. He did know that your family grows grapes for a living. Which is technically farming."

"Yep. Not even my mother had a response to that."

Adam clicks his tongue. "Poor M.K. Sounds like another winner."

"She's set me up with worse."

"Maybe she just doesn't know your type."

"Are you seriously taking her side?"

"Of course not. But you know, Boss Lady, your type is indeed a mystery. If Paulo isn't it for you, then who is?"

Adam has no idea that an image of Clay's smile floods my thoughts.

# Clay

"I DON'T LIKE THE blue."

Rashida frowns, waving the mock-up of the new packaging for FoodMart's brand of frozen dinners with obvious irritation. "It's the same blue as all the others."

"I don't like it." I know I sound rude, but Rashida's been part of my team for long enough to know not to take offense.

"Should you have maybe mentioned that when the packaging for the line was being designed?" she asks as politely as an annoyed graphic designer can be.

"I did, and no one listened." Huffing out a sigh, I take another close look at the offensive blue. The blue needs to be fine unless I want to deal with the extra costs of redoing all the packaging. "Pearl, make a note in my calendar for November to look at redesigning the Keto frozen dinners. Please." My voice softens when I speak to my assistant, and she smiles with gratitude as she does what I ask. "Keep the blue for now. That's it, everyone. Thanks for your input and get back to work."

The team files out of my office. I see the resentful glance Pearl gives Rashida as the younger woman pauses to stand by my desk. "Pearl, would you mind terribly running out to find me a gigantic coffee? And get one for yourself." I hand her my Starbucks card with a winning smile.

"I don't think I need a gigantic one, but thanks, Clay. I'll run out now."

"You're the best, Pearl!"

I keep the smile fixed on my face until Pearl leaves then let it fall as I turn to Rashida. "Yes?"

"You've been a real jerk to work with, you know?"

"How so?" She's right; I know she's right, but I haven't been able to pull myself out of the funk that's trying to swallow me down.

Rashida shrugs. "You've been a jerk. What more do you want me to say?"

I might be stung by the pronouncement if it was anyone but Rashida telling me this. But it was one of the reasons I took a chance on giving my friend Imad's wife a job—her no-nonsense refusal to pay lip service to me or anyone. I'm tired of the sycophants in the office playing nice to the owner's nephew. Half of them think Uncle Joe is the one who gave me the job, which means I have to work twice as hard to prove myself.

Sometimes I wonder why I bother. I need a thicker skin so their snide comments and eye rolls don't get to me. I'm good at my job, damn good, regardless of who my uncle is.

I also know I'm only as good as the people who I work with, which is why I've always made a point to collect the very best to be part of my team. Rashida's only been here for six months, but already she's one of the best I've got.

"How have I been a jerk? Pearl was more than happy to run to Starbucks for me. She wouldn't do that if she didn't like me."

Rashida snorts rudely. "The woman is in love with you, just like half of the women in the office."

"Only half?" My grin takes the conceit out of my words. Ever since Karai Marsden announced her love for me in kindergarten, I've always had luck with women. I've had some tell me it's my resemblance to Tom Cruise; others say it's my smile that lights up a room. Most will mention my personality, how it's refreshing to meet such a nice guy.

I am a nice guy, one that happens to look a little like a movie star. It's not a bad thing.

"Pearl's old enough to be my mother," I add. "She's happily married."

"Fifty-year-old women are allowed crushes," Rashida says, leaning against my desk. "So what's got your knickers in a twist?"

"How do you know I'm wearing knickers?"

"See, you shouldn't be able to say that in this day and age, but you do, and you still come across as a nice, harmless guy. Stop it," she complains.

"Stopping." My smile fades a bit at the corners. Rashida's right, but it's impossible to talk to her about my feelings. One—I don't talk to anyone about my feelings, unless my sister-in-law manages to worm something out of me, and two—I'm her boss, regardless that her husband is a good friend of mine.

"You've been in a bad mood since you and Dean got back from that weekend in Las Vegas," she says. "I can see Dean being the one in the bad mood because of the whole being left at the altar, but you? What happened to you there?"

"Nothing happened," I say automatically. "We went for a wedding that didn't happen—thank God if you ask me, but don't because I will deny saying it—and then we came home. End of story."

Rashida cocks her head, her black hair swinging along her jaw. "I think there's more you're not saying."

Once again my mind flits to M.K., the girl from Vegas that wasn't meant to be. We met, we talked for maybe an hour, and then I never saw her again. She had the same haircut as Rashida, albeit dark brown rather than glossy black, and chin length and swinging rather than Rashida's shoulder length.

For some reason, I can't get M.K. out of my mind.

I straighten the papers on my desk and set my cell on top. The movement causes it to wake up, showing me a series of texts on my screen. "Your girlfriends have been texting you," Rashida points out, hugging the mock-ups of the new packaging to her chest. As we watch, another text appears.

"I don't have a girlfriend."

"Ever think that's your problem? For someone who goes through women faster than the kids outgrow their shoes, you've been without a lady for a while. According to Imad."

"I'm so flattered that you spend your off-work hours talking about me," I say sarcastically.

"You should be. I learn a lot."

"You know nothing—"

"Jon Snow. Yeah, yeah, you sound like Dean. I suggest you text back one of those lovely, available ladies who keep lighting up your phone and make a date. You need the company."

I raise an eyebrow. "Are you suggesting what I think you're suggesting?"

"I'm suggesting you go out and have a good time because you, Boss Man, are *grumpy*. And you need to do something about that to make sure this is a happy place to work." She gives me a knowing look and backs towards the door.

"Yeah." I glance at my phone again. "Thanks, Rashida."

"Anytime."

I don't check the texts until she's safely out of my office. I've got two messages from a Natalie that I took out last week. She was a nice girl, fun and sexy as hell. They come across as casual, but is Wondering what u r up to? masking a needy demand?

There are four texts from Heather, sent in the span of five minutes and without even bothering to hide her neediness.

There are two from Dean, probably about the Jays game next weekend.

I frown at the text from an Abby Benjamin.

The name rings a bell, but I have to go back almost a year to remember her clearly. Abby—I had liked her. We went out a few times, both of us keeping things casual and fun. She was a dancer, I remember, with one of those long and lithe bodies that always seem to catch my eye.

For a few months, dancers were my thing.

Abby never got back to me the last time I texted her, and since I've never been the sort who chase women, I gave up wondering after a day. I never heard from her again.

It was too bad. I liked her.

I respond to Natalie, a noncommittal offer to possibly hang out later in the week, and ask Heather out for drinks tonight. Then I spend a much longer time texting with Dean about last night's game.

I've told so many people I'm immune to love that I think it must be true.

Love isn't my thing. Dating women is. As long as they realize I'm not their Mr. Right, things will continue to run smoothly.

*Chapter Four*

♥

# M.K.

I CLOSE PAIN AT four o'clock and once Adam helps me clean up, I shoo him out to bake. Mondays and Wednesdays are for finger pastries as well as the patisserie's namesake: pain au chocolat, or chocolatine, whichever side of the debate you're on; Tuesdays and Thursdays are for muffins and macarons and scones; Fridays, I stock up on croissants and turnovers and Danish; and over the weekend, I bake mini opera cakes and glazed madeleines. I have a schedule, and it works, so I stick to it.

Unfortunately, with Rhoda missing her shift, I wasn't able to bake the macarons this morning, so I have to stay late.

I don't mind baking after hours. While my home kitchen is impressively outfitted, space is an issue. Here I have the entire kitchen to spread out in.

I've been at it for a few hours when the pounding on the kitchen door interrupts. The door leads to the alley, so it can only be Flora. Without bothering to turn down the music, now early '90s Aerosmith, I open the door.

"I saw your car." Stepping into the kitchen, she sniffs appreciatively. "It smells like jam."

"Blackberry." I hand her one of the macarons that I'm carefully packing in plastic containers to be stored in the walk-in refrigerator. "I didn't know you were working late."

Flora shrugs, her mouth full of the meringue-like cookie. "Nothing else to do," she says, dropping crumbs on her shirt.

"We're pretty exciting, aren't we?"

She grins. "Yes, we are."

I've never been the type of person who needs a never-ending social life. I'm a homebody, content with my books and baking and my own company. Flora likes things a little more lively, but when she had been with Thomas, he liked to socialize even less than I do, so she reluctantly got used to quiet time at home.

I should say that Thomas liked to socialize, just not with Flora tagging along. They had kept their friend groups completely separate, which is why I barely knew the man.

No loss.

"Patrick asked if we wanted to go to the Blue Jays game with him on Saturday." Flora still eyes the macarons. I hand her another, and she pops it in her mouth. "Yuck." She makes a face. "I don't like green tea."

"There's vanilla in it, too. You can't spit it out—I worked hard to make it!"

She swallows the cookie, still grimaces. "I thought it was pistachio. How many did you make?"

"Five dozen. They should last a few days." I carefully press the lid on the container and head to the fridge.

Flora grins at me. "We may have boring social lives, but no one can say we don't know how to run a business."

I smile ruefully. "Other than my mother, of course."

"Pshaw. Bitterness will only give her more wrinkles. What are you doing after this? Want to come hang at my place?"

The invitation warms my heart even though I shake my head to decline. When she was with Thomas, Flora had rarely invited me over, preferring to hang out at my place or at restaurants. "I'd like to, but I'm going to stop off at the farmer's market first, and the cats will be wondering where I am."

"At least we have our furbabies." She sighs. "Cappie is in the car, so I'd better go. So, you good for the ball game? I think he's going to ask Adam, too."

Now it's my turn to sigh. "It's about time. The two of them need to figure things out. Adam likes Patrick. Patrick likes Adam. Enough already!"

"I agree, but it's not like it's any easier for us." When I meet her gaze, I can tell she's thinking of Dean. I noticed last night that she looks wistful when the subject of Dean comes up, resigned and regretful when she's talking about Thomas. It's a slight difference, but we've been friends forever, so I can tell.

Just like I'm sure she can read my bitterness when the topic of Clay, Las Vegas, or Ruthie comes up.

I don't feel like bringing it up. We talked ad nauseam about it last night, and there's nothing that can be done. There is a man out there that might be perfect for me, but I was too busy being transfixed by his smile that I forgot to get his last name, or number. Or anything else about him that might help me find him on social media.

It's not surprising, considering the lack of luck I've had in the dating front.

"Call if you need me," Flora says at the door.

"You call me, too," I reply with a wave of my hand.

· ♥ · ♥ · ♥ · ♥ · ♥ ·

I decide to stop at home and grab my basket before walking the few blocks to the local farmer's market. The late August evening is still bright and warm, and there are people everywhere; kids racing along the sidewalk on bikes, fathers pushing baby strollers. It's like the date on the calendar is a warning that summer is over soon, and everyone wants to take advantage of the nice weather.

I pass the ball diamond, and the crack of a bat pulls my attention. Cheers follow as I smile as a young boy sprints around to second base. Despite Flora's countless pleas over the years, I never played the sport. It was one thing I never challenged my mother on. She thought all sports were unfeminine and unbecoming and refused to allow me and my sisters to join any team.

Instead, I was enrolled in dance classes by the time I could walk, and recitals and competitions filled my weekends when Flora was playing softball.

Maybe it's time to change that. I've gotten pretty good at rebelling against my mother's demands and beliefs. Maybe it's time to finally learn how to play baseball.

I shake my head ruefully and continue on to the market. I barely have time to watch a game, let alone learn to play.

The market is busy. I go straight to my usual vendors, filling my basket with peaches and kale, and a few cobs of corn. I stop for honey, and linger at the mushroom stand before filling a bag with tiny creminis.

What would they taste like in a scone? I could fry them with shallots and butter and lots of fresh thyme before adding them to the batter. Scones always sell well, and it might be nice to have a few savory ones as well. I could try a sun-dried tomato and maybe a spinach and feta and—

My mind racing with recipe options, I happen to glance up in time to see a man in a blue shirt pass by the side of the stand. I only see part of his profile, but something about him grabs my attention. I crane my neck to see where he's going as I pay for the mushrooms.

The set of his shoulders, and the back of his head remind me of Clay.

I shake off the thought. How would I know what his shoulders look like? He was sitting the entire time we were in the bar, and I definitely never saw the back of his head. Plus his hair was darker.

And he wasn't that short.

But I still follow him, winding my way through the vendors trying to pack up and people racing to pick up one last thing before they close. The shirt is a cobalt blue, tucked neatly into slim-fitting khakis.

It's not Clay. It can't be Clay. Why would I even think it's Clay? Just because I've been thinking about him today?

He stops at the same honey stand that I did. I halt in my tracks, pulling my full basket out of the way just as a harried mother rushes after a screaming toddler.

Who would let a child loose in a place like this?

I watch the maybe-Clay pick up a jar of honey, the same one that's in my basket.

So what if it's not Clay? Something about him interests me. Attracts me. It's been a while since I've felt an attraction to anyone.

Other than Clay, of course.

That had been instantaneous. Intense. A once in a lifetime moment. It's not going to happen again.

But it might. Less intense but still good.

I take a step closer, wondering what to say, how to start a conversation with a stranger because I like his shoulders.

We buy the same kind of honey. Other than that, I've got nothing. But I still take another step, and another, until I hear his laugh.

It's loud and flirtatious, just like Paulo's this morning.

I don't need a man like that.

My basket thumps against my leg as I turn and walk away.

# Clay

I SURREPTITIOUSLY CHECK MY watch to find out that only four minutes have passed since I last checked. Heather has been talking the entire time.

Why did I agree to meet her? Boredom? To prove Rashida wrong, that I am capable of having a meaningful relationship that lasts more than one night?

Only I'm not capable of it with Heather.

At least I said to meet for a drink, not for dinner. It's my usual way, to meet for drinks with the opportunity to prolong the evening with dinner and maybe a late night snack. At her place. But as I listen to Heather drone on about who knows what, I shudder at the thought of spending more than forty-five minutes with her.

I glance at my watch again. Forty-four minutes since we were seated.

Heather pauses in her recitation to drain her chocolate martini. I can tell if a woman is my type from her drink order. Beer or wine—a sure thing. A woman who orders a beer with a man has a rough and tumble side that gets me every time. Wine shows a certain level of sophistication and intelligence that is mandatory, except for a white zinfandel. I'm not proud of the fact I did a runner from a woman who downed four glasses of white zinfandel in under twenty minutes.

I did have the bartender call her an Uber from my account, though.

Martinis are usually fine, especially since they can easily begin a conversation on vodka versus gin, shaken versus stirred, leading to discussions of one of my most favourite movie franchises. I've run into trouble with women who've ordered apple martinis, but nothing serious. In my opinion, anyone who orders a chocolate martini is looking for a free meal and willing to do whatever it takes to continue the freebies. It's like ordering dessert before they've even looked at a menu.

"So." Heather gives me a smile that is aiming for sexy but comes across as sly. She looks like a fox with the reddish-brown hair and narrow face. Interesting eyes, though. Hazel, with gold tints. It's what caught my eye in the first place.

"Should we look at a menu?" she continues.

I have five seconds to react, and I rise to the occasion. "Heather, as much as I'd love to, I have to take a rain check for that. I've got a big presentation at work tomorrow. The bosses are coming in and I have to be on my game. I'm going to have to call it a night to run over everything again. A few times." Technically, this isn't a lie, rather a rewording of the truth. I do have a big presentation coming up, only it's not until next month.

"I could help you." She is pretty, but maybe a bit too needy.

I smile at her, a little wider than normal because I can sense the escape opening. "I think you'd be a little too distracting. I need to focus, and to get a good night's sleep. We'll do it again."

"When?" Make that a lot needy.

"Let me get this presentation out of the way first. I'll text you." I motion to the waiter for the bill, and as if sensing my desperation, he brings it right over. Then with a polite hand on the small of her back, I walk Heather out of the bar, right to where she parked.

One chocolate martini equals three ounces of alcohol; Heather ate most of the bruschetta flatbread that I ordered to share, so she'll be fine to drive home.

"This was a lot of fun," I say. Again, not technically a lie because it was fun seeing the heads turn when I left with Heather. She is very pretty.

"I thought I'd have longer." She pouts.

"Duty calls. I'm really sorry." I peck her on the cheek and take her keys from her hand to unlock her car door, then stand and wave as she drives away, still with a pout on her pretty face.

I whistle as I walk back to the office to pick up my car. Tempted to head in for another hour of work, I talk myself out of it with the promise of food. Good food, not takeout; good food made myself. It's been a while since I've cooked.

I put the not-so-great date with Heather out of my mind as I drive home. Hopefully, she doesn't turn clingy. I like assertive women, but there's a fine line with going after what you want and becoming needy. To me, a needy woman is a recipe for disaster.

When I pause at the stop sign, I happen to glance over. I pass by a little strip mall a few times a week, and every time I do, I promise myself I'm going to stop into the French bakery.

I squint at the sign in the window. Pain au Chocolat.

It's closed.

Instinctively, I slow down when I pass a ball diamond. I'm not sure why—just to see a game, wondering if I know anyone there. The teams are young boys, but a few of the guys from our team have sons about that age, including Imad and Rashida.

I'm glad I slowed down because the farmer's market is beside the diamond. I pull into a parking spot, remembering that I'm almost out of honey, and I like the elderberry kind from Niagara they sell here. Maybe I can find something to make for dinner.

Families and singles mix and mingle through the vendor stands. They have a great selection of organic produce as well as arts and crafts and I glance at a few things on my way to my honey.

"Just in time," the honey lady says. She's older, with graying hair and tired eyes. "You'll be my last customer tonight."

I smile widely at her. "Does that make me your very favourite or your least?" I'm glad to see my question brings a smile to her face. "Because I really like your honey."

"Keep smiling and talking about my honey, and I'll stay open all night for you."

I reach over to grab an extra jar. "I'm going to stock up, so I'll make it worth your while."

"But then it'll be longer for you to come back and visit."

"Don't you worry, I'll be back to see you."

"Promises, promises." She gives me a wink as she takes my money.

"I always meet my promises. You have a good night and drive safe to wherever it is you're going," I say as I take the heavy bag.

"Oh, it's far out of your league."

I laugh with delight and give her a quick salute before making my way back to my car.

Tiredness is beginning to set in, making me doubly glad I backed out of extending the evening with Heather. The quick banter with the honey lady is enough for me tonight. It's been a while since I've had a quiet night at home, and I'm not embarrassed to admit I'm looking forward to it.

Because nothing at the market inspired me to cook, I run through a list of takeout choices as I make the quick drive home. I'm debating on Thai or pizza when a woman on the sidewalk catches my eye. She's carrying a red basket that reminds me of Little Red Riding Hood. In fact, give her a red coat, and she'd fit the bill perfectly.

The radio quiets as a text comes in and as I push the read button on the dashboard I miss the chance of seeing Little Red Riding Hood's face.

It's from Heather.

> Already missing you. Call if you need a break from work or decide you really don't want an early bedtime.

It sounds even worse spoken by the robotic car voice.

I heave a sigh. I'm going to have problems with Heather.

*Chapter Five*

♥

# M.K.

THE CATS GREET ME at the door, as excited as any puppy. Anyone who says cats are not social has clearly never met my three.

"Get out of the way, Gulliver," I chide as the big orange cat almost trips me in his haste to race me to the kitchen. "I didn't get anything for you, so don't get so excited."

Scarlett gives a loud meow of protest. I like to think they can understand me so I don't feel too embarrassed when I talk to them.

They always listen; they never talk back or complain or criticize. Perfect conversation.

As I flip on the kitchen light, I see the flashing light on my phone. I still believe in having a separate home line, especially since my cell was the phone for Pain for a while. I check the message with a sinking feeling.

My mother is the only one who ever calls me.

"Moira Margaret, this is your mother." She's the only one who refuses to call me M.K. as well. "I haven't heard from you this week, and neither has your sister. It's rude of you not to call her and congratulate her on the baby—"

Another baby in the family. My second eldest sister Molly had announced her pregnancy via Instagram last week with a picture of her eighteen-month-old twins each dressed in matching pink and holding the American Girl dolls my mother bought them. *New doll coming soon,* Molly had posted. *#Impregnantagain!*

Because my mother acts like her own self-worth is dependent on her daughters getting married, Molly is the new favourite, having eclipsed the wedded glow of eldest sister, Millie, with a quick engagement to the son of a rival winery, announcing the news while Millie was still on her honeymoon. Her wedding took place six months after that, and then ten months after the wedding came the twins.

Since Molly had informed social media before me, I haven't felt the need to call to congratulate her. Besides, the only thing I really want to say to her is to beg her to pick better names. The twins are Misty and Magpie.

The girls will eventually grow to hate her for that, and I smirk at the thought. In fact I'm so busy smirking that I miss the rest of my mother's message. I delete it rather than replay it. It's easier just to call her back.

But I take my time, feeding the cats and heating up Sunday night's leftover pasta for myself. And then I prepare some of the mushrooms, sautéing them with shallots as I ready the batter for the scones, sprinkling in the fresh thyme at the last minute.

It's not until I pop the dozen scones into the oven that I remember to call my mother, but it's better that I waited. She doesn't like it when I'm doing something when I talk to her.

Margaret Donnelly always demands the full attention of anyone she deigns to speak to.

"You haven't called your sister," my mother accuses after the perfunctory greeting.

"Which one?" I bluff.

My mother clicks her tongue with disapproval. "Molly, of course."

Of course, Molly.

There's no way I'll be able to compete with her with another baby. What do I have? Only my own business, my independence, and three cats.

"Your sister is waiting for your call." Mom gives a disappointed sniff. "What have you been doing that's more important than your sister? Have you met someone? Were you on a date this week?"

I ignore the question. "Well, Molly's not going to appreciate me calling her now," I say drily. "I'll call her tomorrow after the lunch rush."

"The babies will be sleeping by then," Mom points out.

"Then it'll be a good time for Molly to talk."

"You need to call your sister." Mom sniffs again, and I'm tempted to ask if she has a cold.

"And I will," I promise. "I'm sure Molly has had her phone ringing off the hook for the last day. She won't miss me."

Part of me wants her to protest, that of course my sisters miss me, but of course she doesn't.

"I was busy today," I say to fill the awkwardness. "Someone didn't come in."

I regret the words as soon as they slip out.

"Your father always had staffing issues," she says with disapproval. "He was too lenient, always coddling the employees. They work for you, I'd always tell him. Their schedule is now your schedule."

"You've told me that." She's given me a lot of advice with the patisserie, most of which I disregard. The winery under her rule may be a success, but I want to run my business my way.

"Rule with an iron fist. That's what I always say," she adds. "Aren't things much better since I took over the winery?"

It's ironic how my mother is so consumed with us finding husbands when she has proven, and is proud of the fact, that she's better off without one.

I shake my head. "Okay, well, you didn't call to give me advice on the patisserie." Because you never mention it unless it's to criticize, I add silently.

I love my mother but she's a difficult woman to like. I thought living two hours away from her might have helped, but it really hasn't done much except make her nitpick my life even more.

"How can you say the patisserie is so busy? What do people in that city do all day? I can't expect you get much business with so few tables. And your hours! You're only open until four o'clock. What about the evening business? Dinner?"

"I've gone for the breakfast/lunch crowd, and I'm pretty busy with that."

"Is anything else new?" Mom asks.

"No, Mom." I sigh. "I told you I haven't met anyone."

"What's wrong with the men in that city?" she frets. "I don't wonder if you should move back here."

"I'm not moving back to Niagara to find a husband. Has it occurred to you that I don't particularly want to find a husband?"

"Of course you want to find a husband. It's time for you to settle down like your sisters. You're not getting any younger you know, Moira."

My mother is the only one who calls me Moira, and I cringe every time she says it.

"It doesn't matter how old I am, I'm still not getting married. Now, I really have to go. I've got something in the oven."

"You need to go on those dating sites," my mother orders, ignoring anything and everything I've said. "I've heard they're a good way to meet men. I want you to put yourself on that Meethimher."

I pull the phone away from my ear and check the number. It is still my mother. "You want me to go on Meethimher?"

"I think you should try. Maybe you'll give someone a chance since you never give anyone I introduce you to a second glance."

I bite my tongue to not mention a few of the winners she's tried to set me up with. The vegetable guy was the best of them.

"You're not getting any younger, Moira," she finishes. "And it's been two years since Ben. It's time to move on."

Her mention of Ben throws me. It has been two years since he died, and it's been seven hundred and twenty-six days since my mother uttered his name. The last time was to pronounce that *she* had never trusted him, and certainly never liked him.

Even though we had been engaged for six weeks, his death negated any points I might have earned.

I take a deep breath. "Thanks for the reminder."

I'm twenty-nine. Even if I was forty-nine and still single, I wouldn't put myself on Meethimher or any other dating site. But I'm not about to tell my mother that.

"So you'll sign up?"

"Sure, Mom. I'll get right on it. And I'll call Molly later. But—" The buzzer sounds with perfect timing. "I really have to pull that out of the oven. I'll call Molly tomorrow and anyone else who happens to be pregnant in the family. Which is definitely not me."

"Someday soon," my mother sings. "I'm going to make it happen for you."

And that's the problem right there. She's not going to give up, even if I find my own Prince Charming. Ben proved to everyone that I had poor judgment when it came to men.

I end the call, my mother's squawk of displeasure still ringing in my head, and pull out my mushroom scones.

"These are good," I say to the cats as they wind around my ankles, driven crazy by the smells. "I'm good. Mushroom scones are good. She doesn't know what she's talking about."

But like always, my mother's barbs have hit home.

# Clay

I'M SO HUNGRY BY the time I get home that I've lost my appetite for cooking anything creative, and make do with Cup-a-Soup. But as I wait for the kettle to boil, my gaze settles on my bright blue KitchenAid mixer in the spot of honour on the counter.

I'm the only man I know who is proud of his kitchen toys.

I'm proud of all my things. I like my condo, like the crisp lines, the easy, uncluttered space. Once, when I brought a girl back to my place, she asked if I was a real estate agent.

"No, why do you ask?"

"Because it doesn't look like anyone lives here. It looks like one of those model condos agents bring people through."

"No, it's mine." I like the minimalist look, but not spartan. I like to think there's a little bit of personality in my home.

"It's cool if it wasn't," she continued. "Or, you know, if you were a real estate agent and this was someone else's place."

"I'm not a real estate agent."

"Okay," she said with more than a hint of disappointment in her tone. "Because that would be kind of kinky, you know."

After our drink, I'd called her an Uber.

I like to cook, and not just barbeque. But I prefer to bake, and I'm good at it. So good that my mother begs me to bring cupcakes whenever there's a family dinner. So good that employees will happily stay late at work if I bribe them with sweets. So good that when women discover my baking talents, they—

Let's just say they get excited, and leave it at that.

Baking is fun and it relaxes me. It also gives me a creative outlet, something that's been lacking since I took on the VP position. I have my graduate degree in marketing and I love it, but some days I wish I was back being a simple graphic designer without the responsibilities and people working under me.

Other days, I love the power and control.

But there is stress to any job, and baking is one thing that helps me deal with it. So as I stand at the counter sipping my soup, I flip through my Martha Stewart cookbook to inspire me.

The jars of honey I bought do their part as well.

An hour later, the soup is gone, I'm halfway through a bottle of cabernet sauvignon, and a dozen honey-vanilla cupcakes are cooling on the counter. But as I set out ingredients to make a honey-cream cheese icing, I prop my iPad on the stand and FaceTime Liv.

She moved to London four years ago and we keep in touch with FaceTime chats. I don't feel bad that it's the middle of the night in England because the baby is still waking up every three hours, so there's a chance Liv might be awake. And if she's asleep, nothing will wake her.

A heavy-eyed smile greets me as FaceTime connects. "Please tell me you were already awake," I say quickly. Even seeing her bleary-eyed and half-asleep, my heart expands at the sight of her.

Liv laughs quietly. "I was. I doubt your brother would appreciate waking up to the sight of you." Two years of living abroad has given her the slightest lilt to her words, almost like she's pretending to have a British accent.

Maybe she is. Liv has always been dramatic. I would have never picked her for my older, more serious brother Clarence, but somehow they work together. Rance is now a professor of Russian literature at Cambridge and Liv is a freelance graphic artist. When I'm annoyed with my brother, the thought that Liv is better suited for me sneaks in, but I push it out just as quick.

It's hard enough that I compare every woman I meet with Liv, and they're never able to measure up.

I know what I feel for Liv is something stronger than the usual sister-in-law feelings, but I can't help it. I fell in love with Liv the day my older brother brought her home for the first time, and nothing I can do will shake it. Over the years, I've managed to convince myself it's only sisterly, brotherly love, and none of the *Flowers in the Attic* brother-sister stuff that she used to read, but it hasn't stopped Liv being one of my best friends.

"How's the baby?" I ask, cutting up the block of cream cheese.

"I hope you're not referring to your brother. Because he's got a cold, and I don't know who's more miserable, him or the baby with the bit of diaper rash he's got."

"Diaper rash doesn't sound pleasant."

"Neither is Clarence with a cold. What are you doing home tonight, all by your lonesome? Did you stash your latest lady friend in the closet to come call me?"

"No lady friend tonight. At least, not anymore." Liv knows everything about my dating history. She gets a kick out of hearing the PG versions of my dates, chides me if she thinks I've led a woman on, and generally tells me to settle down.

"You're thirty-two years old, Clayton. It's time to stop playing and settle down," Liv always says. She's the only one who calls me Clayton, just like she's the only one who calls Rance, Clarence.

As I press the softened cream cheese into the bowl, I tell her I'm looking, but I'm not sure for what. Or for whom. There are too many Heathers out there who catch my eye for me to think about anything serious.

"So you already had your date and are talking to me. I'm guessing it didn't go well."

"She sends too many texts." I sigh.

"Says the man who once sent me twenty-seven texts before I could respond." Liv's eyes crinkle at the corners when she grins.

"I had something important to tell you," I protest.

"Maybe she does, too."

"Trust me, she doesn't." I mix icing sugar into the cream cheese, adding vanilla and a dollop of honey, using my spatula and arm muscles, so I don't have to turn on the mixer. "None of the women I meet have anything important to tell me."

"What do you want them to tell you?" Liv asks, rubbing her eyes.

"How their day went, without trying to impress me. What they want out of life, without assuming I want to be part of it. I don't know, Liv. I want someone real, not fake."

"Clay." Liv sighs. "You want a relationship."

"I have relationships."

"No, you have three-or-four-night stands. It's no wonder you can't find anyone special if women keep flashing in and out of your life. Stop dating."

"How am I supposed to find anyone then?"

"Let them find you. She's out there; just be patient."

My mind flashes to the weekend in Las Vegas, to dark eyes and a blue dress. "What if I already found her?"

And then lost her.

How do I find M.K. again?

*Chapter Six*

♥

# M.K.

MONDAY MORNING I MAKE pain au chocolat. I fell in love with the pastry when I was ten years old during the summer that my parents divorced. Of course I had no idea my family was about to be destroyed when my mother sent me to stay with a distant cousin outside Paris, like some sort of depressing children's novel.

It had been depressing; I'd been lonely, sad, and very confused. My mother had sent my sisters and me to different family members for the summer. Millie was sent to Sudbury, and never forgave me for being the one who got to go to France. Molly went to Toronto, furious with everyone that she didn't go farther away from home. And Meaghan, the youngest, cried all the way to Vancouver. During a time we should have come together for comfort, we were ripped apart, and the sisterly relationships never recovered.

But there had been good times that summer. Cousin Edith was unmarried and liked weekend road trips to little French villages. She also took a liking to me, and we explored the South of France together. I fell in love with everything France that summer as I learned about champagne, French architecture, and the way lavender smells when you press it between your fingers.

It also began my love affair with French food, the most important relationship in my life. I loved the savory cuisine, but it was the pastry that got me excited.

It had been Edith who arranged to get me cooking lessons Sunday mornings in any patisserie she could find. It had been Edith who ate everything I made, even when the pastry had been chewy or hard as rocks. She complimented and praised and encouraged, and I lapped it up.

It was a rude awakening when I returned at the end of August to find my father gone and my mother—

My mother is nothing like Cousin Edith.

I'm already elbows deep in puff pastry when Rhoda arrives, this time only ten minutes late for her shift.

"I'm not good with mornings," she apologizes as she rushes in through the back door. "I tried two alarms but couldn't remember where I hid the second one, and ripped my bedroom apart trying to find it."

I continue to place the grated chocolate in a neat pile before folding the puff pastry and wonder how to fire her. Not now, because I really need the help to open. "Could you get the apple turnovers out?" I ask politely. "With the madeleines I made yesterday?"

"Ooh, I love your madeleines," Rhoda says, apparently thinking she's forgiven.

She's not. While the thought of telling her she's finished here ties my stomach in knots, I value punctuality too much not to do something about her. Just not now.

Once Adam arrives a few hours later, I stay in the kitchen to finish the croissants and make rugelach crescents and palmiers, sorting out schedules in my head and wondering where I can find a new barista who can also bake.

Or at least follow instructions.

My hands ache by the time I emerge, my shoulders sore from rolling out pounds of dough, but I'm smiling with satisfaction. There's enough puff pastry in the freezer for a few weeks, all the tables in the patisserie are full with happy, eating customers, and already the tray of fresh pain au chocolat is half empty.

"Smells delicious," Paulo says with a wink as I take my place behind the cash, grateful that I had time to change into a pale green shirtdress and put on lipstick today.

"I made the good stuff today."

"All *boa*." He smiles. "*Excelente*. You make it easy for me to go to work. I need to work off all this butter."

Thanks to Google Translate, I now have a basic understanding of the Portuguese words Paulo drops into conversations.

"Everything is better with butter," I say, keeping my tone polite and professional despite the flashing white smile and deep-set eyes, the same brown as the chocolate I used earlier. Paulo is almost *too* good looking, which keeps sending me into thoughts of *what if*, rather than *definitely not*.

"*O sim*, of course it is." Another smile, this one practically a leer. Adam brings Paulo's large coffee and gives the white bag with his croissant an extra fold before passing it Paulo with a hopeful smile.

He gets a wink in return.

"He's so pretty," Adam murmurs as we watch Paulo saunter to the door.

"*O sim.*" I mimic Paulo's accent. "But how can he make everything sound sexual? Like butter. It's just butter."

Adam looks at me with pity, and gives me a pat on the shoulder. "Oh, my Boss Lady. You really do need to go out more."

With a shake of my head, I turn to the next in line and look up with amazement because he looks like Hagrid stepped out of Hogwarts and into my patisserie. "Can I help you?" I ask the antithesis of Paulo—tall and broad and very hairy.

"The a pain au chocolat." He jerks his bearded chin toward the display case. "Never had better, not since France."

I might need Google Translate for him as well. Scottish, I think, but his accent is thick and rolling and it takes me a moment to understand.

"Thank you," I say with a smile. "It's all in the butter."

"How many turns?"

"Five." I stare at him with amazement. None of my customers ever ask about the process of making puff pastry, and I can't imagine many of them even knowing there is a system of wrapping the butter in dough, then rolling out, and folding to make the layers. It has to be turned and the dough chilled in between, a long progression between the flour and water becoming buttery, flaky goodness. "I chill after two." He gives a solemn nod, like I've told him a state secret. "Do you bake?"

"Home, in Edinburgh. I ken what goes into a simple croissant and a bit more." He smiles, the corner of his mouth barely visible between his beard and mustache.

"Where do you work now?" My heart begins to race, thoughts quickly forming in my head.

He shrugs massive shoulders. "I dinnae, just got off a boat, doin' a bit barista-ing. Mebbe add a bit o' cinnamon." He pushes the bowl-like mug across the counter to me, drained of his café au lait. "Makes it nice."

"You're a barista. Who can bake?" I ask, unable to hide my eagerness. I glance at Rhoda, leaning against the back wall scrolling through her phone.

"Well enough. You wouldn't be needin' anyone, would you?"

"When can you start?"

· ♥ · ♥ · ♥ · ♥ · ♥ ·

A few hours later, the early morning rush has slowed down, and Adam is manning the cash as I ready for lunch, still feeling the high of hiring Reuben. I invited him into my office for a more thorough interview and asked for references. If they pan out, then I have myself a new employee, one who really seems to know the ins and outs of a patisserie. I gave him a tentative start day of Thursday, never hiring someone so quickly before.

Reuben could open for me. I could have a few days off without worrying myself sick. I'm still giddy when Flora bursts in.

"I just sent Imogene with your coffee," I say with confusion, the scent of the lemon Danish on the tray making my stomach growl. I didn't have time to eat this morning. But I forget about my hunger as I take in Flora. She looks a mess, wearing dirty cutoff shorts and sneakers, her hair tangled like she's scrubbed her hands through it.

"I'm sorry," Flora cries, wringing her hands, still with dirt under her nails. "Dean was here but now he hates me but I'm going to find him and fix it so you can fall in love with Clay."

"Dean?" I clutch the tray of pastry so hard my knuckles turn white. "What are you talking about?"

"Dean came into the shop," Flora says miserably.

"Dean? Here? And Clay? Is he in Toronto? Here?" Hope blooms in my chest bigger and brighter than any of Flora's flowers.

"It'll be okay." Flora's face scrunches like it does when she's about to cry. I hand the tray to Adam and rush around the counter. "Flora, what's going on? You look like you're ready to burst into tears."

And then she does start to cry, standing in the middle of the patisserie, oblivious to the stares of those sitting at the tables or waiting in the line.

I hustle her into the kitchen. "Tell me what happened."

It's hard to understand her through the crying and even more difficult to comprehend.

Dean came into her store looking for flowers.

"He lives in Toronto?" I demand. "And Clay, too?" But Flora refuses to answer my questions, continuing her halting recap of how Dean was in the store, and somehow Thomas was there, too, but the worst thing was that Thomas had somehow married the woman who left Dean at the altar and Dean had stomped off, furious with Flora.

"I don't know what to say." There's a throbbing in my temples as I try to follow her story. Dean and Thomas and another woman? But what about Clay?

All I want to know about is Clay. The disappointment and regret that I've felt since Ruthie got us thrown in jail, missing the "date" with Clay rolls away like the end of a storm, leaving a surge of hope and anticipation in its stead.

"I don't know what to do!" Flora wails, fat tears still rolling down her cheeks.

Adam pushes the door open a crack. "Is everything okay back here?" he asks in a theatrical whisper.

"Everything's fine," I tell him with a wave to leave us alone. Adam gives Flora a sympathetic glance and lets the door swing shut after him.

"I should go." Flora sniffles. "I'm scaring your customers."

"Maybe just keep your voice down?" I grab a wad of napkins from a dispenser and hand them to her.

"What do I do now?"

"That's my line. But I think you need to go find Dean," I say firmly, trying to tamp down my excitement at the thought. She has to find him because finding Dean will lead me to Clay.

And I have a feeling Clay is something special.

"He hates me," Flora moans. "I ruined his life."

"*I'm* going to hate you if you don't go find him," I say in all seriousness. "This is my one chance to see Clay again. Go get me my man."

# Clay

I START WORK ON Monday morning nursing a headache from Mrs. Gretchen's schnapps. That's the last time I'm drinking with Dean's neighbour. I don't think ninety-year-old women should be able to drink like that.

The pain in my head doesn't get any better when Pearl drops a pile of paperwork on my desk, along with my morning coffee.

"Sorry to be the bearer of bad tidings on a Monday," she says with an apologetic smile. "Your uncle needs you to go over these reports first thing. You have a ten-thirty meeting with him."

Uncle. I fight the urge to wince. How many times have I wished I could have a job with no family relations? Even new hires are quick to notice the coincidence of their new boss having the same last name as the company president, the face of FoodMart, Charles McFadden.

And McFadden isn't a common name, so there's no way to explain it away.

"Thanks, Pearl," I say over the throb of my head. "I'll get right on it. And thanks for the coffee. You got one for yourself?"

"I actually stopped into this little French bakery this morning. I got you something." Hesitantly, she sets a plain white paper bag before me. "It's a pain au chocolat, made fresh this morning. The place smelled incredible."

"You didn't have to do that."

"My kids loved the cupcakes last week. It's the least I could do."

I grin. "Someone has to eat them. I'd have to go to the gym a lot more if I ate everything I baked."

Pearl shakes her head with wonder. "They were amazing. I can't believe you bake like that. You just..." She gives a wave of her hand at the office. "You don't seem the type."

"My sister-in-law taught me. Helps me relax. I'll remember your kids like them, if you don't mind bringing more home."

"Anytime." Pearl beams. "Enjoy your snack."

I sniff the bag appreciatively. "This smells great." I look up with a grateful smile. "You're a lifesaver, Pearl. I might be able to get through the morning now."

She gives a quizzical smile. "Is everything all right?"

"Have you ever drunk schnapps?"

"Only peach schnapps. I quite like a Fuzzy Navel now and again. Vodka, orange juice, and peach schnapps," she adds quickly, like she thought I might be thinking about her own navel.

I'm not. I've taken Rashida's warning to heart and I don't want to encourage Pearl, even indirectly. "This was nothing like the peach stuff. This was hard core and appley."

Pearl nods knowingly. "Hair of the dog will help."

I give a surprised laugh. "That sounds like you know from experience."

"Just because I'm over fifty doesn't mean I don't know how to have fun," she says with a pert smile.

"Maybe I'll start with the coffee and my treat." I reach for the cup, the scent of Starbucks dark roast already clearing away the cobwebs.

As Pearl leaves, my phone signals a text. I groan again.

Heather. Again.

We'd gone out for drinks again after work on Thursday night and this time I didn't need an excuse not to prolong the evening. I had a baseball game at nine that I had to get to, so drinks were all I had time for. Heather had pouted, dropping comments as though I couldn't tell from the pursed lips that she was annoyed I wasn't giving her enough time.

Apparently, she's over her sulk because she hasn't stopped texting me all weekend. I've kept up a weak back and forth with her, mainly until I can figure out how to end things.

I didn't know how things had begun. In my mind, two dates don't make a relationship, especially when I've only spent a grand total of ninety minutes with her. Plus I met Amy on Friday night at the gym, and she doesn't seem the type to pout, so sayonara, Heather: hello Amy.

I make a note to text Heather to let her down gently, and begin to wade through the papers Pearl gave me. It isn't until I'm halfway through that I remember the pastry.

I've never had a pain au chocolat. It seems like a fancy name for a croissant but as I take the first bite, I close my eyes with enjoyment. Buttery, flaky pastry like no croissant I've ever tasted, the centre of chocolate adding a richness that I want to savour. As I finish the last bite, I study the bag. It's plain, white, with no name on it. I make a mental note to ask Pearl where she got it.

I'm going to need another one of those.

· ♥ · ♥ · ♥ · ♥ · ♥ ·

The meeting with Uncle Charles runs into the three-hour mark and even with the morning snack, my stomach is aching with hunger by the end of it.

Braving the lunchtime rush crowding the sidewalks in downtown Toronto, I make it to Hero Burger and back to the office in twenty-four minutes flat. I step out of the elevator, my burger and fries leaving a stomach-growling smell.

"Did you bring something for me?" Rashida asks, eyeing my bag with the telltale grease stains as she passes me on her way to the elevator.

"Was I supposed to?" I shake my head. "Brutal meeting, it went so long."

"Did he go for the changes?"

I take a sip of the Pepsi. "He loved them—eventually. I made sure I told him about your contributions. He's pretty impressed."

Her cheeks pink with pleasure. "You told the president of the company about me? Thanks, Clay. I really appreciate that."

"You do a lot for me, and I appreciate that. You deserve credit for your work." I grin. "It doesn't hurt that I get credit for finding you in the first place."

"You're being so nice. Maybe I shouldn't have told you last week that you've been a grump to work with."

"I am a nice guy, and I was a grump. I think I've snapped out of it."

"Who is she?"

"Why do you assume she's a woman?"

Rashida cocks her head. "Because it's you."

"Well, it's not this time. I mean, I met someone, but she's not special. I'm sure she is, but maybe not to me."

"Poor Clay. Don't you think it's time you find someone special for you?"

"You sound like my sister-in-law," I grumble. "I keep getting the lecture from her. It's not my fault."

"Well, who's fault is it that you can't meet anyone?"

"Fate?" I suggest. "Destiny? Someone's out there for me, but it's not our time yet."

"You really believe in that?"

My phone rings before I answer. It's such a surprise that I almost drop my bag. No one calls me, not even my mother. Texting is the way to go for me.

I juggle my food and Pepsi in an attempt to pull out my phone. "Can you grab it for me?" I plead. "Jacket pocket."

"It's probably a telemarketer. I love dealing with them." She drops her hand into my pocket and pulls my phone out to read the screen. "This one has a name. Moira Donnelly."

"Who?"

"How would I have any idea? Want me to answer?"

"Just give me a sec—" I expect her to follow as I hurry down the hall to my office but she stands by the elevator with my phone to her ear.

"Hello? Clay McFadden's phone."

"Who is it?" I hiss with a backwards glance.

She waves me away, listening intently with a cocked eyebrow. "Las Vegas, you say? With Dean? I know Dean."

"Who are you talking to?" I demand. By the time I drop my food at my desk, Rashida is strolling down the hall with a smile on her face.

"No, he's great. I work with Clay. I guess you can say he's my boss, although he doesn't always act like it," Rashida says, turning her shoulder to me and ignoring my outstretched hand. "Right. I know."

"Could I have my phone?"

"My husband plays ball with them," she continues. "I've known Clay for years. So you were there for the non-wedding?"

"Who is on the phone?" I make to grab it, but Rashida dodges. "I better give him the phone. I think he might want to talk to you," she says with a laugh. "Nice talking to you. She says her name is M.K.," she adds as she finally hands me the phone.

My mouth drops open. An image of a dark-haired woman in a blue dress sitting across from me in a crowded Las Vegas nightclub fills my mind with rising excitement. Dark blue with a shy smile. "M.K.? Really?"

"Who is she?"

"Give."

"Say please." Rashida laughs, obviously enjoying my reaction.

"Give me the phone," I growl. Practically grabbing it from her hand, I don't even glance at the name before I slam it to my ear. "M.K.?"

"Is this Clay?" asks a tentative voice. "Clay—Dean's friend."

"We met in Las Vegas. This is me. And you're M.K. Blue dress? Really you? I can't believe you called!"

Rashida laughs from the doorway. "I knew there was something more you weren't saying," she sings as she backs into the hall.

I fight the urge to give her a finger gesture as I find my chair. "How are you? *Where* are you?"

M.K. laughs, and my heart literally flips over from the sound. "I'm in Toronto, can you believe it? Dean walked into Flora's flower store this morning. Of all the flower shops in the city, he picks Flora's because he lives right around the corner. I thought I'd never see you again, and now I find out you're so close." She laughs again.

Even though she speaks so quickly that I barely understand, I laugh with her. Stretching out my legs, I prop them on my desk, forgetting about my food or my empty stomach. "I have no idea how you got my number, but I'm glad you did. And my head's a bit jumbled from hearing from you, so can you explain again, please?"

I can't keep the smile from my face.

## *Chapter Seven*

♥

## M.K.

I'M GOING TO SEE Clay tonight.

I turn the music up loud, but not too loud because Pat and Paul who share the wall between the semi-detached houses have a new baby and I don't want to wake him up. Although two-month-old Gilbert isn't as considerate, crying with loud wails that break through the wood and plaster to invade my sleep.

Babies are inconsiderate.

I dance around the room to Whitesnake. I may look like a quiet mouse of a girl but inside I'm all rocker chick. My youth flew by, punctuated by the songs of the '80s and '90s; the hard rock, metal bands like Def Leppard and Poison, Mötley Crüe and Skid Row. Bands with big ballads and even bigger hair. I grew up knowing the words to every Guns N' Roses song, worshiping KISS like some girls loved NKOTB. I could debate David Lee Roth versus Sammy Hagar for hours and had pictures of Brett Michaels with his glam-rock pout plastered on my wall.

When my father left us, his collection of vinyl remained, and I secreted them in my room in milk crates. I recorded the vinyl onto cassette tapes and listened to them on his old Walkman.

My mother hated the thing because I would never tell her what I was listening to. "You wouldn't like it," I'd say, which had been like waving a red flag at a bull. How could I enjoy something she didn't like? It made no sense to her.

These days, of course, Apple Music and Spotify make it easier to listen to my music, as well as Sirius radio, but I still have the crates of vinyl tucked away in the crawlspace in my basement, my only connection I have to my father.

My first rebellion growing up was to save my babysitting money and buy a secondhand drum kit, which I set up in the loft above the garage, far away from my mother's unbelieving ears. I had been a decent drummer for a time. Dropping out of the oenology and viticulture program at university to work for the restaurants at other wineries was bad enough; my mother had been under the impression I was studying to be a sommelier rather than a pastry chef. She wouldn't have survived if I had followed my first love and became a musician.

My air drumming is interrupted by the chime of my FaceTime notification. I prop my phone up against my mirror as I finish applying mascara.

"You're nervous," Flora greets me.

I widen my eyes, stilling the excited shake of my head before I poke out my eye. "Why would I be nervous?" I bluff, dabbing at my lashes with the brush. "And how can you tell, even if I was?"

"You're listening to Whitesnake," Flora points out. "It's your *gettin' ready to get sexy* song." She growls the words in attempt to sound masculine.

"I don't have a sexy song because I am the least sexy person I know."

"I'm not sure you're the best judge of that. You should ask Clay tonight."

My stomach once again ties itself into knots at the thought of seeing Clay tonight. Of talking to him. Of getting to know him. Of maybe...

I shutter the thought.

"Are you nervous?"

Onscreen, Flora runs her hand through her hair, preparing to pull at the ends, but she's stymied from her recent short cut. "There's no reason for me to be nervous. Dean says he thinks it's a good idea to be just friends. Which implies he thinks it's *bad* to be more than friends."

"He just got out of a relationship," I remind her. "As did you."

"Yes, but Dean and Thomas are so different that I'm sure I would have no trouble compartmentalizing my feelings for them."

"So you have feelings for Dean?"

Flora laughs hollowly. "You know what they say—women sleep with men because they love them, men sleep with women because they want to fall in love. I don't think that applies to either of us."

"You had a one-night stand in Las Vegas of all places. That doesn't mean you have to marry him. I don't think you should even think about marriage for a very long time. Or ever. Remember what we promised each other? That we'd never get married?"

"We were seventeen," she reminds me.

"We were very wise and mature seventeen."

"And I had just gotten my heart broken." Flora pauses, and I glance at my screen. "It doesn't feel like I've gotten my heart broken this time."

"Maybe it's already healed."

"Maybe. Are you almost ready?"

"You said we were meeting at seven thirty. I still have ten minutes before you pick me up. Are you ready?"

"I'm picking you up?"

I bite back my sigh. I love Flora dearly, but I don't understand her lackadaisical organizational abilities. "Yes, I thought we agreed you were picking me up," I say patiently.

"I better go! Text you when I'm outside." Flora hangs up before I can say another word. I carefully finish applying my mascara, trying to ignore the fact my hands are still shaking. I blink, the mascara accentuating my blue eyes and reach for my lipstick.

Clay is just a guy. I shouldn't be so nervous about meeting a guy.

There haven't been many other guys for a while.

Not since Ben.

I probably shouldn't tell Clay that it's been two years since I've been in a relationship. He might think I'm desperate. Am I? I met a man, talked to him for maybe an hour, and now I've built him up to the next best thing? He's probably looking for a fast hookup and I'm looking for...?

What exactly am I looking for?

# Clay

I'M GOING TO SEE M.K. again.

I glance around the restaurant/bar where we're meeting, the same place where the team had met last week for beers after the game.

Dean stands and waves from the table across the floor, like he isn't noticeable enough with his height and his hair.

"Hey," I say, pulling out the chair opposite him. "They're not here yet?"

"No," he says shortly.

I frown at his tone. "What's up?"

"I think this is a bad idea."

"Why? We're just having a drink with a couple of girls we met when we were away for a weekend. That's it. You need to chill." Maybe calming him down helps with my own nerves. I'm nervous. I'm never nervous.

The chime of my phone makes me jump and I grab it like a lifeline.

It's Heather. Again.

What r u up to tonight? I'm lonely...

I stuff my phone back in my pocket without answering. I don't have time for Heather. For once I want to focus on one girl.

"Call them women." Dean stares across the bar. "Evelyn always hated being referred to as a girl."

My mouth tightens. "Evelyn would really hate what I call her now."

Dean turns and gives me a ghost of a smile. "It's not her fault."

"Oh no?" I shake my head. "I'm not getting into that here or now because you're freaked out. But she better not run into me anytime soon because I have some choice words for her."

"Thanks, man, but it's not worth it. Seeing her today..." Dean trails off with a shake of his head. "I don't want to do that again."

I look around for the waitress. "You're going to have to see her again. You've got to figure out the house...stuff like that. You've been together for two years. You have things. A house."

Two years with the same person seems like a lifetime to me.

"At least I'd want some advance notice. Seeing her hand in hand with this Thomas guy, with a *ring* on her finger." He drops his gaze to the table.

"That is messed up. Evelyn, with Flora's ex." I'd heard the story from M.K. earlier and again from Dean and still found it hard to believe. "You going to be okay?"

"Yeah." He draws in a shaky breath. "But this is why I can't let anything happen with Flora again. If this is how I feel, imagine how messed up she is from it?"

"Maybe she's not," I suggest. "Maybe it was for the best for her, and she's ready to move on. And maybe it's the shock of seeing her again that's messing you up. Maybe tomorrow you'll wake up and realize it was all for the best." I frown, thinking of what Dean had said. "What do you mean—again?"

"I didn't tell you." At least Dean has the grace to look guilty. "I hooked up with her in Las Vegas."

"Who—Evelyn?"

"No, Flora. I didn't say anything to you, because well..."

"When was this?" I demand.

"That night. You were sleeping but I couldn't, and I was walking around and bumped into her on the street. We had pancakes and she was crying, and we ended up back in her hotel room. She didn't see the note I left."

"Why did you leave her a note?"

"Because I got your text in the morning, about Evelyn stopping by. I went to find her."

"You left the cute girl you hooked up with in her hotel room to go find the woman who just dumped you?" I ask with disbelief. "Bro, get your priorities straight!"

"I know. It's messed up."

"And now your ex and her ex are married?"

"Yeah," he says in a heavy voice. I don't ask how he feels about that because I'm not sure he'd tell me. Plus I can imagine how he's feeling.

"So what's going on with you and Flora?" I ask instead.

"Nothing. I can't—not right now. I told her we could be friends. Just friends."

I laugh. I can't help it. I remember the way Dean looked at Flora in the bar that night and that was before they hooked up. "Good luck with that." I check my watch. "They're late. Let's get a beer. God knows you need one."

Even with a cold beer in front of me, waiting for M.K. to walk through the door is the longest ten minutes of my life.

I tap my fingers on the table. This is like I'm on a blind date. I really have no idea what M.K. is like.

But I have an image of her in my mind and I really think it fits. She may outwardly look tiny and delicate, but I saw a few expressions and heard a few comments and think she's tougher than she lets on. And she loves her friend. She and Flora had some sort of mental telepathy going on that night.

But this was three weeks ago, and I could be imagining all of it. She may have agreed to this out of obligation.

And then I think of her blue eyes and the way she smiled at me when they left the bar that last time I saw her. There had been promise in those eyes.

I'm not sure what kind of promise, but there was something.

Even as I talk with Dean while we wait, I keep my eyes on the door.

My heart jumps into my throat when they walk in.

"Look, they're here." I jump to my feet, fighting the urge to run across the floor—M.K., smiling and pretty with her dark hair crisply cut and brushing against her jaw. She's shorter than I remembered. Cute, so cute, with a tiny waist and a great smile.

There's something about this girl that makes me lose my cool. M.K.'s smile widens as she catches sight of me, and my chest puffs out like a proud rooster. I elbow Dean as he stands beside me. "I'll tell you one thing, Deano, I'm looking for more than friendship with that one."

Dean frowns. "Clay, maybe...you know, take it easy on her? Lay off the full-court press? She seems nice. They both do."

"Are you kidding? A week ago, I thought I'd never see this girl again, and I still can't get her off my mind. She better take it easy on me."

I watch with bated breath as they cross the floor.

"Hi!" Flora stops before the table. "Sorry we're late. Actually, M.K. was on time—for your information, she's *always* on time, but I don't always have the same punctual prowess, so this is my bad. And then we couldn't decide whose car to take because we live close but in the opposite direction from each other."

Flora may be talking but my gaze hasn't left M.K.

"Hi, Flora," Dean says when she pauses for breath.

"Hi." I wrench my gaze away from M.K. Flora is cute, looking like the girl next door with the blonde hair and big green eyes but —

M.K. smiles, and I barely acknowledge Flora's greeting.

Dean doesn't try to hide he's checking Flora out. "How many pairs of those shoes do you have?" he asks gesturing to her feet.

"I've actually lost count," Flora says with a mischievous smile

M.K. finally speaks. "You notice shoes? Impressive."

"Your shoes are lovely," I say quickly with a wave at her basic black flats. "I've never seen anything like them."

M.K.'s laugh breaks any awkwardness and we sit down.

I like her smile. I like her smile even more than I did in Las Vegas.

## Chapter Eight

♥

## M.K.

"M.K. EARTH TO M.K." The next morning, I shake my head to clear the fog when Adam's singsong voice breaks into my thoughts. "What do you need?" We're ten minutes from opening, and I slide the last tray under the glass. Croissants, the slick pastry gleaming in the light. I smooth my apron over my hips. I've already changed into my dress, makeup is in place—everything is ready to go.

"I need to know what's gotten into you this morning." Adam has a grin on his face as he points at my feet. I realize with horror that I'm still wearing my kitchen shoes.

I race back to my office, leaving Adam laughing behind me.

Last night went so much better than I expected. Not only cute, Clay is smart and funny and *nice*. I like nice guys. I've never been into bad boys or brooders. Ben was—

"Nothing has gotten into me," I say as I return, proper shoes in place. With a glance at the clock, I head to the door as Rhoda swings open the door from the kitchen. I'm in such a good mood that Rhoda's lateness this morning didn't even faze me.

"How was last night?" Adam asks pointedly. "Was it a good *date*?"

Rhoda perks her head up. "You had a date last night? I didn't know you dated."

I blink with surprise. "I date. Of course I date."

"When's the last time you've been on a date?" she asks with a younger woman's confidence.

"It wasn't that long ago."

Adam coughs. "Two thousand and nine," he says amid the coughing.

"It hasn't been that long," I protest, my hand hovering over the Open sign.

"Are you going to tell your mother about him?" he asks eagerly.

"Why would she tell her mother?" Rhoda demands in horror.

"Haven't you heard her and Flora talking about the reincarnated Mrs. Bennett?"

I had no idea I'd been so outspoken about my mother. I vow to keep more of my thoughts to myself, or at least when Flora and I are alone. I flip the sign, unlock the door, and head back to the cash.

"She's not that bad." Even from me it sounds like a lame protest. "The date was fine."

"Just fine?" Adam wears a mask of sympathy as he ties his white apron around his waist.

"Fine's not good. Neither is okay," Rhoda says, taking her place at the coffee machine.

"You want to go for at least good," Adam adds, smiling at the first customer.

"It wasn't a date!" I hiss.

"You just said the date was fine," Rhoda corrects.

"It wasn't a date, per se. It was four people who are slightly acquainted getting together for a drink to get to know each other better."

"And did any of the four hook up?" He whispers the word as Mr. Cullen rolls up to the cash. "Because that's a great way to get to know each other." Adam makes a clucking noise when he sees my expression. "Okay, that's too much to ask. Did any of these four make another date?"

"I'm, ah, actually going out with Clay tonight."

Adam jumps on my words. "I knew it! You're all hot and bothered by this guy, and you can't keep your mind on anything but how cute he looks in his jeans, right?"

"The only thing hot and bothered are those Danish if they don't come out of the oven." I glance pointedly at the kitchen door, and Adam takes the hint and disappears through the swinging door. "And he didn't wear jeans," I whisper.

It's not until the early morning rush is over that I can run over to Flora's. I've wanted to talk to her all day to see if she thinks I should be as excited as I am.

Regardless of what I told Adam, things went great last night.

I bring Flora her favourite coffee and an apple juice for Imogene. "Morning!" Imogene greets me with a wide smile. "Are you here to tell me about last night because Flora won't tell me anything. 'We're friends.'" She mocks Flora's cheerful voice. "Friends aren't going to keep her warm at night."

"I think she's got enough blankets for that."

"She needs someone to help her get over Thomas," Imogene insists.

"I agree with that, but I think she's doing okay on her own." I lower my voice. "Is she here?"

"She's in the back playing with her flowers." She leans as close to the counter as her belly will allow. "What did she say?"

"It's what she didn't say." Even though I don't appreciate the fact that Adam and Rhoda most likely began gossiping about me the moment the door closed, I have no qualms discussing Flora with Imogene because I know Imogene loves her almost as much as I do. "She hasn't said much about Thomas these last few weeks."

"Maybe she thinks you're sick of hearing about him."

I shake my head. "She listened to me go on and on about Ben for over a year, so she'd say that I owe her to listen to every single thing about Thomas that goes through her head, even the stuff I really don't want to hear about."

"He was a nice guy, wasn't he?" Imogene frowns. "I hate thinking about her with a not-nice guy."

"They weren't well suited," is all I say about the subject.

But thanks to Dean and his ex, Thomas is out of Flora's life. Ancient history. It's my opinion exes should remain in the past.

"What's this Dean guy like?" Imogene asks, rubbing a hand absent-mindedly along her burgeoning stomach. "Is he nice? He's definitely cute...and tall. Big...and cute."

"You said that." I smile. "He seems great."

"Good. And his friend? Oh—!" Imogene clutches her stomach with an expression of surprise.

"Are you okay?" I cry.

"Just a kick," she says. "A big one. Want to feel?"

"I'm not in the habit of—" Imogene waddles out from behind the counter to where I stand and grabs my hand, placing it on her belly. "Okay, then."

"Push down. Can you feel it? Harder." It feels as if Imogene is shoving my hand into her stomach, and I want to pull back.

"I don't want to hurt you."

"You won't. Say hi." We stare down at her belly until a movement inside makes her top flutter. "There! Feel it?"

It feels like something is pushing at my hand, and my mind has a hard time comprehending that it's a little hand or foot. "I feel it."

"It's amazing, isn't it?"

"I guess." Imogene looks surprised at the reluctance in my voice. "I don't think I'm the maternal type. I've never had a thing for babies."

"Have you had much to do with them?"

"I have three nieces," I admit. I pull my hand away.

"So you've had a bit to do with babies. That's okay. Not everyone has to be a mother."

"Tell that to my mother. My worth would definitely go up if I gave her a grandchild."

"Don't we always want to make our mothers proud?" Imogene asks. "And mothers-in-law are even worse. I gave Scott's mother her first grandson but she still makes me nervous."

"You like being a mother?" I ask awkwardly.

"It's the best thing in the world," Imogene says over her shoulder as she heads to the back room. "I'm going to tell Flora her coffee is here."

I stare at my hand that touched a baby appendage. Thinking of it like that makes it easier than imagining a tiny creature curled up inside Imogene waiting to be pushed out into the world.

The bell over the door chimes as a woman with reddish brown hair steps into the store. "They'll be right out," I say as she looks around with a curious expression.

"That's okay. I don't need anything. I'm here for an interview," she said.

"Then you want to see Flora. She's owns the place."

"Actually, it was an Imogene who set up the interview. I think that's what she said."

"She works here, too." I smile inwardly at how Imogene must have taken it on herself to find her replacement for when she went on maternity leave.

The door to the back opens, and Imogene waddles out, followed by Flora, still with one of her AirBuds in. I smile and point to her ear. She pulls it out with a grin. "Hey, thanks for the coffee. I'll come over when I'm finished, for a debriefing."

"Don't bother," I groan, heading for the door. "Adam has big ears today. We can save it for tomorrow."

Flora laughs and turns her attention to the woman. "Hi, and welcome to Fleur. Oh, M.K.," she calls as I pull open the door. "Have fun with Clay tonight if I don't see you before."

"Thanks. You, too. Not with Clay," I add, flustered at the thought. "Have fun with Dean."

"Clay?" the woman says with confusion. "Clay McFadden?"

Flora turns to me with her own confusion in her gaze. "I don't know. Is that his last name?"

"Why?" I ask more sharply than I intended.

"Clay and Dean..." she says. "They're kind of uncommon names. You're dating Clay?"

"I wouldn't exactly say dating," I say hesitantly with a nervous glance at Flora.

"Why?" Flora asks the woman with a hard edge to her voice. "Are *you* dating him?"

The woman laughs bitterly. "Clay doesn't date. Or at least he doesn't do relationships. We went out a few times, and I thought things were great, but now he won't return my texts. Nothing. He's ghosting me."

It takes three swallows before I can reply, my heart breaking like the cup Rhoda dropped earlier. Clay and this woman with the hair and amazing hazel eyes? Clay and other women? My Clay? "Ghosting?"

"Pretending I don't exist. He's done it before to a couple of girls I know, but at least he was nice to them. I sent him a bunch of texts and now nothing."

"I'm sorry to hear that," I say faintly and walk out of the shop without meeting Flora's eyes.

# Clay

AS SOON AS M.K. opens her door, I know I made the right decision giving up my ticket for tonight's Jays game.

She's wearing a navy, sleeveless dress that makes her eyes even bluer and her waist tinier than I thought possible.

But she's frowning, her eyes filled with worry. It's the twist of her lips that stills the hug I'm about to give her.

"You look amazing," I begin. "I've been—"

"Are you seeing someone else?" she demands, folding her arms across her chest. Her blue eyes flash with anger.

"No! Are you?"

"I met someone who has been texting you." M.K. takes a deep breath. "She says she went out with you a bunch of times and now you're ghosting her. I don't even know what that means." Her frown deepens and a tinge of concern sparks.

"It means...Don't worry about what it means, because I don't do it. And I'm not dating anyone." Now it's my turn to frown. I don't know M.K. very well, and therefore don't know what she considers dating. My hanging out with Heather was last week so —"Was it Heather?"

"Was what Heather?" M.K. remains in the doorway, leaving me on the step below so we're the same height.

"Is that who you met?" I glance down to see a movement at her feet. A gray cat winds its body around M.K.'s ankles. "A cat."

M.K. raises an eyebrow. "I have three cats."

"That's a lot of cats." I laugh awkwardly, knowing I'm sinking fast.

"Do you like cats?"

I feel like this is a very important question, more important than the usual favourite animal query. "Who doesn't like cats?"

"Do you?" Her voice cools several degrees, and for a moment my knees quake.

"Not especially," I admit, steeling myself. "But only because I'm allergic."

"You're allergic to cats?"

The disappointment on her face cheers me. "Only a little bit. And I always have Claritin."

"You have allergy pills with you now?" she asks skeptically.

"Never leave home without them," I brag. "I'm like a Boy Scout that way. So, are we ready to go?" I step back in hopes she'll leave the doorway.

No such luck.

"Not so fast," M.K. says quickly. "I think I need to know more about this Heather. Are you dating her?" Her voice is cool and calm, but I can't read the expression on her face. She might be teasing, or she might be deadly serious. She might be getting ready to slam the door in my face or set one of her three cats to attack me, laughing as I sneeze myself into misery.

I really wish I'd texted Heather back.

"Let's get this clear. Was the girl—woman—you spoke to tall with long brown hair? Lots of earrings? And she wears this mauve-coloured lipstick that really doesn't go with her colouring?"

"Sounds like you know a lot about her."

"I'm observant. I have a thing about lipstick. Like yours." I reach out and touch the corner of her mouth with a hesitant finger. "I like the shade—enough pink so that it's not technically a nude, but I think you could even go a shade or two brighter, to make your lips stand out." I gently swipe my finger under her bottom lip. "You have really nice lips. As I was happy to notice last night." I smile carefully at her, wondering if I went too far.

M.K. draws in a shaky breath. "You're trying to distract me."

"Am I? Am I distracting you?" This time I grin at her, seeing the coolness in her face dissipate.

I'm surprised how much I really want this to work.

"No. I'm not dating anyone," I say slowly. "I went out with Heather a few times. The last time was last week, but I never gave her any indication that it was anything other than casual. I wasn't into developing a relationship with her. It was fun; she's a nice girl."

"But you didn't text her back. That's rude."

"It is." I pull out my phone. "But if you look here..." A few touches has my list of messages open and inviting her to look. "Heather texted me yesterday and again last night." I hold my phone up. "I got them yesterday right before you called me. And last night it came in just as you walked in the door." I smile at her.

"You kind of distracted me. Not that it's your fault, of course. I should have gotten back to her."

"But you're not dating her?"

"My relationship status is single. But I'm hoping to change that after tonight."

• ♥ • ♥ • ♥ • ♥ • ♥ •

It takes almost the entire drive to the restaurant before M.K. relaxes, and even then I sense the questioning sideways glances she gives me. But she does give me a smile, albeit a tight-lipped one, when we walk into the restaurant.

How did things go so wrong? I enjoy the company of more than a few women so it's not impossible that my past and present overlap but never before have they collided like this.

I hope M.K. is past it, but nope, she's only just begun.

"Are you a player?" she demands as soon as the hostess leaves us with the menus. But M.K. doesn't wait long enough because her head whips around when she hears her comment.

"Define *player*," I counter, dropping my napkin in my lap and fighting the urge to open the menu. Not that I care about eating right now, but it might be a good defense should cutlery start flying.

"You date a lot of women." It's not a question.

I take a deep breath. "I do." There's no sense beating around the bush. And besides, I already get the impression M.K. isn't one for withholding the truth.

"Why?" M.K. rests her chin on her fist, her dark gaze searching my face. On closer look, I realize her eyes are a very dark blue, almost navy. And her nose turns up a bit at the end.

"Why what?" It's not that I'm avoiding the question, but studying her face actually distracts me. Her lips are a perfect bow, the bottom lip full, and the little dip on the top is adorable.

"Why date numerous women? Why aren't you looking for a relationship?"

"Who says I'm not?"

I've never had a girl look at me like M.K. is—like she has the ability to read my soul.

A woman—M.K. is a definitely no girl.

I think she might have the potential to be a scary woman too.

As M.K. stares at me, I toy with my fork; moving, adjusting. Fidgeting.

Like I'm afraid of the question.

"When I meet a woman, the first thing I do is tell her I'm not looking for anything serious. I say I'm looking for fun and want to keep it casual. My way of thinking is that people will accept anything if you're upfront at the beginning, so that's what I do. I never tell women that my first serious relationship was in my senior year in high school and on the night of the prom, I found out she had been sleeping with my best friend all year. I don't tell anyone about the woman who I dated in university who had changed my mind about getting serious until I caught her with my roommate." I grin ruefully. "I also don't introduce many dates to my friends."

M.K. swallows. "Is this the part where you tell me you're not looking for anything serious?"

"I would have told you that last night. Before I kissed you, too." The memory of her lips against mine brings a smile to my face.

"Oh." The corners of her mouth turn up, and I hope she's having the same memory.

I glance at my watch. "It's twenty-five minutes into this date and I've already told you more than any woman I've dated in the last year. I date a lot of women because I enjoy women. They're fun. They're fun to be around. And I haven't been looking for a relationship. And right now, I think that's been a really smart move on my part."

"Why is that?"

I reach my hand across the table and touch her fingers. "Because then I wouldn't have been ready to meet you."

## *Chapter Nine*

♥

# M.K.

WHEN I LOOK AT Clay, I will myself not to melt. Because he's very good looking—even more once I realize he's not the sleazy player Heather made him out to be. He's like a blond Tom Cruise, with that contagious smile and even a tiny dimple in his cheek.

He smells better than freshly baked pastry.

Maybe it's naïve, but I trust Clay more than Heather right now. He showed me her texts; he gave all the right explanations and despite how he's trying to smooth it all under the table, I believe him.

I really want to believe him.

I open the menu and search for the wine list. "Does anything look good?" Clay asks politely.

"I think I just want—I really need a drink right now," I admit with a smile. "This—this night hasn't gone as well as I'd planned."

"So it's not just me?"

At the sight of his hopeful smile, I do melt a little and give him an apologetic smile. "I should apologize for attacking you like that."

Clay shrugs. "I should have texted her back, and then we wouldn't have had the problem. Just out of curiosity, where did you meet her?"

"She came in to Flora's for an interview when I was there. Flora said something about you; I said something about Dean and Heather—if that's who it was—put two and two together."

"She never even met Dean. Maybe I mentioned him..."

"Maybe she's observant."

"You mean like a stalker?"

I laugh, and then Clay laughs, and then it's like the whole world is laughing with us.

This is going to be okay.

Maybe better than okay.

"Since you've had the Twenty Questions about my dating life, do I get to ask you any?" Clay asks, resting his hand on the table. It would be easy to reach out and touch it, touch him. I can't believe how much I want to.

"There's no need," I say ruefully, tugging on my earlobe. "My last actual date was seven months ago, courtesy of my mother trying to set me up. It went horribly, as expected."

Clay winces. "You let your mother set you up?"

"Trust me when I say I really had no choice."

"Sounds like my mother. Actually, no, because Mom would never try to set me up. But she's strong and tough. She makes sure I give women the respect they deserve."

"My mother is the strongest woman I know." My admission surprises me. "My father left us when I was ten, and she had to raise me and my three sisters, as well as take over the winery because my father gave that up, too."

"Winery? Like a Niagara winery?"

"Four Leaf Clover wines. It's outside Niagara-on-the-Lake. That's where both Flora and I grew up."

"Four—named for you and your sisters?"

I laugh again, my shoulders relaxing bit by bit. "You'd think. No, my grandfather started it, named it. It's a family joke that my mother had the four of us to fit the name. Apparently my father only wanted two—two boys probably."

"Boys are overrated. Girls are much more fun." His hand still rests on the table and if I reach just a little bit, I can touch his fingers.

I fold my hands in my lap instead. He smells incredible. "How about you? Any siblings?"

"Two older brothers. Clarence and Clyde."

I bite back the smile. "They're interesting names."

"You can say that. I'm not sure what my parents were thinking." Clay points to the menu. "Look, if you grew up with wine, you can pick the bottle, and then tell me what you're doing in Toronto instead of tending the grapes."

"I can't just pick wine for you without knowing what you're going to eat," I protest.

Clay gives me a blinding white smile. "It doesn't matter what I order; I'm not going to be able to taste anything because I'm so full of you."

My heart lurches.

He wrinkles his nose at me. "Was that too cheesy?"

"Maybe a little," I admit with a shy smile. "But I think I like cheese."

I order a bottle of Gamay Noir and tell Clay about taking culinary classes at night before following Flora to Toronto; name dropped the restaurants I worked in before realizing I needed to open my own place before I went crazy taking orders from arrogant chefs.

"I didn't want to run a restaurant because of the hours," I admit, after tasting the mouthful of wine and nodding to the waiter who brought it. "I've always been more of a morning person. Flora gave me the idea for the patisserie. She had already opened Fleur, and there was a pub that was for sale. She said she didn't want a bar there because we'd drink too much, but someplace that had coffee that could compete with Starbucks would be great. It's ironic because we had been drinking at the time of this conversation," I finish with a laugh.

"So you up and bought the place? All by yourself?"

"Flora helped. It was a tough go at the beginning, but I managed."

"I don't think your mother is the strongest woman you know," Clay says with admiration. "You must be one tough cookie."

"I like making cookies," I say.

"I'd like to try your cookies," he says lightly.

"That might be arranged." He holds my gaze until I dip my chin self-consciously. "So what do you do?"

"Nothing nearly as exciting as you."

As I listen to Clay tell me about his marketing duties with FoodMart, I feel my heart pounding. My rule is four dates, four substantial dates before any physical contact. I don't do casual sex.

I need a degree of developed intimacy before I allow myself to take that step. It's a hard rule for me, one that will protect me from the confusion and uncertainty an impulsive physical relationship can lead to. It also protects my heart. I don't do sex with men I don't know well enough to trust.

When I look at Clay, I wonder if it's time to break the rule.

· ♥ · ♥ · ♥ · ♥ · ♥ ·

We linger over dinner. Every comment seems to lead to a new conversation train.

I don't remember the last time I laughed so much.

Clay pours the last of the wine in my glass. From the heated flush of my cheeks, I know I've drunk my fair share of the bottle, but Clay is driving, and it is a nice bottle. "I'm not ready for tonight to end," he says, sounding surprised.

I circle the rim of my glass with my finger. "Why do you sound so surprised by that? Do your dates not last?" I glance surreptitiously at my Fitbit. "Wow, it's already after ten o'clock!"

Clay looks sheepish. "I don't remember the last time I had a three-hour dinner with a woman."

"When's the last time you invited a woman to dinner?" I ask then shake my head. "Don't answer that. It's none on my business."

"It could be your business," he says casually, but the words send a childish thrill through me. "I think you've figured out that I date a lot of women. You can call me a player if you want, but I enjoy the company of women. I think the female species is fascinating."

"I don't think I've heard that one before."

"Well, it's true," he says with a rueful grin. "You, especially, are very fascinating."

I motion with my hand for him to continue and Clay laughs. "You're not falling for any of my bullshit, are you?"

"Is that what it is?"

"I like to compliment. Is that so wrong?"

"As long as you mean it."

He holds my gaze for a beat. "I do. I mean every word. There's something about you, M.K..." He shakes his head. "What's your real name?"

"Moira. Moira Margaret."

"Moira." He rolls my name between his lips and never before have I appreciated it more. "What's the K stand for?"

"That's a long story, and one you might not understand. Have you ever seen the movie *The Cutting Edge*? It came out in the nineties."

"I have a vague recollection of the nineties." Clay grins. "And I remember sitting through that movie more than once. It's the one about the skaters, isn't it?"

I laugh at his admission. "You must have been forced to watch it with a girl."

He nods. "My sister-in-law, actually. She wanted to be a figure skater. Liv." Something passes over his face that I don't recognize. "Rance's wife."

"Rance?"

"Clarence. My brothers are ten and eight years older than I am, so Liv's always been like a big sister to me."

"That's nice."

"So—movie," he prompts. "We seem to go off topic a lot tonight."

"We do," I agree. "Anyway, I watched that movie with friends and since there was another Moira in the class, they started calling me M.K. because I looked like the actress in the movie, Moira Kelly."

He cocks his head to the side. "I can see it. But I think you're better looking."

"I thought we agreed no bullshit?"

"It's not." Clay reaches across the table and tucks my hair behind my ear, displaying the ragged, whitish-pink scar. "That looks like it was painful. How'd you get it?"

He's the only man who has ever noticed my scar and not said it looked ugly. I swallow past the lump in my throat.

"Biking accident," I say lightly. "I was sixteen and Flora and I got pushed off the road by a truck. I fell into barbed wire; she dislocated her arm. It ended any hope of her career in softball."

He traces the jagged line with a gentle finger. "And what did it do to you?"

I shrug. "It's not pretty."

"But you still are. Beautiful, actually."

I'm the first to drop my gaze again. When I glance back at him, Clay is looking around the restaurant. There are only two other tables still there, both who came in long after we did. "We've been here a while," I offer.

"Maybe I should take you home," he says. I'm happy to hear the reluctance in his voice.

"I guess so. I mean, they probably want us to go." I gesture to the waiter hovering nearby.

It's a quiet car ride home as I argue with myself about what to do next.

"This has been a great night," Clay says as he pulls up in front of my house. "Is it wrong to say I'm really happy Dean and Flora didn't marry who they went to marry?"

I laugh. "Do you know we've barely talked about them at all tonight?"

"Well, I don't normally go around talking about Dean, but I can see why I would tonight. But there were lots of other things to talk about. And I'm going to keep talking as I walk you to your door. Can I park here?"

"Maybe go around the corner," I suggest. It's on the tip of my tongue to add *So you don't have to rush,* but I don't say it. Because I don't know if I want him to rush away. Maybe I do.

Maybe I want him to stay.

The night air is crisp and cool for summer.

The scent of the flowers in the containers at the door brush my nose. Flora uses my porch as advertising for Fleur, arranging plants and flowers in more creative ways than she would at the store. This month she has filled the black urns with shades of orange; zinnias, marigolds, and petunias in a variety of shades, calibrachoa and nasturtium tumbling over the edges.

I pluck off a dead flower before unlocking the door.

"You could come in," I blurt. "For a bit. For a drink maybe. Or something. But that's it." I swallow, feeling like my words have tangled up like a bag of yarn. I invited Clay in, but for what? Even I don't know. "I have to get up early."

"I'd like to come in for a bit." Clay smiles and I relax. "To meet your cats even though I'm not a cat person."

"They're nice cats."

"Of course you'd say that because you're a cat person."

Will I ever get used to his smile? It's so wide and white and if I'm not careful, I'll find myself panting a little when he uses it on me. "But I need to tell you something." Clay takes my hand. "I don't want to sleep with you tonight. Obviously, I do," he corrects as my eyes widen with surprise and more than a little disappointment. "I really, really do, but don't let me."

"Don't let you have sex with me?" I repeat.

"Please."

"Please? I think this is the time I get offended." I pull my hand out of his grasp. "And rescind my invitation to come in."

"Ninety-five percent of the dates I go on, I end up having sex with them," Clay says in a rush. "I know I'm not saying this the right way."

It's the first time I've seen him flustered but it doesn't help. "That's so nice for you. Look, thanks for dinner but—"

"I want to wait for you," he says, the words tripping over each other in his rush.

"Pardon?"

"I don't wait for women. I'm not saying I force them or anything, but it happens. I want to wait for you, for when it means something." He grabs my hand. "I seem to be doing everything I can to mess up this date, but it's the last thing I want to do. It's been amazing getting to know you, M.K., and I want to see you again. Soon. Really soon."

"Then why do you want to wait?" I ask quietly. "I don't understand. I like you. I think you like me and—"

"I don't want to leave here with you thinking this was a one-night thing for me," Clay interrupts. He cups my cheek with his hand, and before I can stop myself, I lean into his hand. "Because it isn't. I already know I want more with you, and I want to prove that to you. Because I think you're going to mean something."

"Okay," I whisper.

"And I would like to kiss you goodnight, but not out here," Clay says with a relieved laugh.

"Come in and have a drink." I pull away from him when every part of me wants to move closer. "And meet my cats."

# Clay

THAT WAS THE STUPIDEST thing I've ever done.
I want nothing more than for M.K. to invite me in and for us to see what the rest of the night will hold but no, I have to come up with the most idiotic rejection ever.

I want M.K. as much as I've wanted any other woman, but not tonight. She's special, and I want to make it special.

I want to make *us* special.

"So how did you get three cats?" I ask, hoping M.K. can't tell that my voice is a little shaky. I really want to kiss her. It would have been easy to lean forward and touch my lips to hers and—

"I never meant to," M.K. says, pulling me out of my stupor as she unlocks the door. "After Ben died—"

"Who's Ben?"

It's the way she says his name. There has only ever been one woman who has ever said anything to make me jealous, so the sensation is an unusual one. I still recognize the sharp stab of pain in my stomach. "You haven't mentioned a Ben before."

"Long story," M.K. says stiffly as she opens the door. "Cats."

"Dead Ben," I retort. Thankfully she laughs, so I don't have to explain that I need to hear about him and any other men in her life more than I need to meet any cat.

"I'll tell you about him," she promises. She gives me a strange look. "For once I really want to tell you about him. But right now the cavalry is coming." The pitter-patter of paws sounds down the hall as all three cats come running. "This is Gulliver and he's always first for everything." M.K. sets her purse on the side table and reaches down to pick him up.

"Because he's the biggest." I take in the long-haired, orange cat as well as the narrow hallway leading into what seems like a living room. M.K.'s house is small and semi-detached. Maybe it's the cats, or maybe it's because I'm used to the space in my condo, but it seems cramped. Cozy, but cramped.

"Twenty-seven pounds. He's a big boy," she agrees, holding the cat, so he can check me out.

"Gulliver, for Gulliver's Travels?" I give him a cursory scratch on the head.

"Exactly." M.K. beams like I've won an award, and I smile in return. Her whole face lights up when she smiles.

She sets Gulliver down and wiggles her fingers to tempt the sleek gray, already winding her way around my feet. "That's Scarlett, and she's a flirt."

"I'm good with flirting." I bend to pet her. "Who's a pretty kitty?"

"I thought you didn't like cats?"

"I didn't say I don't like them, only that I'm not a cat person. I'm more into dogs."

"You'll like Flora's dog, then. She's got a bulldog named Cappie."

"Captain America?"

"You'd think, but no. Her grandmother named him Captain Jack Sparrow because she liked the pirate movies, but Flora shortened it when she took him after she passed."

"Interesting pet names."

M.K. laughs as she gestures down the hall to find a tiny white cat lurking. "That's Pennywise."

"Pennywise—from *It*?" I ask with disbelief. "The scary clown?"

"You must be a reader. I like that." She leads me down the hall and Pennywise skitters away. "He's shy, so don't be offended."

"As long as he doesn't try to pull me down into the sewer, I'm good. You like to—" The word is cut off as M.K. switches on the lamp in the living room, and I see the shelves reaching to the ceiling, packed with books. "You like to read," I finish.

"I do," she says proudly.

"It's like a library in here." I head for the shelves, Scarlett still at my heels. "This is great." I finger the spines reverently like a true reader does. "Really great. You've got quite the collection."

"I've had some since I was a kid," she admits, looking at me carefully. "My mother was very happy to get them out of the house. She's never understood my book fetish."

I turn, eyebrow raised. "A fetish?"

Her cheeks redden and I smile. "I like books."

"I like that you like books." I hold her gaze before turning back to the shelves. I like looking at M.K., but even more, I like making her look at me. It's like she's trying to hide at times, to duck inside herself.

What are you hiding?

"My sister-in-law forced me to read all these books growing up," I say as I study the shelves. "She told me it would help me relate to women. Understand them more. Of course I was into that, and therefore was the only twelve-year-old male to read the entire series of *Sweet Valley High*, thanks to Liv."

M.K. laughs with delight. "You're kidding!"

I grimace. "Unfortunately not. Todd and Elizabeth forever." I raise a fist in a mock cheer.

"Then you need to see this." She moves along the shelves, books carefully arranged by genre, then alphabetically, and pulls out a book with a red cover.

I groan as I recognize the blonde twins on the cover. "You're kidding me. They wrote another one."

"They did. I won't spoil it for you."

"Because you know I'm going to have to borrow that." I shake my head, wondering if Liv knows about the adult *Sweet Valley High* book.

"Be my guest." She hands me the book and as our fingers touch, I swear there are sparks.

I step away with a laugh. "Was that our electricity, or did you just give me a shock?"

"Shock," M.K. says weakly and points to the floor. "Carpet. It happens all the time."

"And here I thought I was special." I hold her gaze for a moment longer before turning back to the shelves. "What other treats do you have here?" My fingers trail over her collection of cookbooks. "Wow. You'd think you like to cook or something."

"Or something," she echoes.

"I have this one." I point to Nigella Lawson's *How to Eat*. "And all of Jamie Oliver's books. Liv got them for me. She thinks I should have been the Canadian version of Jamie."

"You like to cook?" M.K. asks with surprise.

"I do," I admit, my gaze still on the books, tipping her edition of Martha Stewart's *Baking Handbook* to display the cover. "But I really like to bake."

"You're just saying that because I own the patisserie," M.K. bursts out.

I shake my head with a grin. "It's not the most masculine hobby to have, so I don't admit it to many people. What do you think the guys on the baseball team would say if they knew I make cupcakes in my spare time?"

M.K leans closer. "Then you need to see my kitchen," she whispers.

My grin widens. "Anytime." She leads me into the next room, and I whistle even before she turns on the light. "This is going to be fun."

M.K. might not have a lot of spare space in her place but she makes the most of what she has. Her cupboards are open, and the shelves are impeccably organized, the cheap laminate counters spotless, save for a thick wooden cutting board beside the oven.

And the stove... "This is a beauty." I tap the stovetop, admiring the double oven in the Bosch. "I don't even have one of these, and I have all the toys."

"I know, right? I got a great deal for it, but I had to pay the moving guys almost as much to get rid of the old stove. It's not gas, though. My next place, I want to run a gas line." She opens a bottom cupboard door to show me what looks like an advertisement for KitchenAid appliances. "These are the rest of *my* toys."

Mixer, food processor... Is that a pasta maker in there? She's so excited talking about her appliances that I don't want to burst her bubble and tell her about my gas stove.

"What's your favourite kind of cupcake?" M.K pulls down a mixing bowl. I watch openmouthed as she grabs measuring cups and takes out a spatula.

"Are we making them?" Out of all the ways this night could have ended, I never would have come up with this scenario. But I like it. It's spontaneous—another side of M.K. I never expected.

"We don't have to," M.K. says apologetically, taking a big step away from the counter. "I just—I like baking at night. The house always smells so good when I wake up in the morning."

"I'm all for good smells. Let's do it!" I roll up my sleeves, wondering how to ask for an apron without sounding too fussy. "What's your favourite thing to make?"

"Are you sure?" she asks doubtfully.

All night long, I've gotten the impression that M.K. has been giving me little situations or scenarios to test me, like she wants me to prove I'm worthy. This is another one and by far the easiest. "You saw that little itty dessert they gave me. You think that was enough?"

M.K.'s smile is like the last flash of sun during a sunset. I have a pang of fear about when, not if, I'll eventually disappoint her.

Or maybe I won't. Maybe after all this time, countless attempts and relationships that I've shied away from, maybe she's the one.

I'm not sure if the sensation is excitement at the thought, or fear.

"I don't make a lot of cupcakes," M.K admits. "I mean, I do in my spare time, but these days, anything I make will usually make it to the patisserie."

"So what do you make for the patisserie?"

"Pastries, obviously and muffins, but I've been playing around with breakfast bars. There's this one I want to try with oats, flaxseed, with chia and pistachios."

I picture it in my mind. "You need some fruit in it or it'll be too heavy," I suggest.

"That's what I thought, too," she says eagerly. "I can't decide if I want cranberries or dried apricots."

"Too predictable. What about blueberries? Or bananas?"

She's so sweet when she's excited. And adorable. I've passed this test with superpower speed.

We spend a few minutes gathering ingredients, M.K. pointing out where everything is. As I peel my first banana, I glance over to see her studiously measuring flour. "You know, if this was one of those romantic movies, you'd spill all the flour, and we'd have a food fight about now," I say casually.

M.K. takes a pitch of flour between her fingers and aims it threateningly at me. "I can't do it," she says with a gasp, her shoulders slumping. "I can't even think of messing up my kitchen like that."

"Good," I say with a shudder. "Because I haven't even asked you for an apron."

Two hours later, we've gone through half a bottle of wine while we wait for the cupcakes and my bars to bake. The kitchen is full of enticing smells that have the cats standing guard at the door. M.K. won't let them enter the kitchen. Twelve perfect cupcakes sit on the cooling rack as M.K whips up a caramel icing and I carefully cut up the tray of breakfast bars—banana oat with Nutella and flakes of coconut sprinkled on top.

"These aren't going to be up to your standards, but they're not bad." I taste a corner. "Try. They're still warm." I'm proud of the Nutella inspiration.

"Mmm," she says appreciatively after I pop a small piece into her mouth. "That's good."

"That's going to be so good," I say as she finishes the icing. I swipe a finger along the edge of the bowl. "Mmm. I have a bad sweet tooth."

"I'll have to remember that." She's quick to ice the cupcakes, showing a lot more talent and technique than I do. I watch as she pulls out boxes.

"You need to have customized packaging," I say.

"You mean like with Pain au Chocolat on it?"

I nod. "Your logo. Your brand."

"I don't really have a brand," she confesses.

"You need a brand. Do you do orders at the patisserie?" When she nods her agreement, I continue eagerly. "What do you use?"

She points to the plain white boxes. "Them."

I shake my head. "You need something more. You're wasting the opportunity to advertise. You need to—" Suddenly I stop myself. "Sorry. Got caught up in work stuff. That's what I do—packaging and branding, and marketing."

"That's stuff I'm not very good at." M.K. takes a deep breath. "Could you maybe give me few pointers? If it's not too much to ask?"

"I'd love to. Can I stop by your patisserie tomorrow?"

"That'd be great." As she carefully packages half the cupcakes and most of the breakfast bars for me, I glance at the clock to see it's after midnight.

"Wow, I didn't realize it was so late."

M.K. grimaces. "I'm going to have a hard time getting up in the morning. I have to go to bed."

"I'd better go," I say automatically.

"I didn't mean that." Her cheeks flush prettily. I like it when she's flustered because I doubt it happens too often. "I don't want —I have to sleep but I don't want you to go. I mean, if you want to go…" She fidgets with the corner of the box and I take her hands.

"I've had an amazing time tonight."

"Me, too," she says breathlessly.

"I haven't kissed you all night."

"No…"

"I wanted to. Driving up to pick you up, that's all I could think about. When I could kiss you again, when it's not in front of people in a bar."

"Me, too," she whispers.

"And then that stuff about Heather and the texts and then here with your books and your baking…Do you know why I haven't kissed you yet?"

"I…maybe…I wondered."

I lean down and kiss her forehead then her nose. "Because I'm having so much fun with you."

"You are? That's good?"

"That's great. At least it is with me. I've never had this much fun with a woman. I've never come back to someone's place and talked about my love for *Sweet Valley High* and cupcakes. This is new for me."

"I've never talked about it with a man either." She laughs weakly.

"I'm glad I haven't kissed you yet tonight," I say in a low voice. "Or anything else."

"You are?"

"Because now it'll mean something, not just be a time waster."

"Kissing women is a time waster for you?"

"It has been before, but not with you." I touch her lips softly, gently feeling them move under mine.

She tastes like caramel.

I enjoy it for a long moment, her hands snaking around my neck, my hands firm at her waist. I want nothing more than to sweep her in my arms and run a touchdown dash to the bedroom, but I know moving too fast will scare her.

Feeling the way I do about her is beginning to scare me.

I draw away reluctantly, pressing my lips against her forehead, still with my eyes closed. "I wanted it to be like this," I murmur. "I hoped it would be. The first time I saw you, the way you smiled..." I pull back and open my eyes to find M.K. staring at me, wide-eyed and tremulous. "I knew it could be."

"Me, too," she whispers.

"Is that all you're going to say tonight?"

"Right now it's all I can say."

"Me, too." I kiss her again, and it's a long time before I manage to get out the door to go home.

## Chapter Ten

♥

### M.K.

**S**IX WEEKS LATER....

Clay groans as I slip out of his arms. He's a cuddler, something I never thought I'd get used to, but now I sleep so much better when his arms are around me.

I hover by the bed in case he wakes up, lingering as long as I can before I need to get dressed and to the patisserie.

His eyes stay closed, the dark lashes brushing against his cheek.

It's been six weeks, but my heart still gives a squeeze when I watch him sleep.

The first date, as terrible as it began, was only the beginning.

Six weeks and I haven't gotten past the giddy excitement of knowing Clay is mine. He dealt with the uncertainty and confusion of that first dinner by texting any woman he'd been seeing, or talking to, or even gotten their number in the last two weeks.

I was surprised at how many there were.

But Clay went through the list and told them all he was taken; that he'd met someone and was focusing on her. That it had been nice meeting them, but he was a one-woman man now.

He got a surprising amount of texts in return; some with laughing emojis, some with disbelief, all of them with an undercurrent of disappointment.

Since then he'd been honest and upfront when women approached him, or when they texted him.

"There's no one you have to worry about," he constantly assures me.

I'm not worried, or jealous, but I can't seem to bring myself to truly believe that this man—this amazing, funny, kind, respectful, and *hot* man wants to be with *me*.

Me.

I brush the hair off Clay's forehead with the hope he might wake up, but no such luck. Reluctantly, I head to the washroom.

I prefer to stay at my place because of the cats and because Dean has been staying with Clay, but his place is so comfortable, especially his bed. It's still hard to get up at four thirty to get to the patisserie by five, almost impossible if Clay wakes up, but I'm getting better at it.

For the last six weeks, we've been together every night; sharing a bed for the last five.

We had promised to take it slow after that first night, but my slow and Clay's are two different speeds. The whole relationship has been in fast-forward since we met. It's a literal whirlwind, and I love it.

I love him.

Using the light of the washroom, I slip quietly into the clothes I laid out the night before. Clay gave me a drawer in his bedroom and space in his closet. He made room for my face wash and moisturizing creams in the bathroom, which makes the counter cluttered because Clay has quite a few of his own products.

Luckily, the condo has two bathrooms because while it's been interesting to start a relationship with Clay and having Dean right in the middle of it, it might be a different story if we all had to share a bathroom.

If it was anyone but Dean, I might have had more of an issue, but the truth is that I adore him. He's become the brother I never had, the brother-in-law I've always wanted.

Thankfully, Flora finally woke up and realized what an amazing person she has in front of her. And it happened after we spent the evening at the karaoke place and right in front of all of us.

I felt like cheering when she kissed him.

Flora wanted to make sure Dean was over Evelyn, and from the few comments Dean made, I think he was unsure of how Flora felt about him, but The Kiss seemed to clear the air between them. It seemed like it knocked Dean's socks off.

Now Flora and Dean can move forward, and maybe catch up to Clay and me.

Dressed in my stained kitchen pants, with the tiny burns from a caramel accident last month dotting the fabric, I lean down and kiss Clay's forehead.

"Don't go," Clay mumbles with his eyes still closed.

"I have to. The patisserie won't open itself." Actually it might soon. Rhoda finally left on her own and even though it stretched the budget, I hired two new employees. Nikki is a cute, second-year university student whose perkiness delights the morning rush, and Reuben, my Scottish highlander, who can make the best cup of coffee I've ever tasted.

Business has been great since their arrivals. And Reuben has hinted he would be willing to start opening, which will give me a few more hours sleep.

And more time with Clay.

I'd love the time with him, but I'll be happy if he sleeps more. Regardless of how carefully I slip out of bed, he still wakes up, and most days he doesn't go back to sleep.

Clay's green eyes blink sleepily at me, and my heart tugs with guilt. "Go back to sleep," I plead. "It's Saturday morning."

"I'm up now." He yawns. "Early bed tonight."

"You say that every night." I've had years to adjust to the early morning, early bed routine, but often as I crawl into bed, he is still wide awake and ready to play.

I lean down again and kiss his forehead, his nose and finally his mouth. "You're already dressed." He sulks, his fingers tugging on the bottom of my black T-shirt.

"I'm very quick in the morning."

"I wish you weren't. I wish you were the laze-around-in-bed type."

"Not in the morning," I remind him. "But I can laze around in bed tonight."

Even this early, even half-asleep, his smile is blinding. "It's a date."

"You won't want to go somewhere?" I know I've completely turned around his life. Early mornings, instead of sleeping late and rushing into the office ten minutes late. Quiet evenings at home instead of late nights at the latest hotspot.

Commitment.

From what Clay has shared about his past, I know that's been the biggest change for him, but he keeps assuring me it's the one he's the happiest about.

I have to trust him. I have to believe him, and it's easy to when I'm in the moment, but it's when the insecurities start dripping into my head like the coffee machine, that I have problems.

Of course I don't tell him this. It's the one thing I've kept from him—how I feel about him and how it scares me more than anything. He hasn't told me he loves me yet, so I don't think he's ready. Or that he just doesn't love me. Maybe he's waiting for someone better, more suited to his energetic lifestyle, to come along.

"I'll make you dinner." As Clay sits up in bed, the sheets slide down and my gaze flickers to his smooth, bare chest. In the last few weeks, I've noticed changes there too, because early mornings means he goes to the gym before work. I was happy with his body the first time I saw it, but I have to admit, everything is just a little more defined now. "I've dragged you out for the last few nights, and I thought you'd appreciate a quiet night at home."

At home.

"You're going to cook?" I ask teasingly, without letting on the thrill that goes through me at his words.

"I thought I might bake, too." His hand fists and gives my T-shirt an insistent tug. Somehow I manage to pull away but he doesn't let go.

"The way to my heart is through my stomach," I say with a rueful smile. "You're stretching my shirt."

"I'll buy you a new shirt."

"I like this one."

"Don't you like me better?" He gives me a pleading smile, and reluctantly I kneel on the bed.

Clay's hands slide under my shirt as he circles my waist. "I like how you try to make me late."

He pulls me closer. "Good. The last thing I want to do is make you mad at me."

I ruffle his sleep-tousled hair. "I haven't found anything to get mad at you about. Should I look harder?"

"Don't bother." He grins with sleepy eyes. "I'm sure I'll find a way to mess it up."

"Don't say that."

"Are you afraid I'll jinx it?"

"Do I seem like the superstitious type?"

His hands tighten around my waist, and for a minute, I wish I had more time to linger. "You seem like my type."

After meeting Heather, after hearing stories of bad dates and Dean's jokes about how an old girlfriend stalked him, I think I'm the furthest from Clay's type, but I keep those thoughts to myself. "Good," I say instead.

"I suggested that Dean try and find other arrangements tonight," Clay says, pulling me onto his lap. Despite the ticking clock and the list of what I need to do at the patisserie, I bury my nose into the sensitive skin between his neck and his collarbone and inhale his Clay scent.

I like the way he smells. I like his cologne, his deodorant, even his soap.

I like him so much.

I pull away reluctantly. "Do you think he'll stay with Flora?"

"After last night? What do you think?"

"I hope so. I want them to be as happy as we are."

"Are you happy, M.K? Do I make you happy?" Clay's gaze is intent, serious and for a moment I think he might have the same insecurities I do. This is good, but it's happening fast, and what if we're doing something wrong? What if we're breaking some rule that will make the good deflate like a bad soufflé?

"Yes," I say simply, unwilling to give into my thoughts. "I'm happy."

# Clay

IT'S DIFFICULT, BUT I manage to fall asleep for a couple of hours after M.K. left. It still amazes me how much I miss her when I'm in bed without her. It's like she's a variation of the stuffed giraffe I had as a little boy. I refused to sleep without it, would barely let the thing out of my sight. It was horrible when my mother had to wash it.

I'm a thirty-two-year-old man and Gerry the Giraffe has been reincarnated into M.K.

When I wander, bleary-eyed, out of the bedroom, Dean is already awake and dressed. "Where you off to, dude?" He turns and I see he's in the process of rubbing sunscreen on his face. "You've got a streak there," I say, pointing to his cheek.

"I'm helping Flora with her garden job today," Dean says, eagerness loud and clear in his voice. But I don't think he's looking forward to digging in the dirt.

"Is this the same cute blonde who planted that kiss on you last night?" I raise an eyebrow as he runs a hand, still greasy with sunscreen, through his red hair. "The one that everyone in the parking lot saw?"

"I guess," he says, his cheek pink from embarrassment and the rigorous sunscreen application.

I scratch my stomach as I stretch. "So what's going on with the two of you?"

For weeks, Dean has been insisting his feelings for Flora are purely friendship, but after last night, it's clear to everyone that he feels differently. And I'm pretty sure Flora does, too.

Dean shrugs with a bemused grin. "I have no idea."

"Well, maybe you should figure that out. A day together has got to help with that. You looked pretty good together last night. You sounded pretty good, too. Singing," I add when he raises an eyebrow. "I have no idea how your kiss sounded. I wasn't paying that close enough attention."

"Apparently Patrick was." Dean pulls out his cell to show me a series of texts that Flora's nephew Patrick sent him last night. I laugh out loud.

I think Patrick is her nephew. They seem more like cousins or even brother and sister. M.K. tried to explain Flora's family to me one day when she was baking cookies, but I liked the sight of her in an apron so much, and one thing led to another, and well, she burnt the cookies.

"Are you doing something with Flora tonight?" I ask, heading into the kitchen for coffee. Dean is a good roommate in that he always puts on the coffee and always makes sure he leaves enough for me.

Dean follows me. "I'm not sure."

I glance up at the hesitation in his voice. "Do you really not have any idea what's going on with the two of you?"

"No. We're friends, but now I don't know. I don't know if last night changed things."

"Trust me, bro. Things have changed. And it's about time."

"You think?"

"C'mon, if you saw the two of you going at it, you'd know. She's into you."

"That might have been just last night."

"If you're worried that she's already friend-zoned you, forget about it. From the looks of things last night, that line has been jumped over. You're good to go." I shake my head as I pour myself a coffee, the scent of the brew forcing my senses wide awake.

"But what if she's not over Thomas?"

Now I can hear the fear in his voice. He's got it so bad for Flora, and that's a good thing, if he can pull it together. "Look, bro, I don't know Flora very well, but what I do know, she seems like a pretty cool girl. And from what M.K. says, she's been over that Thomas arse for a while now. I don't think you have anything to worry about. I don't think you *had* anything to worry about when you came up with the friend stuff."

"You think?"

"I trust my girl." Pride seeps into those four words. I trust M.K. I love M.K.

I love her.

And I'm going to tell her tonight.

"Your girl, huh?" Dean grins. "Have to admit, that sounds a bit strange."

I smile widely as I lift my coffee. "I know, right?"

"But good. Nice. I like her." Dean pulls the to-go cup from the cupboard and fills it with coffee, adding milk and sugar.

I hand him a few of the power bars he lives on. "So do I."

"More than like?" he asks with a raised eyebrow. Before he stayed with me, there was no way we'd ever have this conversation. Being roommates has done interesting things to our friendship.

I shrug, unable to stop the goofy grin spreading across my face. "I was going to tell her tonight. It's been two months since we met in Vegas."

"Has it been that long?"

Reminding Dean about Las Vegas means reminding him that it's been two months since Evelyn dumped him at the altar. I hope that doesn't mess him up with whatever is going on with Flora. Because if something happens with them, it's going to affect M.K. and me, as much as we'll try not to let it. I want to see Dean happy, but even more, I want to stay happy with M.K.

I've never felt this way about a woman before.

"You're thinking about her, aren't you?" Dean demands, interrupting my thoughts.

"Who?"

"M.K. You've got this look on your face." Dean laughs as I give an offhanded wave. Yes, I was thinking about M.K. I'm always thinking of her, wondering what she's doing, wanting to tell her something that's happened in my day. Wondering what's going on in her day.

"Go," I say, pointing to the door. "Flora's probably waiting for you. Don't screw it up."

He takes the cup and the bars. "Let's hope not."

Once Dean leaves, I wander around the condo, picking up his things. He's already taken the sheets and blankets off the couch and folded them neatly. The pile sits beside the couch with his pillow resting on top. It's not that Dean's a messy guy, but I'm a bit of a neat freak, and I like to keep things put away. I know he's trying, but both of us know it's impossible to keep up to my standards.

I've never had a roommate before and it took some getting used to him, but I haven't minded having him here as much as I thought I would. He keeps saying he won't stay for long, and I know he's looking for a place.

What choice did I have? I couldn't let him stay on the street after Evelyn kicked him out of the house. And if my place is impersonal, hotel living would be worse.

Besides, he says my cupcakes make up for sleeping on a couch.

I head to the kitchen. A few touches of buttons floods the space with music from my Spotify list, the latest from Drake, Post Malone, and Khalid. There's a ton of things I should be doing, from getting a jump on the next project at work, to going to the gym, but I feel like baking for my girl.

I like to bake for M.K. because no one else ever makes her anything. She's an amazing baker, an incredible cook. She's my kitchen goddess, and in the weeks we've been together, I've learned so much from her.

Our first date ended with cupcakes, so tonight I'll start with them.

While I set up the ingredients for a simple vanilla cupcake with brown sugar and bourbon icing, I set up my iPad to FaceTime.

"Do I have the time difference straight? This is really early for you, Clayton," Liv says when it connects. It's the middle of the afternoon in London and she's at her PC, wearing her glasses and a heavy sweater that droops off her shoulder.

"I like early now," I say with a grin, trying desperately to keep my eyes off her bare shoulder.

Liv leans into the screen until her nose touches it. "Is this really Clay? King of sleeping in with his latest hot girlfriend tucked in beside him?"

"You know I don't do sleepovers." At least I didn't before M.K. I had rarely brought women home to my place because I preferred to sleep alone in my own bed.

Liv grimaces. "Well, no I don't, but thanks for the information."

"Well, I might be doing more sleepovers now," I say with a bigger grin. "I met a girl."

"You've never had trouble meeting girls, Clayton." Liv sighs. "It's what you do with them after you meet them that causes the concern."

"Yes, but this one is special. And don't tell me they're all special, because you know that they're not."

"Actually, I don't know anything, because you've never called to tell me about a girl before. Or woman. How old is this extra-special female?"

"Twenty-nine."

Liv picks up her mug. I'm sure it's tea—weak tea with a generous spoonful of sugar. Her tea drinking began when she and Rance moved to London. Before that, she had a serious coffee addiction. "Ah, the marrying age. I remember when I was that age. All my friends were jealous that Clarence had been so quick about putting the ring on my finger. Good times!"

"You make it sound like it was so long ago." I begin to measure flour and baking powder, dumping it into the mixing bowl.

"Twenty-nine was a long time ago for me," she reminds me.

"Forty isn't that old."

She leans closer again. "Can't you see my crow's feet? All these wrinkles that keep popping up."

"You're still as beautiful as the day Clarence brought you home," I say loyally, my heart giving a tug. I'll always remember the first day I met her, how my eight-year-old self was in awe of the coltish fifteen-year-old who had taken over the kitchen with her free-spirited beauty.

Liv smiles widely. "And that's why you're my favourite brother-in-law."

"No, it's because Clyde is an ass," I say ruefully.

She laughs. I love making a woman laugh. I look at this as the first round of foreplay. But not for Liv because that would be wrong. Very wrong.

"So tell me about her." I see her settle back into her chair, her mug of tea in her hands. "Does she like your cupcakes?"

I add the vanilla bean, the seeds sprinkling on the flour. "She loves my cupcakes. I'm making some for her now. She owns a patisserie and bakes even better than I do."

"Well, it's always nice for a woman to do something better than her man. What's her name?"

"M.K." Liv gives a groan of disappointment. "Moira Margaret," I relent.

"What's the K stand for, then?"

"It's a long story."

"Aren't you glad I have nothing better to do than to listen?"

## *Chapter Eleven*

♥

# M.K.

IT TAKES ME TWO cups of coffee that morning before I start to feel like I'm functioning properly. I've always been a morning person, so the early hours of the patisserie never fazed me. But I do need at least seven hours of sleep at night and these days I'm lucky if I average five. I need a day to lie around in bed.

Preferably with Clay.

At least I have Reuben with me this morning, and I make a point of asking him to do most of the kitchen set-up while I sort out the paperwork in the office. If he's ready to open, I need to be able to trust him to do it. Maybe I'll give it a try in a couple of weeks.

Once we open, the line of customers is steady, full of smiling couples enjoying the weekend, fathers with young kids bribing them with treats, and the usual older couples stopping in after their morning walk. Despite my tired eyes, I smile and make a point to say a few words to all.

I escape back into the kitchen after a few hours in desperate need of coffee.

## CHAPTER ELEVEN

"You look a wee bit peaked," Reuben says, offering me with a warm croissant on a plate.

"What exactly is peaked?" I ask after thanking him for the pastry. I'm not sure if he thinks I should eat, or he wants me to sample the croissant, which he made this morning. In any event, I'm quick to devour it.

"Tired. Hungry. Not yourself," Reuben explains in his thick accent.

"I do need sleep," I admit, punctuating the words with a yawn.

"Your new beau keeping you up all hours?" Suddenly Reuben's expression is one of horror. "I'm not supposed to say things like that, am I?"

"It's fine," I tell him. "We're all friends here. And you've heard Adam digging for details. He's the worst of them."

"He's a fun lad."

I smile. "I think he'd appreciate the description."

"Take a moment; we've got it covered."

"Thanks, Reuben."

I'm still back there, leafing through my macaron recipes when Adam pushes open the door. "Boss Lady, your *man* is here to see you."

Wiping my hands on my apron, I can't stop the smile that spreads across my face. I had left Clay's place only a few hours ago, but already it seems like forever. My insides go all melty like a stick of butter does when it's left too close to the stove when I see him standing at the counter.

"What are you doing here?" My gaze flicks to the customers nestled into the tables dotting the room. Too many for me to sneak a kiss.

But Clay has no such qualms and snakes a hand along my neck to pull me close, dropping a chaste-but-not-chaste kiss on my eager lips. "I missed you."

"You just saw me." But I can't stop the smile from widening. I love how Clay is so open with his feelings and his affections. There's no brooding, or sulking, or me wondering what's on his mind. If he has something to say, he says it.

He kind of reminds me of Flora in that extent, but that's it. The last thing I want to do is date a man who reminds me of my best friend.

"I think I'm allowed to miss you." That smile. The way it crinkles the skin around his eyes…The naysayer in me says Clay will have so many wrinkles and laugh lines when he's older but the soft, gooey centre in me loves the way his eyes twinkle when he smiles.

I've got it so bad.

"You missed Dean heading out bright and early to hang with your girl," Clay says, tearing me away from thinking about how his eyes will look when he's older. "He wouldn't say much about the lip-lock last night."

"That's a gentlemanly thing, but is it bad that I really want him to open up about how he feels about Flora? This has been going on long enough."

"It's pretty painful to make us go through this," Clay agrees.

For my second date with Clay, we spent most of the evening talking about Flora and Dean and their situations that brought them together and then apart. After all, it was the two of them who brought us together.

Since then, we've watched things unfold with a detached sense of interest, like the non-fans of *Game of Thrones* must feel watching the final episodes of the series. Both Clay and I do agree that Flora and Dean have wasted enough time and need to get it together. They're perfect for each other.

Not as perfect as Clay and I, but pretty close.

Clay moves to the side to let me serve the next customer. When that's done, Adam brings Clay a dark roast with sugar and a white takeout bag. "I think we can all assume this is on the house." He winks at me. "Favourite customer and all."

Clay clutches his chest as he flashed his smile at Adam. "I'm your favourite customer? Aw, thanks, Adam."

"You should thank the boss lady," Adam simpers as he skips away.

"I'll thank the boss lady later tonight," Clay says, dropping his voice in a way that tickles me to the tips of my toes.

It's never been this way with a man before. Even with Ben, who I thought I loved more than life itself, I was never this excited with him. Clay makes everything bigger, brighter, better.

I think I love him.

I know I do.

It's the only thing we haven't told each other, and I don't know what we're waiting for.

I know what I'm waiting for—for him to say it first. Because no matter how much I can tell Clay cares about me, there's the little voice in my head that reminds me that Ben cared about me too, and he cheated on me.

Clay peeks in the white bag, not realizing the turmoil in my head. "Pain au chocolat?"

"I don't think you've had one before," I say. "At least not from me."

"Do you know," he begins slowly, "I think I have. My secretary brought me one once."

"That was nice of her." Clay has told me all about how Pearl and Rashida run his office life.

"You know what?" Amazement spreads on his face. "This bag. She gave it to me the *day* you called me. That first time after Dean and Flora met again."

"Really?"

"It's like it was fate. Somehow I would have found my way to you, even if it was through your very delicious pastries. It's like we're meant to be together."

I smile. Clay talks about fate sometimes, that we were destined to be together. I don't like the thought of leaving things to chance, but even I have to admit it was a lucky set of circumstances that brought us together.

Clay glances around to make sure there's no one behind him in line before he opens the bag and breaks off a piece of pastry. "Fate tastes great." I laugh, and he leans in to kiss me again. The customer waiting in line beside him smiles indulgently at us. Clay gives him a grin and holds up his bag and coffee. "I'm going to go because you're busy. And I'm going to eat that in the car. Or maybe when I get to the office. Because I'm pretty sure I'm going to make a mess, and I'm not ready to do that in front of you."

"You can make a mess in front of me." I laugh.

Clay shakes his head. "Nope. You're the only one I know who can make a pot of spaghetti sauce without getting a drop on you, so I can't let you see that side of me yet."

Clay is joking, but his words jolt me. "I want to see all the sides of you," I say quietly.

His expression sobers and he sets down his cup to reach for my hand. "You do. I was joking."

"I know but...is it wrong that I want to know everything about you? It's not stalking or something, is it?"

Now he lifts my hand and kisses my fingers that still smell like melted sugar. "You do know everything about me. I'm an open book. Now you, my lady of mystery, are a different story."

As much as I'm trying, I know I'm still holding part of myself back. I'm naturally reserved and prefer to keep things close to my chest. I know that. Flora tells me that at least once a month as she begs me to tell her what's going on inside of my "inscrutable face." That's what she calls it because I can keep a poker face better than anyone I know.

What I don't tell her, what I can't, is that I'm afraid if I open up about something small and silly, a whole bunch of other stuff is going to bubble over. Once I start, I'm not sure I'm going to be able to stop.

"Ask me anything," I say bravely, knowing that Clay won't ask me anything difficult, at least not then and there. I know he's only stopped in on his way to work for a couple of minutes and should be there by now, so there wouldn't be time to get into anything serious.

There's a lot I have to tell him, but not now.

"Will you move in with me?"

I snatch my hand away.

# Clay

I DIDN'T MEAN TO ask her *then*.
I was saving it for tonight. After my stint at the office, I'd planned on heading to the hardware store to get a key cut for M.K. She's already given me one, but lately we've been spending more nights at my place, even with Dean there.

Something about how my bed is a little more comfortable than M.K.'s.

The truth is that it's not just the bed. M.K. lives in a tiny two-bedroom house that's nice enough, but there's a new baby on one side of the wall, and on the other side, they're building a brand new house. Except for the first night when we baked, I've never once been in her house without the sounds of crying, or hammers, and the shouts of the workers seeping through her thin walls. I don't know how her cats handle the constant noise. I've thought more than once about taking them to my place, but besides my allergies, Dean's not a cat person.

He's actually frightened of cats; big, strong guy's legs turn to jelly whenever there's a cat sniffing at him. It's pretty funny to watch.

I had an idea in my head about how to ask her tonight—what I would do and how I would ask her. I like grand gestures. If I ever propose—when I ever propose—I'm going to do it right.

So it surprises me that I blurt it out like that.

I can't read the expression on M.K.'s face. But I hear the quick intake of breath. "You want to live together?" she asks in a quiet voice that makes me nervous.

"We're together most nights anyway." Not only does it seem simple to me, I really want her around all the time. I miss her when she's not there. "We can talk about it tonight," I concede, hating to see the indecision in her eyes.

"We don't have to," M.K. says with conviction. "I think moving in together would work. I'm only trying to figure out where."

The tangle of nerves in the pit of my stomach suddenly untangles, leaving me sagging with relief, and blocks out the shock that M.K. agreed so quickly. This is M.K., the woman who plans things three days in advance and has lists of pros and cons for every major decision. There's no way she can make a choice that quickly.

But she just did.

"Really?" I laugh loudly with stunned happiness. "I thought maybe—I should have waited until tonight."

Her eyes dart around the patisserie. "Maybe. But it's fine."

"I should have waited, but you asked if I had anything to ask you, and I've been thinking about this for a while. I got excited." Her smile widens and I know then it's going to be okay. "Maybe I was nervous."

"You were nervous asking me to live with you?" she asks.

"Me? No," I scoff. "Maybe. Maybe a lot. I've never done something like this before. From sleepovers to roommates." I heave a sigh and then another. "It's a lot."

"We don't have to," M.K. assures me. "We can slow down."

"I don't want to."

And I don't. It's only been weeks, but I know in my heart that M.K. is who I want. I want a future with her. A place of our own, a life together. It's like I've unlocked a secret box that is unfolding into infinity with choices and decisions and M.K. at the end.

"Neither do I," M.K. admits with a shy smile. "But I'm not sure where we'd live," she muses aloud. "Your place is nice but small and you don't like my place—"

"It's not that I don't like it—"

"Babies and hammering and the cats—"

"I love your cats. They just make me sneeze a bit. But I'm okay with sneezing."

I love the affection in her eyes. "We'll buy stock in Claritin. But maybe we should look at finding a new place together?"

For a minute my heart stops. "Buy a place together?" I hadn't gotten further than thinking about exchanging keys and giving her more drawer space and Dean moving out, not about real estate agents and lawyers, and a binding commitment.

My thoughts must have flown across my face because M.K.'s smile falters. "It's too soon. Too much."

"No..." I reach for her hand and the touch of her soft skin centres me. "No, it's not. It's just that I never thought of that. Yet. But why not. Neither of our places really work for us. They're not big enough."

"But we can make it work."

"Or we can make something new work. With a really big kitchen." I see the wheels working in M.K.'s mind, and I know by the time I get to my car, she'll have a plan for this etched out. "And a gas stove."

I know it'll be a good plan. A solid plan for our future.

I can't seem to catch my breath. "We can talk about this tonight," I say, pushing back from the counter. "You need to get back to work."

She frowns as she glances over her shoulder. I know her business means the world to her, and I'm proud of what she's accomplished. And she's done it all on her own.

That thought creates a funny feeling inside, like the first time I saw Dean hit one out of the ballpark. I'm happy and proud but... jealous? I want to be able to do that. Accomplish something on my own.

"I should but I have another minute..." Another glance, and I smile, any residue of envy wiped away.

"Go. We'll talk tonight."

I kiss her goodbye, conscious of the customers watching with fond smiles. She's created something really special, and I can't help but be proud of her. I kiss her again, and with a wave at Adam grinning from behind the cash register, I leave.

And walk down the sidewalk to Flora's store. Flowers would be perfect for tonight.

I forgot all about Heather working there until I open the door and see her standing behind the counter with Imogene.

Imogene greets me with a wide smile. "Hello, Clay."

Heather is not smiling. In fact, her foxlike face is pinched with annoyance. "Clay."

I regret ever coming up with the idea to buy M.K. flowers.

"Hi." Still, I turn on the smile, wondering how I can get around this. I need to smooth things over with Heather so she won't bad-mouth me to Imogene and Flora and do it without leading her on. "Small world, isn't it? How are you?"

"You'd know if you had texted me back."

My smile tightens. "I did text you back and told you I wasn't able to see you anymore."

"I think there was more than a few you didn't respond to. I don't like being treated like that."

I wince. "About that." Excuses fly through my mind, but that wouldn't be fair to M.K. "I did get your texts, but a lot was happening at the same time." I glance at Imogene who is watching intently, one hand on her belly. "I got her text a minute before I got a call from M.K. The first one."

"Ah," Imogene's face relaxes.

"Who is this M.K.?" Heather asks with a note of irritation in her voice.

"Flora's friend. She works at Pain au Chocolat," Imogene supplies. "You met her when you came in for the interview."

"I take it you got the job." I glance between them. "Congratulations."

"Tomorrow will be her first time on her own," Imogene says, her hand still resting on her stomach. "Not soon enough for me. This little guy feels like he's about to pop out any minute."

"You look great," I say automatically. Heather clicks her teeth and my heart sinks. Who knows what she's going to say about me? At least I'm telling Imogene the truth. "Pregnancy suits you. There's a glow, just like they say."

"They also say you get your energy back in the final trimester. They lie."

I smile. "Good luck with everything." My smile falters as I glance at Heather. "I—uh, I need some flowers."

"Of course you do," Heather says under her breath.

"And here I thought you came in to see me." Imogene smiles.

"I always come in to see you." The easy banter I've developed with Imogene feels awkward in front of Heather, who is now standing with a sour expression and her arms crossed across her chest. "M.K. is my girlfriend," I explain quietly to Heather.

"A girlfriend?" she asks skeptically. "A real, live girlfriend? From the king of anti-commitment?"

"People change," Imogene says. "Love does strange things."

"I know—it seems impossible, doesn't it?" I say, wanting Heather to stop scowling at me. "But we met in Las Vegas two months ago, for about an hour, and I couldn't stop thinking about her. I didn't know her last name, where she was from and I had no way of getting in touch with her. But fate stepped in and we found each other."

"Literally right around the corner from each other. It's a nice story," Imogene says dreamily. "Almost as good as Flora and Dean's, *if* they ever get together." She pushes away from the counter. "I'll get your flowers. Do you have a preference?"

"Something pretty," I say weakly, at a loss to even name a flower right then.

Imogene laughs and waddles over to the refrigerator where colourful blooms sit inside buckets of water.

"I'm so happy for you," Heather says sarcastically. "That you've found true love."

"I didn't mean to hurt you." I hold her gaze. "I had no idea I'd ever find M.K. again."

"Even if you hadn't, it would have never worked out with us." Heather rolls her eyes. "You made that perfectly clear."

"I don't think I made anything clear," I say. "Except that I wasn't looking for anything serious."

"Until now."

"Until M.K.," I correct. "I think we were looking for two different things."

Heather tosses her head. "It doesn't matter now. You don't matter, at least not to me. But some people..." Her tone changes, becomes sly. "Do you remember my friend Abby, who you also went out with?"

I take a step back. Abby. Abby of almost a year ago; fun, sexy. Dancer. "Of course I remember Abby."

A memory nudges me. Didn't Abby text me a couple of weeks ago? When I first met Heather? "I didn't realize you were friends."

Heather smiles knowingly and I feel the first prickle of fear. Obviously I crossed signals with her, and now I have to suffer. But there's nothing she can say or do—it's not like I promised her anything.

It was just drinks.

"It's a small world, isn't it?" Heather says mockingly. "I bet you don't remember that Abby was trying to get in touch with you, too."

"I saw that. But it was at the same time as—"

Heather cuts me off with a wave. "I know. M.K. Love of your life. But you should really get in touch with Abby. She has some big news."

"I doubt she'd want to share anything with me," I say ruefully, looking to see if Imogene has finished with the flowers. She has a bouquet in her hand but keeps adding to them.

That's enough flowers for today.

"Oh, I think she would." Heather gives me a sly smile.

"I'll have to text her, apologize for not getting back to her." Is that what Heather wants? For me to grovel to every woman I've ever known?

"Apologize? That might be a start."

I narrow my eyes. "A start to what? As far as I remember, Abby and I left on good terms. No hard feelings there."

"Yes, but how good is your memory? Seems to me that you've forgotten a few things. Basic courtesy, the fact that Abby had your baby…"

I drop the bag holding my pain au chocolat.

## *Chapter Twelve*

♥

# M.K.

I RUSH INTO THE kitchen as soon as Clay walks out the door of the patisserie. Did the customers hear that? Was the elderly man at the corner table with his paper and café au lait listening to every word?

Did I really hear Clay say he wants to move in together?

I did. I really heard Clay say those words.

Were the two women in their running outfits who stopped in to get the full-sized latte, with an extra squirt of vanilla wondering how I could have agreed so quickly?

Did I really agree to move in with Clay with no plan or schedule in place? And buying a place together? Did I really suggest that?

When I bought my house, I took a week to decide, spent two sleepless nights and almost gave myself an ulcer. Why would I want to do that again?

Because Clay asked me.

I lean against the wall beside the swinging door and hug myself. "He wants to move in together," I whisper. How can I keep quiet when all I want to do is shout, scream, sing and tell the world I have a man who wants me.

I can't do that with a patisserie full of customers but I can dance.

I flick the volume of the radio and am rewarded with an AC/DC song playing.

AC/DC was a personal favourite of my father's.

I dance around the kitchen, shaking my head, my hips, my ass with moves that would make a stripper proud. Grabbing a spoon off the counter, I mouth the words with abandon, wishing I was alone in my car so I could sing loud and proud.

Clay wants to move in with me. Clay wants to live with me.

Clay wants me.

Suddenly sober I stop mid-step, still holding the spoon as a microphone. How can Clay want to live with me so soon? It's *too* soon. We've only been together a few weeks; there's no way he can be ready to make such a decision. There's no way that *I* can be ready.

My shoulders slump as Pink Floyd replaces AC/DC on the radio. I can't move in with him. Because what happens if I give up everything, and Clay figures out that it's too soon, or he's not ready, or meets someone else...

"He's not Ben," I hiss. "He's *Clay* and he loves me."

He loves me.

Does he? He hasn't even said it. And what if he does? What does that mean? Where is this leading?

What do I do now?

Adam bumps open the door with his hip, a questioning smile on his face. "What is going on back here? I heard music. Are you— it seems...you're *dancing*."

"No, I'm not, it's just—"

"You were dancing," Adam corrects. "You only dance when we sell out of croissants or you get an office-party gig. It means you're happy."

"I—yes," I admit. "I'm happy. I think."

"Why do you have to think about it? What did The Man say to get you so giggly?" Adam carefully closes the swinging door and leans against the counter. From the expression on his face, he's not leaving anytime soon.

"I—" I clap a hand over my mouth to muffle my giggle. Why can't I finish a sentence? A thought. Why can't I blurt out to Adam what Clay said?

What happens if Clay takes it back?

"M.K.?" Adam crosses his arms with an expectant glare. "Moira Margaret? What's going on?"

"I should have never told you my full name," I mutter, turning away from Adam's eagerness.

"I would have stolen your wallet to check if you hadn't. It's a tease when you go by initials. And so is this conversation!" He tosses his head and then is suddenly distracted by a container of macarons I pulled out earlier. Carefully selecting a mango cookie, he pops it in his mouth.

I watch him, feeling the words bubble inside me like a pot boiling over. "Clay asked if I want to move in with him," I confess in a rush.

Adam blinks, his mouth full of macaron. "Is that all?"

"Is that all?" I parrot.

He chews and swallows, taking time to choose his words. "Well, yes. You spend every night together as it is. Plus it would save on rent."

I shake my head. For all his exuberance about life, Adam has a practical streak that constantly surprises me. "I guess."

"What's your problem, then?"

"I don't have a problem."

"You totally do. You were in here dancing and I'm sorry I missed that because obviously you've gotten it in your head and talked yourself out of being excited about it. Probably gave yourself a talking to about how Clay is going to meet someone else and renege on the whole thing."

Now I'm the one blinking with surprise. "How do you know that?"

Adam waves his hand before pulling a bag of milk out of the walk-in refrigerator. "Please. I've been working here for two years, five months and sixteen days, and while you don't offer much in terms of backstory, you do tell me some. And when I get a nugget, I can go to Patrick and ask him because, in case you forget, he has known you since he was born."

I frown. "What exactly did Patrick tell you?"

"Nothing bad. Nothing you wouldn't have told me yourself, given a chance and a bottle of tequila.

My shoulders sag. "You know about Ben."

"Yes." There is no hesitation in his voice. Adam may be a lot of things, but he's exceedingly truthful.

"You know about my father?"

Another wave. "That's old news, and nothing to be ashamed, or angry, or offended about. Or anything else."

"You should get out front. I'll be there in a minute," I say in a low voice.

"Which means I've offended or angered you, and you don't want to talk. Look, M.K., you're clearly freaking out here, so why don't you run and talk to Flora? She's always able to talk you down, and I can hold down the fort here."

"She's doing a garden today. I'll talk to her later."

"Make sure you do." Adam touches my shoulder. "The two of you are really cute, you know. You and Clay, as well as you and Flora. I like the two of you. Don't mess it up by being in your head, or I'll make a move on him, okay?"

The thought of that brings a faint smile to my lips. "I'm not sure that's the best idea."

"What are you talking about? If Patrick and I really used the mojo, I'm sure we could convert both Clay and Big Dean. Once you've had gay, you'll always want to be my Bae," he sings, and my laughter bubbles out. "That's better." Adam smiles with satisfaction. "Get out of your head. Things will be just fine."

# Clay

Flowers forgotten, my phone is in my hand as the door of Fleur swings shut behind me. At least I picked up my pastry bag.

A baby?

Abby had a baby—my baby?

The timing works. I hate to say it, but it works. Abby and I dated for six weeks—a relationship length of time for me—a year ago. I remember because I went to my parents for Thanksgiving and didn't invite her. Liv had been furious with me, but Abby took it in stride, or so I thought. We mutually ended things soon after.

Thanksgiving was last week.

I liked Abby. She was cool and liked things casual. I liked her as much as I could like someone who isn't M.K. But—a baby. She wasn't pregnant when we broke up. I would have known.

What do I do now? What am I supposed to do with this information?

I don't bother texting Abby. This calls for person to person, or at least voice to voice to begin with. I find her name in my contacts as I stalk to my car, the bag with the pain au chocolat crumpled between my coffee and my hand.

"Clay?"

Abby's voice is hesitant as she picks up. I stand frozen by my car at a loss what to say. "Did you have my baby?" I blurt.

"What?"

"I just saw Heather, and she said you had a baby, and it's mine. Is it?" I hold my breath, not knowing what I want her to say.

Do I have a child that I never knew about?

"I tried to tell you," she says defensively.

My breath whooshes out in a huff, and I sag against my car. "You had my baby?" I whisper hoarsely. "My child."

"I tried to tell you," Abby echoes.

"You didn't try very hard!" I glance around, not wanting anyone to hear this conversation, not wanting M.K. to hear. "Jesus, Abby, how can you just throw this on me?"

"I'm not throwing anything on you. You're the one who called me. I wasn't even going to tell you."

"*Why not?*" My voice raises enough that a customer walking into Pain turns to look at me. "Look, we need to talk about this. I need to know things—a lot of things. And not here on the phone. But now."

"Are you sure about this?"

I pull my cell away from my ear and stare at it like it's about to self-combust. I'm about to self-combust. How could Abby keep this from me?

"Of course I'm sure. This is a *baby* we're talking about."

"My baby," Abby corrects.

"*Our* baby," I insist.

"If this is really what you want. I'll meet you at your apartment in an hour."

· ♥ · ♥ · ♥ · ♥ · ♥ ·

It's the longest hour of my life.

I forget about going to the office, my plans with M.K. for that night. All I can think about is that I have a child.

And it's not like the news has destroyed my world or anything. It's like Abby telling me she had my baby makes everything clearer, more concise. I'm a *father*.

I'm pacing the condo after picking up everything small enough to fit in a baby's mouth when Abby buzzes. I doubt I'll ever remember where I put my car keys.

I have the door open at the sound of the elevator chime.

Abby greets me with a cool smile as she walks down the hall. "Clay."

I don't say anything, just stare at the car seat she's holding. "Is that—?"

"Something smells good," she says, walking in. A blanket covers the car seat so I can't see the sleeping baby.

I don't even know if it's a boy or a girl. How could I not ask that?

Would it matter? "Abby," I warn, "is that—?" My throat is tight and drier than a bottle of fine Chardonnay.

"This is Theo. Your son."

A boy. I have a son. My chest puffs with pride as I shut the door behind her. "Theo. My son."

"Hope you like the name." Abby strolls into the condo, her gaze flickering to the couch, the kitchen, the table. We spent a fair amount of time here during the weeks we were dating.

At the open bedroom door.

We spent a lot of time in there, too.

She sets the car seat on the coffee table and sinks onto the couch.

"Can I—can I see him?"

Abby rolls her eyes as she folds back the blanket. "Don't wake him up."

My heart clutches in my chest as I set eyes on my son. Theo is asleep, his hands fisted in his lap, his downy, blond hair ruffled. I search him for signs of myself. "He's mine?"

"I'm happy to do a paternity test, or you can trust that I was only sleeping with you during that time. You know as well as I do that we had a good thing going, and I wasn't about to mess it up. Even though neither of us wanted a commitment."

I turn my gaze to Abby, at her cool smile, her unblinking brown eyes. I remember how it was with us; I know she's telling the truth. Theo is mine, the result of a miniscule margin of failure in birth control. "Looks like we've got some commitment now."

"And some issues."

"How old...?" I try and do the numbers in my head and fail miserably. I lean forward and study his face intently. Is that my nose? The wisp of hair falling onto his forehead is a darker blond than mine. My hand reaches forward on it's own volition, stroking a gentle finger along his fist resting on his leg. He's wearing gray jogging pants and a blue shirt. One of his white socks is falling off and I carefully adjust it.

"He's eighteen weeks old. Almost five months. He's a good boy—sleeps well and growing bigger every day He's twelve pounds now. He eats well." I can't help but notice that Abby tells me this without the tired but proud smile of a new mother. I've seen that smile so many times on Liv's face. Even Imogene lights up when she talks about her pregnancy.

But there's no light in Abby.

"How was the pregnancy? The birth?" Why didn't you tell me? I want to scream, but I know the answer. Abby was—is—independent to a fault. It's something that drew me to her. She never needed me, never

needed anyone. She would have had the baby by herself just to prove that she could.

"The pregnancy went well. I was able to keep dancing until I was six months, and then I spent the next two months training my replacements."

"Was that healthy for him?"

She gestures coolly to the sleeping baby. "As you can see, he's just fine."

"I don't know that he's fine because he's sleeping. And I can't tell that he's fine because I've never seen him before!" The hold on my anger slips, and the words erupt like gunshots.

Abby only shrugs. "You should have texted me back."

"That was six weeks ago! You had months to tell me."

"I was away. You knew I was touring—that's why we ended things. Which you were happy enough to do."

"You didn't give me a choice. And there are things like phones, texts—you could have sent me a bloody email!"

"I actually don't know your email."

I grit my teeth. "Are you going to give me any explanation for why you didn't tell me that I have a child?"

Abby shrugs. "Can I get a drink of something? You might need one, too."

This time I grind my teeth. "It's barely noon."

She smiles blithely. "It's happy hour somewhere in the world. And you don't have to judge me because I'm not breastfeeding."

"I'm not judging anything. I just want to know why."

"Which is why you might need a drink. There are a few things we need to discuss, Clay."

"I think there's more than a few things, Abby." But I rise and head to the kitchen, taking the time to settle my temper, curb my impatience. Why? How? What's going to happen? How will it change things?

M.K.

My heart sinks as I remember her, my first thought of her since I opened the door to Abby, since I heard about my son. The woman who had constantly been in my thoughts since I met her had been completely overshadowed by a twelve-pound baby boy.

My baby boy.

I pour two shots of ice cold vodka in glasses, drain one and then refill it. I add soda to Abby's, leaving mine as a shot.

I'm not sure what good it's going to do, but I need something. With a deep breath I head back into the living room.

"So." I hand Abby her glass. "Tell me. Everything." I sink into the couch, staring at Theo, who is still asleep. I
finally turn to Abby, trying to keep the glares of resentment to a minimum.

She sips delicately before meeting my eyes. "This was over a year ago, you have to remember."

"And a lot of things have changed since then. But Abby, you should have told me."

"Do you even know why I started dating you?"

Her abrupt question throws me. "You liked me?"

Abby snorts. "You never bothered to ask about my past, you know. You had no idea that, before you, I'd been with a man who wanted me to quit dancing and settle down to marry him. He wanted serious, but I wasn't ready and we broke up. Then I met you, and it was nice and easy because I didn't love you. I wanted nice and easy because it had been intense with David. I loved him, and you had no idea."

"Why are you telling me that? I know we weren't serious. It was fun and—"

"We weren't intense," Abby interrupts.

"Because neither of us wanted that. We were nice. Fun."

"Because that's how you kept things. Always. With everyone you date. Fun and nice."

"Nice got you pregnant," I point out.

"Yes, nice did, which was unfortunate."

I rear back and stare at her. "Unfortunate? Are you going to sit there and tell me Theo was a mistake? You regret giving birth?" Theo's hands twitch in his sleep, fisting like he's grabbing on to something. I lower my voice. "You had options, Abby. Not ones that I would agree with, but options."

She toys with her glass as she watches Theo settle himself. "What would you have done if I'd told you I was pregnant?"

"Married you." I don't even have to think about the question. It's how I was brought up—to take responsibility for my actions. It's what I would have done then, and what I should do now.

My heart sinks at the thought.

"You would have married a woman you didn't love?" Abby asks skeptically.

"I would have wanted to give my son a family. A father."

She sighs, the sound frustrated and annoyed. "I didn't want that. I didn't want that with David, so why would I want it with you?"

"Because there was a baby involved. Theo..." My voice softens as I say his name.

But Abby shook her head. "Theo doesn't make marriage an option. That's why I didn't tell you because you would have forced me to do something I didn't want. To be honest, he was a mistake, a regretful mistake. I didn't realize I was pregnant in enough time so I could deal with it and when I did, it was too late."

"How's that possible?" I ask with disbelief. "You're a smart woman, Abby."

She shrugs. "Dancers' bodies can be irregular. A new tour, I was overworked, exhausted. Or I thought I was because of the new tour."

I tap my fingers angrily on the table. "So you had the baby and didn't tell me because you thought I would want to marry you?"

"I didn't think, Clay; I knew it. I knew you well enough. I had the baby, alone. It happened. Get over it. We have other things to discuss."

I jump to my feet. "How can I possibly just get over it? He's my son, who I just found out about. Why did you text me a few weeks ago, if you didn't want me to know?"

Abby lowers her head. "I shouldn't have done that. It was a bad day. Anyway, it's over."

I'm amazed by her coolness. How could I have ever found that attractive? I ignore the little voice telling me, before M.K., Abby was exactly the type of woman I looked for. Not warm and funny and sweet—cool, and controlled, and contained.

I'd missed out on so much.

"If you won't talk about that, what do you want to discuss?" I ask coolly.

Abby takes a healthy swig of her drink, her gaze darting around the room, never once meeting mine. Never once glancing at the sleeping baby.

"Well?"

She drains the glass in one final gulp, setting the glass on the table beside the car seat. The baby stirs in his

sleep, his face contorting like he's having a bad dream. I fight the urge to gather him into my arms,

surprised at how much love has opened up inside me for such a little creature.

It's like he filled a hole I never knew was there.

He has my full attention, so it's a moment before I realize Abby hasn't replied. Tearing my gaze away from Theo, I glance back to see her stand up. "Where are you going? You can't just leave. I only found him."

"You want him? Great. Because I need you to take him."

## Chapter Thirteen

♥

# M.K.

I'M STILL SMILING WHEN I leave Pain. Adam and Nikki shoo me out right at when we close and for once, I listen to them. I've also taken Adam's advice and stopped worrying about things. Clay wants me. Clay wants to live with me. That's all I need to think about.

I need to make a plan.

The cats greet me by the door. I haven't been home in a few days, save for quick trips to feed and water them and I spend some time making up for my neglect, sitting on the floor with Gulliver in my lap, telling him and Scarlett about my plans to decide on a real estate agent, and what I need to do to the house to make it ready to be sold.

I love my house, but I love Clay.

Pennywise sits a few feet away. He's very stingy with his affection, especially if he's mad. I wiggle my fingers at him, trying to get him to come closer but no luck.

"Clay really likes you," I say to the tiny white cat. "You'll go with us. But maybe not sleep on my bed. I don't know if his allergies can handle it. Should we get a new bed?" I ask Scarlett, as if the cat will answer. "Flora got a new bed after Thomas and it helped."

Maybe Clay and I should get a new bed.

I'd really like to call Flora, but I know she'll be working in the garden until the sun sets, trying to get it ready for the Canada Blooms contest she's entering. I don't want to bother her, but if I don't tell someone about this, I might scream.

I hear the baby's cry from next door. I should make sure real estate agents only show the house when the baby isn't there. I won't miss the crying when I move out.

With a resigned sigh, I get to my feet, Gulliver tumbling out of my lap with an offended meow. There's only one person other than Flora that I need to tell my news to, and I'm not sure what the reaction will be.

"Hi, Mom."

It's been a few weeks since I've spoken to my mother, mainly because I haven't wanted to tell her about Clay. It was too soon, too private—and if I'm honest with myself, I didn't want to jinx it.

But now if we're planning on moving in together…

My hips do a happy sway as I cradle the phone against my shoulder.

"Moira?"

"It's me," I say.

"What's the matter?" she demands.

I stifle my sigh as I hit the speaker button. "Why does something have to be the matter?"

"Because you never call me." Her voice fills the kitchen and even the tinniness of her tone over the speaker can't mask the maternal guilt she's so good at throwing on me.

"Well, I'm calling you now."

"Do you have a reason? Because you never call just to chat."

She's in fine form today. I need to bake to get through this. I pull my mixing bowl down from the shelf along with my measuring cups. Double-chocolate muffins with hazelnut and pecans, I decide. I need something decadent.

"I do have some news I thought I'd share with you. I met someone," I say quickly before she starts to play the guessing game.

"A *man*?" I can picture the gleam in her eye.

"Yes, a man." For a moment, I wonder what she would say if I said a woman. I've been tempted more than a few times over the years to tell her that I met a nice girl who was cute and funny and smart, just to stop her from tormenting me on my lack of a love life. But the fallout from that wouldn't be worth it. "His name is Clay."

"*Clay*? What kind of name is that?"

"It's a name, Mother. Clayton McFadden."

"Why don't you call him Clayton? It's a much nicer name."

"He goes by Clay."

"I'm calling him Clayton."

"You'll have to meet him to be able to call him anything." And the way this is starting out, it's not going to happen for a while.

"When will I meet him? When did *you* meet him?"

"I met him—" I can't tell her I met Clay in Las Vegas because then I'll have to go into why I was there, and that would give her more ammunition against Flora. "I met him through a friend of Flora's."

"What kind of friend of Flora's?"

"A nice friend. Dean is very nice. He's a baseball player."

"Is Clayton a ballplayer?" The scorn in her voice is as loud as the thump of the flour container on the counter.

"Clay plays baseball, but Dean is a professional." Almost. "Clay works for FoodMart. He's a VP of marketing," I add quickly before she can screech a question about me dating a man who returns the carts to the store.

Not that there's anything wrong with that, except to my mother. She wouldn't be satisfied unless I was dating the head of the company. And even then, the company wouldn't be good enough.

"Hmm," she says after a long pause. "How long has this been going on?"

"A while," I say carefully. "I didn't want to tell you until there was something to tell."

"And my daughter spending time with a man isn't something to tell? The fact that your romantic life has been nonexistent, according to you, because you spend so much time at your little bake shop—the fact this has changed isn't a worthy reason to call?"

"I'm telling you now. And I call it a patisserie. Pain au Chocolat patisserie, in case you've forgotten the name."

"Don't be pert, Moira. So what does this *Clayton* think of it? I'm sure he won't want you to spend so much time there."

"He loves the idea that I run my own business."

"Hmm, he'll get tired of sharing you with it. Just like your father."

"Not every man is like Dad."

"Hmm. I'll find out soon enough. When will you bring him home? You missed Thanksgiving, you know."

"It couldn't be helped. And I have no plans on bringing him down yet," I say, hoping my voice stays firm. "I'm only calling to tell you I met someone. And that we'll be moving in together."

"Moving in!" Her screech sends Gulliver racing from the room. "Why on earth would you do that?"

"It makes sense since we spend every night together."

A long, dangerous pause comes from my phone. My mother can't honestly believe that I'm still a virgin, but she's never been one to openly discuss sex. Every other part of a relationship is fair game but never the physical aspect of it.

This is another ramification of my father's affair with a younger woman.

"Moira Margaret Donnelly, you know I don't like talk like that. It must be Flora's influence."

Blaming Flora only adds fuel to my fire. "Flora has never once influenced me to have sex with a man. I do just fine on my own."

"Moira Margaret!"

"My name is M.K., Mom! Call me that."

"No, because it is *not* your name. It's childish, and I don't understand why you insist on it."

This time I don't bother hiding my sigh. "Well, I wanted to call and tell you about Clay."

"When will I meet Clayton? And have you talked about the wedding?"

I run a hand through my hair looking at the ingredients spread out with dismay. Why did I ever think I could do two things at once? Talking to my mother exhausts me. "I don't know." I ignore her question about the wedding because I can't stomach that argument tonight. Or any other night.

"I expect you to bring him to the house for dinner soon. Your sisters will expect it. Have you told them?"

I give a bark of laughter. "I thought I'd tell you first." Like there wouldn't be hell to pay if I told Molly first.

Sometimes I imagine doing just that, like I pretend telling her I'm a lesbian. It helps during the more tedious conversations.

But I'm a good daughter, so I've done nothing of the sort. "I'll pass on the invitation and let you know what day works for Clay." I already know there won't be a good time. My visits to Niagara-on-the-Lake have been few and far between and take place during my days off. I haven't had one of those in a while, and I don't think I'll want to waste it on a trip to see my mother.

The good daughter in me bristles at the thought. I should make more of an effort. She's not going to be around forever.

"I'll talk to Clay and let you know," I concede.

"Do you love him?"

This is a surprise question because my mother talks about love even less than sex. It's been like that since my father left, like her heart was turned to stone as soon as he walked out the door. I've forgiven him for a lot of things, but not that.

Which is why I answer honestly. "I do."

"Hmm. Bring him down," she instructs.

# Clay

I have a son.

Abby leaves Theo with me.

I protest halfheartedly, not because I don't want him, but because I don't want the baby to be upset when he wakes up and finds her gone.

"You take him for tonight. Get to know him. I'll stop over tomorrow with his things."

"You can't just give him to me."

"Well, I can't take a baby on this tour, and I'm not giving up this chance."

Abby's been offered a job in the national tour of *The Lion King*. She'll be moving across Canada for the next twelve months: an impossible task with a baby.

I close my mind to her selfishness and open it to gratitude that I will be able to get to know my son.

I refuse to consider what I'm taking on, how my life is going to change. The impact this will be.

I only think of Theo. Everything else will work out.

## Chapter Fourteen

♥

# M.K.

I MAKE THE MUFFINS while I wait for Clay to get back to me.

He knows I close at four, that I'm usually gone by four thirty unless I make puff pastry. Talking to my mother and recovering from the conversation, as well as the muffins, keeps me busy until almost five thirty.

I hop in the shower at five thirty. He doesn't call, doesn't text.

I give him until six.

> What time should I come over?

There's no response. I wait until six thirty, thinking that maybe he's planning something, that his planned dinner has gone awry.

> Is everything ok?

Six forty-five.

Are you working?

I get to seven o'clock by staring at a baseball game on television and sitting on my hands so I don't text. I'm worried, I'm annoyed, and I'm disappointed.
Plus I'm hungry.
I make it to seven oh five.

Are we still doing something tonight?

I get a response to that ten minutes later.

I'm sorry, I lost track of time. I'm not feeling great and laid down for a bit. I have to cancel tonight. I don't want you to get sick.

My heart sinks—not only that I won't see him tonight, but because it's probably the lack of sleep that's made him sick, caused by me.

Of course, rest and feel better. Do you need anything? I can bring soup, juice…whatever.

I'll just sleep. I'll be ok in the morning.

No I'll miss you. No xos. Just that he'll sleep.

Since I have no choice, I grab one of the muffins and settle in with the cats. I find a series on Netflix and empty the bottle of red wine left over from four nights ago when Clay was here. I pull the blanket over my legs, missing Clay's warmth against me. The house is so quiet without his voice. Even the silences between us aren't really quiet.

I don't want to think about how I'm going to sleep tonight.

I want to text him again to tell him I miss him, but that might sound needy, and he should be resting.

I'm used to spending nights alone. When Flora was with Thomas, he took up most of her Saturday nights, and it quickly got to the point where I didn't miss the bars and going out and meeting people. Flora is much more outgoing than I am, even though she can't compare to Ruthie.

I wonder if Ruthie is in town.

I sip my wine and vow not to call Ruthie, no matter how quiet it gets in the house. And I'm certainly not going to call Flora because after Friday night, I really hope she's with Dean tonight. And I am not interrupting that.

I'm on my second episode of Dead to Me when my phone does ring. Blinking with surprise, I recognize my sister Meaghan's number.

"I hear you got a man," is how she greets me.

I smirk, thinking of how quickly my mother must have called my sisters to tell them the news. "That was quick."

"She didn't waste any time on spreading the news." Meaghan laughs.

"And what news did she tell?" I ask archly. "Did she tell you we're moving in together—not getting married."

"She did not," she says, enunciating the last word.

"I thought she might leave out that little tidbit." I stroke Gulliver's head, wishing Clay was here for me to share a laugh with.

But would he laugh at my mother? I've told him some of the stories, but not everything.

"So tell me about him," Meaghan urges. "All the stuff you don't want Mom to know."

Meaghan is the youngest, but she was the first one to realize how our mother played us against each other. She was the first to notice how we constantly fought to become the favourite daughter of the moment.

I stopped fighting with my older sisters after that, letting Millie and Molly battle it out. I was in Toronto, and it was easy to distance myself from the family drama.

But Meaghan won't let me distance myself. She continues to make an effort to repair our relationship. While I might have felt cut off from my sisters as a teenager living at home, I'm closer to Meaghan now than I ever was.

So I tell her about Clay, about how we met in Las Vegas, the spark between us. I tell her about Flora and Dean because she is the one sister who admires my best friend rather than sharing our mother's resentment of her. I tell her about Clay—how sweet and funny and smart and kind he is.

"He sounds perfect," Meaghan marvels. "If you don't marry him, I will!"

"I don't even want to think about that," I protest. "It's too soon, too fast."

"It's not going according to your plan."

"I don't have a plan for him."

"Maybe that's why it's going so well." She doesn't mention Ben, but the unspoken name hangs between us.

"I think I need to plan something," I say nervously. "Asking me to live with him is so quick, and I'm not sure what to do."

"Again, if you don't want him, pass him on to me!"

"But I'll have to sell this place, and where do we look for another? Near the patisserie? He works downtown, so will he want to go there? What about the cats? Will they adjust?" All the concerns and worries that I've bottled up since this morning pour out of me quicker than how fast I've drunk the wine.

"Slow down," Meaghan says, sounding a lot like our father. It used to bother me when he told me to slow down, but now I know that my thoughts will only pick up speed and spiral out of control. "Everything will work out just fine. It always does, regardless of how much you freak about it."

"I'm not freaking."

"You sound like you're about to. Where is Mr. Perfect tonight? Shouldn't you be doing something fabulous together?"

"We were, but he's not feeling well. He had planned something —I'm not sure what."

"Is it bothering you more that you don't know what it was, or that he backed out?"

I chuckle softly. "Probably that I don't know what he planned. I'm okay on my own."

"You like to know what's going on. And I know this because I'm as much of a control freak as you are. Did Mom tell you I'm seeing a therapist?"

"You—really? For what?"

Meaghan laughs. "Do you really have to ask?"

"Am I that much of a mess?"

"No, and neither am I," she says firmly, "but Dad leaving did a number on us all, and with Mom being the way she is, I find it's nice to talk to someone, that's all. And I don't have a Flora like you do, or a Clayton."

"His name is Clay."

"Well, Mom rechristened him Clayton because that's what she does."

I sigh. "She does."

"I'd like to meet him."

I don't let on how that makes me feel. How Meaghan isn't trying to plan my future with Clay but accepting my present. And wants to be involved with it. "I'd like that. Maybe you could come to the city?"

Meaghan laughs again. "Wouldn't that piss off Mom?"

# Clay

DEAN DOESN'T COME HOME that night so I'm alone with Theo.

I feel a frisson of guilt for lying to M.K., but I'm not ready to tell her about this. I'm not sure how to tell her about it—an old girlfriend has left me with our baby, one I didn't know even know I was the father of. That I didn't know existed?

It's such an un-M.K. thing to do that I know she's going to have a hard time believing it.

"Hello." I stare at Theo, and he stares back at me, his eyes round and unblinking. Green eyes, like me. He's back in the car seat because I'm not sure what to do with him.

I can't believe Abby just left him with me.

"There's enough bottles in the diaper bag until tomorrow morning," she said as she was leaving. "Diapers and a change of clothes. He'll be fine."

"Where does he sleep?" I ask, wishing she'd confirm that *I'd* be fine. I've had experience with babies, but I've never been left alone with one. I've never been solely responsible for their care and safety.

What if I hurt him?

What if he cries?

What if he won't eat?

But as the afternoon wears on, I manage. In fact, by the time I realize I need to cancel with M.K., I'm pretty proud of myself.

I didn't hurt Theo. I got him in and out of the car seat without issue, fed, changed, sat with him on my lap, all without causing him pain.

He did cry, several times, but I got him to stop by putting a bottle in his mouth. And that made him eat.

"Hi," I say as the baby continues to stare at me. "I haven't really introduced myself. I'm Clay. I'm your father."

Father sounds so formal and old-fashioned.

"I'm your dad."

Theo coos and lifts a hand, splaying his fingers. I take that as a good sign. "I just found out about you," I continue. "It was a bit of a shock. A good one," I quickly add. "I've always wanted a baby. A son."

My heart constricts painfully, and suddenly my eyes are wet. "I didn't know you existed, but I'm really glad you do." Leaning over, I quickly unbuckle the straps on the car seat and carefully lift him out before I change my mind. The only time I've held him is when I carried him to my bed for a diaper change. I even fed him in the car seat.

I settle him into the crock of my arm and lean back against the cushions.

"I'm your dad," I say again. "You're my son."

This time Theo gives me a hint of a smile and I reach for the remote on the table. "Let's see what's on TV."

A quick glance at the sports channels gives me a baseball game. "It's the Yankees, but it'll have to do," I tell Theo. "It's the playoffs. Usually I watch the Blue Jays. They're the best team—not really, but they're Toronto and since we live here, we cheer for them. Plus your Uncle Dean—you'll meet him soon—he used to play for them. Well, he started a season, and then he got hurt, but maybe he'll get back there. Wouldn't that be something, going to a game to see him play? You and me? And Flora, of course, and M.K. She likes baseball, too."

I smooth Theo's hair off his forehead, and he snuffles as he tries to grab my hand. I give him my finger to hold, marveling at the strength in the little grip.

I can't take my eyes off him.

"I think you'll like M.K.," I say quietly. "I'm just not sure when you'll meet her. Soon, I hope, but things have to be sorted out with your mom. Is it okay if you stay with me when she goes away?"

Theo pulls my hand into his mouth with a gurgle and I laugh. The baby looks at me in shock.

"It's okay. I laughed. Laughing is good. I like to laugh. I like to make M.K. laugh." My stomach tightens at the mention of her. We haven't gone this long without speaking or texting or seeing each other since we began. I miss her—I miss her smile. I miss her scent. I miss her sitting beside me, dropping her head on my shoulder when she can't keep her eyes open.

I glance at the clock on the cable box. It's after nine; she'll already be in bed. Or at least she should be. If I call her now, I'd have to explain everything, and it'll be hours before she could go to bed.

It's better that I wait until tomorrow. She needs her sleep.

I keep telling myself that so I don't give voice to the worry that she's not going to be happy about Theo.

We watch a bit of the game until Theo begins to wriggle in my arms, finally giving a thin wail that tells me he's hungry again. Keeping him tight against me, I warm the bottle like Abby explained and settle back on the couch to feed him.

It's nicer when I hold him. I think it's more comfortable for Theo, too.

After he finishes the bottle, I hunt through the diaper bag to find pajamas for him, and change him for the night.

By ten o'clock, I'm in bed, with Theo curled into my side with my arms around him.

• ♥ • ♥ • ♥ • ♥ • ♥ •

Abby shows up at nine in the morning, dragging three bags and a playpen. Theo and I have been awake since six thirty, and I've been rationing his bottles.

"This should be everything you need," she says, lugging the last bag into the living room. "I brought you the rest of my diapers and formula, but you'll have to buy more."

"I don't understand." I stand in the middle of the living room with Theo in my arms. "You're really leaving him with me?"

She heaves a bag onto the couch. "I told you, I don't have a choice. If I don't show up on Monday, I'm losing the part. I was going to leave Theo with my mother but she wasn't really keen on playing grandmother, so you finding out about him is perfect."

"I'm not sure I would call this perfect."

"C'mon," she wheedles. "You seem excited about him. This way you'll be able to get to know him, have him all to yourself. It'll be fun."

I close my eyes and will myself not to say the words building inside. "You're seriously leaving your child?" I manage.

"With his father," Abby adds. "Men do it all the time."

"Yes, but—" I stop myself. This isn't the ideal situation, but maybe she has a point. I am excited about him. This will give me a chance to get to know my son.

As if sensing I'm weakening, Abby plunges forward. "I've got a babysitter set up for him already. You can drop him off at eight, pick him up before six. I've got all the information here for you." She drops a spiral ring notebook on the table. "I wrote down his schedule and anything I could think of about his likes and dislikes."

I pick up the notebook. Flipping through, I notice only a few pages are full. Was it because she didn't make the effort or because she doesn't know his likes and dislikes? "Is there a number I can reach you at?" I ask coolly.

"Oh, you won't need me," she says with a wave. "You'll be great. You were made to be a father."

After a few more minutes of instruction/persuasion, Abby says she has to leave. "I have so much to do." She laughs. "Make the most out of babysitters. It'll make your life easier." She comes over to where I stand with Theo in my arms.

Theo stares at her solemnly.

"Goodbye, little man," she says in a singsong voice, dropping a kiss on his blond head. "Mommy will miss you."

And then she's gone.

The only reason I let her go is because I'd be frantic with worry about what she would do with Theo if I don't keep him.

## *Chapter Fifteen*

♥

# M.K.

I DON'T HEAR FROM Clay on Sunday.

All my texts, my calls go ignored, and the silence between us is deafening. I spend the day at Pain, running back and forth to my phone, growing more frantic as each hour goes by. I picture him sick, injured, the victim of a carjacking, hurt. Abandoned.

And then I begin to think the worst.

There's someone else, someone he's met. Someone from his past back to claim him. Someone who isn't me, someone who he wants more than me.

Sunday night I realize Clay isn't calling me back because he's changed his mind.

He doesn't want to move in with me. He doesn't want to be with me. He's ghosting me, just like he ghosted Heather all those weeks ago.

I thought Clay was different. I thought he had changed from the player he used to be.

I spend Sunday night imagining the face of the woman he's with. It hurts more than Ben ever did.

Monday morning, I pull myself out of bed with difficulty, my body tired and achy from lack of sleep. Gulliver trails after me to the bathroom, weaving around my ankles as he demands his breakfast.

"Don't trip me," I snap. "What do you do the mornings I'm not here?"

Clay comes and feeds them. Once I had been late to unlock Pain for Rhoda—the one time she had been on time for work and Clay informed me that it was silly for me to run from his place to mine before going to Pain, just so I could feed the cats.

"I can feed your cats," he'd said. "As long as they'll let me in the house without you."

"Do you miss him?" I ask Gulliver in a wistful voice. "I miss him."

As I glance in the mirror, I'm shocked by my red-rimmed eyes and heavy purplish bags. I must have been crying more than I thought.

"There's no point missing him," I tell the cat. "He's gone. It's over. It has to be over."

My chest is hollow, like my heart has been carved out.

Luckily, Reuben is working with me and makes no mention of my eyes, which makeup does an admirable job of hiding. And he doesn't ask about my monosyllabic answers, my curt requests.

Adam would have been all over me, but luckily he has Monday off.

I think I've managed to compose myself by the time Flora stops by for her coffee. This is the test—Flora, the person who knows me best in the world will be able to see through my attempts at cheerful conversation. And when she asks, of course I'll tell her everything. The words will gush out of me, like spilling a bag of milk on the counter.

But when I look at her, the words dry up because all I see is her happiness. She never notices my eyes.

"Someone's in a good mood," I call through the lump in my throat.

"Yes, I am." Flora sashays through the patisserie, bringing smiles to the faces of my customers. All I can think of is how different it had been weeks ago when she burst in to tell me she'd found Dean again.

A hard part of me, as prickly as a cactus, suddenly wishes Dean had never stopped into the flower shop that day. But I don't let that part of me show. "Good weekend?" I ask.

She's glowing. My best friend is glowing, and I'm about to burst into tears

Flora hugs herself. "Great weekend! Oh, M.K. I didn't expect this at all. Dean was Dean, and I never thought—I'm not making any sense. I'm just so happy. Did you see this coming?"

"Yes." Despite my misery, I can't help but feel smug. "Everyone saw this coming except for the two of you. It was as predictable as a rom-com movie."

"But if this was a rom-com, then the bad stuff would happen. The stuff that tears the couple apart."

Is this what's happening to me? The bad stuff that tears the couple apart? If so, *what happened*? How did the bad stuff happen? What did I do wrong?

"Your life is not a movie." I swipe at a spot on the counter so Flora can't see the furious blinking to stop the dampness.

"If it was, it'd be a good movie," Flora says with a giggle.

I take a deep breath. "I'm happy for you. Is it officially more than friends now?" And I am happy. I can't not be happy for Flora.

I'm just not happy for me.

"I think so," she says with a grin. "I want to tell you all about it but I'd better get to the shop. Dean kept me busy all weekend. Talk to you later?"

"Later," I promise.

I won't tell her anything until some of her happiness dims. Until I have something to tell.

I give myself a shake after she leaves before I focus on the next customer coming in. "Hi, Mrs. Gretchen."

Her kindly face frowns as she approaches the counter. "You've gotten yourself into a pickle, haven't you?"

"I don't know what you mean," I stammer.

She points a liver-spotted finger at my face. "Someone's made you sad."

How can this woman, who barely knows me, and Flora, who I've known forever... "Yes," I say softly. "Someone has made me sad."

"Then it's up to you to make yourself happy. Because you're the only person who can make yourself be sad."

I blink with surprise at her commanding tone. "Okay?"

"It's up to *you* to make yourself happy," she lectures. "And only *you* can let yourself feel sadness. So snap out of it."

"Okay," I say with a shaky smile. "I'll try."

"You'll do more than try," she mutters. "Now help yourself to one of those chocolatine things you make so well and paste a smile on your face until it's the real thing."

When Mrs. Gretchen leaves, I take her advice. I don't need a man to make me happy. I don't need a man to do anything. I'm a strong, independent woman with my own business, my own life.

I'm fine on my own.

And then Dean comes in.

"Another one in a good mood," I call to him from behind the counter.

"You saw Flora?" Dean asks eagerly.

I can't help but smile at his reaction. "How could I miss her? She was glowing."

"Yeah." He runs his hand through his hair, his face contorting like he's trying to dim the sunshine of his smile. "How are you this morning?"

I can't help it. "Not as good as you."

"What happened?" Dean asks in a gentle voice.

I hold on to my smile that's probably more like a grimace. "Nothing that a little time and distance can't handle because that's obviously what he wants."

He groans. "Clay messed it up?"

My smile breaks at the sound of his name. "I don't know what happened. Things were so good, and I thought maybe I'd have a chance this time, but over the weekend, he just wasn't there. I haven't talked to him." A tear escapes to trickle down my cheek.

"Has he said anything?" Dean demands. "Maybe something happened."

"He hasn't said anything. That's the problem. He'd been so open, telling me everything. We've talked about his past, his parents. There are no secrets between us. At least there wasn't, but now this. I don't know what to do."

"Don't do anything," he says automatically.

"But what if he's getting cold feet. He asked me to move in."

Dean leans forward over the counter. "Honestly? If he is getting cold feet, there's nothing you can do about it. He doesn't do well with clingy women. Not that you are." He raises his hand to still my quick protest. "But just give him a little space. He loves you. I can tell that, even if he didn't already tell me. Everything will be fine."

"He told you?" Hope swells inside me, kept in check by the worry.

"He can't stop talking about it. It's annoying, actually. But sweet. I've never seen him act like this before."

"So how do you know it'll be okay?"

"Because it has to be," he says simply. "When I see the two of you together, I can't see any reason that you can't make it work. Clay knows this. Maybe he's just scared of what this means."

"What does it mean?"

"That he's looking at forever with you, and that's an awesome, but kind of scary thought."

# Clay

SUNDAY NIGHT THEO WAKES up crying and nothing I can do will make him stop.

He finally cries himself to sleep around four a.m., and I fall back asleep soon after, around the same time M.K. would be waking up.

Of course I sleep through the alarm.

It's eight thirty before I wake up, a half hour after the time I'd arranged to drop Theo off at the babysitters. Because yesterday had been so exhausting, I make the snap decision to work from home today and call the babysitter to tell her Theo won't be there.

After Abby left yesterday, I eventually ventured out with Theo snug in his car seat. I discovered that sports cars aren't the best for transporting babies, and that diapers and formula are expensive.

I also discovered Theo loves people.

He smiles. He waves. He gurgles whenever the attention is on him.

"What a cutie!" the third woman cried as we entered Loblaws and that was before we had even got our cart.

Shopping with a baby was an experience, but I took it slow and we managed. I'd never been approached by so many women in one day.

"You're lady bait," I whispered to him as he smiled toothlessly at another woman. "If I was looking for a lady."

I feel horrible for not talking to M.K. yesterday, but every time I picked up the phone, I realized it was a bad time for her to talk, or Theo needed me.

And now it's Monday, and I still haven't explained.

I've just gotten Theo settled for his morning nap when I hear Dean's key in the door. "Shh," I greet him with a whisper, finger to my lips.

Dean's confusion is obvious as he drops his keys on the hall table. "Who's here? And why are *you* here?"

I scrub at my hair, already mussed from the baby grabbing it and making the same gesture of frustration I've done countless times today. "Long story."

Dean's gaze hits the car seat, the pile of baby blankets I've yet to find a home for, and finally the empty bottle in my hand. "I think you better start talking."

"I've got to tell M.K. about this, so can you wait for her?" I head to the kitchen to rinse out the bottle. How am I supposed to tell M.K.?

"About M.K." My head swivels around at her name. "Why haven't you talked to her this weekend?"

I wave a hand towards the bottles drying on the rack. "I haven't figured out how to explain this."

"Try with me because it looks like there's a baby here and I'm not sure why. Or how. Or whose?"

"Mine," I say heavily. Dean's eyes widen.

"Since when?"

"Since Abby Benjamin dropped him off Saturday. And before that, about four months ago."

"Did you know she was going to be dropping a baby off? Your baby? How's that possible?"

I raise an eyebrow. "If you haven't figured that out yet..." I lean against the counter, my shoulders sagging with exhaustion. I've never felt quite this tired before. "You remember Abby—the dancer."

"I could say, which dancer, but I'm guessing now's not really the time. Tall, dark hair. Dancerlike. Got it."

"Well, after we split up—not that we were ever really together—she found out she was pregnant. It was mine," I add, to offset the next logical question.

Theo is mine. Every time I look at him, I see more of me in his face, his smile. It might be wishful thinking, but he definitely looks like me.

"Ohh—kay," Dean says slowly. "She had a baby and never told you?"

I shake my head. "I heard from her about nine weeks ago, the same day M.K. got a hold of me, so I never texted her back."

"How did you find out? Did she just show up?"

I laugh without humour. "Flora hired a friend of hers to work in the shop. Or Imogene did. The Heather that is now working at Fleur is a friend of Abby's. Oh, and I went out with Heather too."

"She's not pregnant, too, is she?" I give him a disgusted look. "Okay, so she's not pregnant."

"When I was in Fleur on Friday," I continue, "Heather sprung the whole *I know about your baby* thing on me."

"Nice of her."

"I needed to know."

"I'm not saying you didn't, but Abby should have been the one to tell you."

"I agree."

"That wasn't a very long story. So, are you babysitting for her? You missed work because of a baby?"

I heave a sigh. "That's where it gets complicated. She's leaving on a year-long tour on Friday. I'm taking Theo."

Dean's face is still except for the blinking of his eyes. "I think you better tell M.K. about this," he finally says.

## Chapter Sixteen

♥

## M.K.

IT'S THE LONGEST AFTERNOON, with every customer taking their own sweet time ordering, lingering at the tables. A group of new mothers, around two in the afternoon, is the worst. They've been coming in for the last few months, three of them with strollers and sleeping babies: friends who take time for themselves while the babies sleep.

It's something I could see Flora and me doing if I ever planned on having a baby.

Not that it's a hard no, but it's a hard not anytime soon. I've listened to my mother plan her grandchildren for years and the relationship I have with my mother makes me reluctant to give her that satisfaction of getting one from me.

I've had a flurry of texts from my other sisters about Clay today, so I'm not inclined to do anything for her. I can only guess what she's said about "Clayton."

They are actually calling him Clayton, with Molly giving me a snarky sidenote:

Why are you with a man named Clayton?

He sounds old.

"His name is Clay, and I really hope he can explain where he's been all weekend before I freak out," I mutter as I'm wiping the counter at the end of the day.

"You were sayin'?" Reuben asks. Normally, I don't let anyone work longer than six hours, but somehow Reuben got a full open-to-close shift. I'm embarrassed at how my careful planning let me make such a mistake, but Reuben only waves off my apologies and stays the day, despite my assurances that I can finish on my own.

"I was talking to myself and I got loud," I explain, my cheek growing hot.

"Do that often, do you?" he asks with the hint of a grin. "Talkin' to yourself, I mean?"

"More than anyone realizes," I admit.

"Best to say it out loud lest the thoughts fester in your head," he says, cleaning out the frother with a loud hiss.

"Is this your way of suggesting I talk to you?"

Reuben shrugs. "Ye've got friends who'll listen—the FlowerFlora, the red-haired bloke. No need of my ear."

Dean did help, and Flora would listen but I'm sure she's got more of her own happy news that she's bursting to tell me, and I need to get into my great listener-BBF mode before that happens.

"Only me here, though, isn't?" Reuben adds.

"Family issues," I say shortly. "My mother, actually."

"Ah. Mothers. World's best creation, cause of the biggest problems."

I allow a smile. "That's about right."

"And what did your mam do this time?"

"Nothing." I heave a sigh. "And everything. She's always been so consumed with my sisters and me finding a husband. It's so old-fashioned—"

"*Pride and Prejudice.*"

"Exactly!" Some of my foul mood lifts and I beam at him. "I've always thought of her like Mrs. Bennett."

"There's a woman who'd try the patience of a saint."

"Yes! And I'm no saint."

"I take it she's hurrying things along with you and your man? Or is he not good enough for the likes of you?"

"She's never met him, but now she and all my sisters are trying to guilt me into bringing him down to meet them. This is why I never told them about him because I knew I wouldn't hear the end of it. They can't even get his name right."

He narrows his eyes. "They calling him…?"

"Clayton."

"That not his name?"

"Well, yes, but he prefers Clay."

"He'll be quick enough to tell them. Dinnae be too fussed about a name. Pick your battles, my mam always says."

"My mam always says I'm in need of a husband," I say drily.

"But you don't think so."

"No. I don't need anyone."

"I dinnae agree with that, but a husband no a requirement for you. If it be what you want, then get yourself one, for sure, but don't let your mam's thoughts on the matter ruin your day."

"Or my life," I mutter.

"Has it now?"

"I guess not," I admit. "But it makes it difficult."

"The mother-daughter bond is both a beautiful and a terrible thing."

I narrow my eyes at Reuben. His size and somber demeanor had intimidated me when he came in for the interview but vanished once I saw him around the coffeemaker. And watching him with Adam and the customers made me realize how lucky I am to find him.

Talking to him makes me think he's a godsend.

"How do you know all this?" I ask. "Are you a closet psychologist or something?"

He huffs a laugh. "I haven't the book learning. But it's easy to see there's all types in this world. And me mam's a bit of a complicated sort herself." He smiles, his dark eyes warm. "Mebbe talk to your man. That'll help."

"If I ever talk to him again," I mutter under my breath. But when the cleanup is finished, I check my phone to find a text from Clay.

> I'm so sorry!!! Please come over after you're finished and I'll explain everything. I have so much to tell you.

He signs it with xo.

# Clay

I'VE NEVER KNOWN THE meaning of waiting with bated breath until that afternoon. Every noise in the condo has me on edge as I wait for M.K. Theo is as content as ever, so at least he doesn't pick up on my nerves.

What will she say when I introduce her to my son?

In the weeks we've been dating, M.K. and I have never had The Conversation, the one about marriage. Or the one about children. There had never been a good time to bring it up, plus I've spent the past years dodging those exact questions, so I'm unsure of the etiquette. If I ask M.K. about her thoughts about marriage and babies, does that mean I'm thinking of it?

Do I want a future with her?

Honestly, the present has been so good that I haven't given it much thought. Now as I watch Theo sleep in his playpen, I realize my future has changed. Flipped upside down and backwards.

The baby stirs in his sleep, his face scrunching up like he's deep in thought. Or more likely he's pooping.

I already know his pooping face. I've cottoned on to the difference between his *I'm hungry* cry and his *I need to sleep* wail.

Even after only forty-eight hours with him, I know my heart will break without him. This is a new kind of love, one that I never imagined.

I wait for the telltale odor from Theo as M.K. knocks.

"Hi," I say in a hushed voice as I open the door. Even though she came straight from the patisserie with the scent of chocolate and coffee clinging to her, she looks amazing in her swinging, blue dress, her slim legs bare despite the cool day. I pull her to me, loving the feel of her in my arms.

"What's wrong?" she asks against my shoulder.

"Nothing's wrong." I stroke her back, my hand snaking up under her dark bob. "Just changed a bit."

"What's changed?" M.K. pulls away, her face a mask of concern. Twining my fingers with hers, I tug her inside.

"Come see."

M.K. is silent, but I know she's taking in the car seat against the wall, the stack of baby blankets on the coffee table as Dean had done earlier. I lead her into my bedroom where I've set up the playpen.

"This is Theo," I say, unable to keep the pride from my voice.

When I met M.K. and Flora, I remember thinking that for best friends, the two couldn't be more different. M.K. is quiet and reserved, while Flora is outspoken and outgoing. She's a good match for Dean.

If Flora was faced with Dean's surprise baby, she wouldn't have been able to stop talking. But M.K. is taking her time, and making me sweat it.

"That's your baby," she finally says in a quiet voice.

"It is."

"Why am I only meeting him now? Or even hearing about him?" Her voice is so very quiet, and a prickle of fear runs up my spine.

"I only met him this weekend myself."

"How is that possible?" She stares at the sleeping baby with an expression on her face that I can't read.

I give her the quick version of Abby's visit, but when she doesn't respond, I give her the rest, the part I was going to tell her slowly.

"She's giving you her baby?"

"He's my baby, too."

"Yes, but she's the mother. How can she give up her child like that?" Her voice is like ice, and even though I'm annoyed with Abby, I bristle at her implications.

"Abby has her reasons."

"There's no good reason for a parent walking away from their child."

Just in time I remember that M.K.'s father walked away from his family. "Abby isn't walking away. Not forever. Theo wasn't planned and she's made the best of it. She has an opportunity now, and I'm helping take care of Theo. He's my responsibility, too."

"One that you never knew about."

"Again, she had her reasons for not telling me."

"And you're not upset about this?" M.K. suddenly bursts. "This is big, Clay. It's not like she lied about going out with her friends when she was supposed to be with her grandma—she had your baby and never told you."

"I know."

"Aren't you upset about it?"

I stare at Theo. "I haven't had a chance to really think about it. To process it."

"Don't you think you should?"

I gesture to my son. "He's more important right now."

"So you're taking him? This is how it's going to be? That you suddenly have a son?"

I turn at the anger in her voice. "I know it's sudden, M.K., but I don't want to upset you. This won't change anything between us."

"How can it not? You have a child—a child with another woman."

"Who is no longer in my life. Abby wasn't really in my life anyway."

"She was in your life enough to have your child," she said grimly.

"She was, but that's over."

M.K. gives a humourless snort. "This isn't because I'm jealous. Or insecure of some woman I've never even heard of."

"I told you about her," I say reluctantly. "The semi-serious one."

"And that's supposed to help?"

I shrug helplessly. "I don't know what to say that will help. And I want to. I know this is big—I know that I'm springing it on you."

M.K. is quiet for a long moment. As if interrupted by the silence, Theo stirs with a frustrated cry. I rest my hand on his stomach as his hands fist and flail. "It's okay," I soothe as his eyes open fully. "I'm here."

The cry turns into a wail and I pick him up. "You hungry, buddy? Want something to eat?" With an apologetic glance at M.K., I carry him into the kitchen and warm a bottle.

"You're good with him," she says as she watches Theo take the bottle with a grunt of gusto.

"I'm as surprised as you are." I laugh. The kitchen is quiet save for Theo's slurping. "What do you think?" I finally ask.

M.K. takes a deep breath. "I think I've never wanted kids, let alone someone else's," she says sadly.

"M.K.," I plead.

She holds up her hand. "He's very cute, and I'm sure he's sweet, but he's still your baby with another woman. I think I'm going to need some time with this."

And then she leaves.

## Chapter Seventeen

♥

# M.K

**C**LAY HAS A SON.

The words reverberate in my head as I drive home. I regret walking out of Clay's as soon I do it, but I didn't have another option. His news shocked me more than anything ever had.

More than Ben's infidelity.

Because of everything going on, I almost forget Flora and I had planned to get together that night. Luckily, I remember in time and suggests she come to my place instead.

"Smells good in here," she says cheerfully as I let her in. "Smells like—bacon?"

"Bacon maple muffins." I lead her into the kitchen where the fruits of my labour are cooling on the rack, topped with a crumb topping and maple drizzle. "Try one."

"You don't have to ask me twice." She sets the brown paper LCBO bag on the counter before grabbing the muffin, sniffing it appreciatively. "So what's going on? Obsessive baking is usually a sign of something gone wrong, and last time I checked, things were going right with you and Clay."

I pull the bottle of Châteauneuf-du-Pape out of the bag with a rueful smile. There are only certain times we dip into the good wines—when something good happens or really, really bad. There was no way Flora knows about me so…

I swivel, catching her trying to cram half the muffin into her mouth and study her dancing eyes. "You're still glowing," I say finally. "But even more than before."

"I'm eating," she says through the mouthful.

"No, but you are. Is it Dean?"

Crumbs drop into her shirt as she nods, her face breaking into a wide, happy smile. "Lots of things."

I force a smile, happy for my friend even when my life is suddenly in shambles. "You better tell me everything."

We take the wine into the living room where Gulliver hops up, the scent of Flora's bulldog driving him crazy as he writhes in her lap. She tells me about her weekend with Dean, *all* the details including the ones he might not want me to hear. She tells me about Thomas showing up in the shop yet again, this time freshly broken up with Evelyn and wanting another chance with Flora. I high-five her, almost spilling my wine when she gives a play by play about shutting him down.

"It's like he can sense something about Dean," Flora muses aloud, refilling her glass. "Thomas came into the store maybe a half-dozen times when we were together, but twice alone since I met Dean."

"But things are good? Dean doesn't think—?"

"He is so over her," Flora says happily, guessing what I'm about to ask. "And that's the best part, but there's more." And then she tells me about her brothers, and how they want to bring her back into the family nursery business.

My heart swells for her because I know how much it devastated her when they bought her out. All because her brothers never trusted Thomas, which they had a good right not to, but it wasn't easy for her.

"I'm so happy for you," I say, gripping her hand. "Truly. And proud of the way you handled things. Walking out on that wedding was the best thing you could have done."

"For you, too, right?"

I reach for the bottle, feeling Flora's suddenly concerned gaze turn on me. "M.K? What's going on?"

I shrug helplessly. Flora has always been there for me, but at this moment when I need her, I'm reluctant because her life has fallen into place exactly as it should.

"M.K.," she says sternly, the same tone I've heard countless times from her brother Oliver. "Dean's at Clay's now, so I can call him and ask, so don't think you can hide this."

"Oh, there's no hiding this," I say, thinking of how the playpen nestled into Clay's bedroom, the love I saw in his eyes when he presented me with his son.

"We don't hide things."

"No, we don't." I take a deep breath. "Clay has a son."

"Pardon?"

"Clay has a son," I repeat. "A former—the term girlfriend seems a bit loose—a woman he had dated just told him she had a baby."

"When?"

"Four months ago."

*"What?"*

"That's not the best part," I say grimly. "She's left town and wants Clay to raise the baby."

Flora stares at me, eyes narrowed. "And you don't want a baby."

I shrug again, like the weight of a four-month-old baby is weighing down my shoulders. "My mother is going to love this. She'll see it as a ready-made family."

"This isn't about your mother," Flora says gently.

"No, it's about me raising another woman's baby."

"With the man you love."

"What happens if the mother comes back and takes him? Takes both of them?" Even as I say the words, the possibility of losing Clay to another woman looms before me. "He's so honourable and good. Of course he'll want a family with her. Why wouldn't he? And where does that leave me?"

"You don't know that."

"If you got pregnant with Thomas, wouldn't you have tried and make it work with him?"

"But this isn't me and Thomas. This is Clay and a woman he slept with. Not a girlfriend, you said. Where is she? And why did she leave the baby?"

"I have no idea," I say bitterly. "Clay didn't tell me. He just assumed I'd be happy about this and didn't give me any details."

"Because you left, didn't you? Did you let him explain everything?"

"No, but..."

"M.K." Flora's sigh is more affectionate than reproachful. "Have more wine."

"I have wine."

She still pours more. "How long have we been friends?"

"Since kindergarten."

"That's twenty—that's a long time. Have you even wondered why we've never had a fight?"

"We've had fights."

"Not really. Not the ones where we've said exactly what's on our minds and then stuff we don't mean, where we both end up in tears, eating a whole pint of ice cream alone until we figure out how miserable we are without each other."

"Do you want to have a fight like that?"

"Of course not. You never fought with Ben, either."

"No, but—"

"And even when you thought I was crazy being with Thomas, and I know you did, you never once said anything negative about him because you knew I'd defend him and that would cause problems with us."

"I didn't want to hurt you."

"And I appreciate that. In all the years that your mother had been planning your weddings and baby showers and trying to run your life, have you ever once told her to stop? Told her to shut up and let you live your life?"

"No."

"You walk away instead. You tuck your head down and make a batch of fabulous croissants until you settle down. You take this crap stuff and make a plan on how you are going to deal with it, instead of fighting against it."

I stare into the dregs of my glass. "Maybe it's the wine, but I really don't understand what you're trying to say."

Flora laughs. "I don't either. I went on one of my tangents, but it comes down to how you walked away from Clay without knowing everything. You just walked away from this great guy who probably had the shock of his life, because of the slim-to-none possibility that he's going to pick this mystery baby mother over you. This mother who gave her baby away."

"I'm sure she had her reasons."

"Which you don't know. Did you ever contemplate helping him raise the baby? You walked away to plan your life without him. Right?"

I reach for the bottle. "Maybe you're right. I don't like fighting. Conflict."

"You know I'm right. And no one likes conflict. But some things are worth fighting for. Is Clay?" I think of him, picture his face, his smile, how he makes me feel about myself. "You two are good together. And from what Dean has told me, Clay really hasn't had this with anyone else before."

"He hasn't. The longest relationship he's had was about a month. Maybe six weeks."

"And how long has it been for you two?"

"Nine weeks. He said something about moving in together."

"Before or after baby arrived?"

"Before. So that might have changed."

"Or maybe he needs you even more."

I stare at Flora, wondering if I've made a mistake. Feeling terrified and sad but with surge of hope that's beginning to grow. "What do I do now?"

Flora smiles and tips the bottle into her own glass. "Finish this bottle with me. Then I'd go talk to him for a start. Fight for him, if he's worth it."

"How can I fight a baby?"

"Maybe you don't have to."

# Clay

I'D SETTLED THEO AGAINST me on the couch when Dean let himself in. "You wouldn't believe all the stuff that went down today," he calls from the hall. "With Flora, and I talked to—" His foot catches the edge of Theo's car seat, and he accidently kicks it. "He's still here?"

He steps into the living room, taking in me with the baby. "Looks that way. Did you talk to M.K.?"

I nod morosely.

Without a word, Dean turns on his heel to head for the kitchen and the clink of bottles reach my ears. "I guess that's why Flora ran out like her greenhouse was on fire." Dean hands me a bottle of Mill Street, touching his with it. "They'll be into the beer themselves. Or whatever they drink together?"

"Wine, probably. Or maybe this is a time for tequila." My shoulders sag at the thought of another night without M.K.

"It's baby time." He sets his bottle on the table and reaches for Theo. "I haven't seen one of these in years. Hey, buddy." He studies the baby's face, his blue onesie. "He is a buddy, isn't he?"

"Theo. His name is Theo."

"Hey, Theo, little buddy." He holds him up, stretching out his arms to dangle him and my heart stops. Dean is well over six feet and holding Theo like that—I breathe only when Dean tucks the baby into his arms. "He's like a little football."

I drink deeply from my beer. "He's my baby."

The words hit me then, like the time I took a pitch in the leg. It's sudden, and sharp and it hurts. I've been so busy with getting everything I need for my son that I haven't taken the time to realize what that exactly means.

"You're going to raise him?"

"You don't have to sound so disbelieving. I think I'm in shock enough for both of us."

He settles into the chair with Theo in his arms. I watch my friend, noting how comfortable he seems. "You look like you've done that before."

"Older sisters have babies. I was the best uncle until I left." He bounces Theo on his knee. "He smiled! It's probably gas," he adds. "I miss them."

"I hardly ever see my brothers' kids. My mother is going to freak." I'm tired just thinking about explaining things to my parents. I haven't even told Liv yet, and I tell her everything.

"What did M.K. say?" Dean glances around as if realizing she's not there. Where I want her to be. Where I need her. "Uh oh. That's why the call to Flora?"

"I guess. She didn't say anything, just walked out."

"Nothing?"

"Just that she didn't want kids, especially not someone else's." I try to keep the bitterness out of my voice. I can't blame her. I don't know how I'd react if the situation was reversed. If she had a baby that she didn't tell me about.

She would at least have known she had a baby. My mind is still spinning from suddenly being a father.

"What are you going to do?" Dean asks after a few moments' silence.

"I'm going to raise my son. I don't have a choice in the matter."

"I guess not. But what about M.K.?"

"I don't know what I can do. This is my problem. Not that he's a problem. You're not a problem," I say to Theo.

"He can't understand you."

"How do you know? Maybe he's brilliant and understands every word we say?"

Dean lifts up the baby again. "Do you want a beer, little buddy?"

Theo gurgles and reaches out a hand for Dean's beard. "Definitely brilliant."

"See?" Then I sigh. "He's mine, but as much as I love M.K. and want her in my life, I can't force her to take him on. It's a lot."

"But you're going to do it?"

"Again, I don't have a choice. He's the consequence of my actions. He's a really good consequence," I add with a smile. "I never thought I'd hear myself say that."

"Neither did I. You're happy about it?"

"I have to be. I have a *son*. It's kind of cool." My smile fades. "It's actually terrifying."

"Maybe she's just scared, too."

"Maybe. I hope so."

"You love her, don't you?" Dean says gruffly. We've been friends for years; he's my best friend, but we've never talked personal stuff. Being with him after Evelyn left him was the only time I've seen him vulnerable.

"I've never felt this way about anyone," I admit. "She's amazing, and great and smart and driven. She sees things like I don't, sees them in a way that I can't even fathom. She's built this business up by herself, and she's so independent that I can't see how she would ever need me."

"She doesn't have to need you like that. Like a needy woman. But she can need you in her life."

"I need her. It's only been a couple of hours since she left, but I don't know what to do without her. Even with all the chaos about Theo this weekend, I was miserable without her. I don't know what to do without her, how to get through this on my own." I glance at Theo, now smiling up at Dean. "I don't want to do it on my own."

"You've got it bad."

"So bad," I agree. I measure my words, trying to sort out the intensity of my feelings. "It's like my heart was this little peanut before I met her. Hard and covered in a shell. And after I met her, I realized I had a bunch of peanuts, only now they've become peanut butter. All gooey, and sweet, and good."

It sounds insane when I say it, but Dean only nods. "I know exactly what you mean."

We sit quietly for a few minutes, watching the sports plays of the week on TV. If M.K. was here, she would be in the kitchen with me, cooking dinner, laughing together. Or she would be curled up beside me, her warmth giving me comfort that I never knew I needed.

I blink quickly to stop the burning in my eyes. The peanut butter analogy was enough; I can't let Dean see me crying over M.K.

Even though I could be. Easily.

I can't put into words how much it hurt when she walked out, without giving me a chance to explain. To ask.

"I don't think I handled it right," I say suddenly.

"With M.K.?" Dean asks.

"I told her about Theo, without realizing how much of a shock it was. We've never talked about the future, and I liked that after all those women who kept pestering me for a commitment. It's so easy with her."

"Do you want a future with her? Like the marriage and children type?"

I nod slowly and keep nodding. "I do. I didn't understand how much until Theo. It's always been an abstract concept—you see kids, but you never really understand what it would be like."

"You've only had him for two days."

"I know," I agree. "It's just the tip, but I can see how it can be. Not great—not all the time. Probably really hard. But worth it. At least it would be with her."

"But you don't know if that's what she wants."

"I don't. And I'd like to. Because that changes things."

"Maybe she loves you enough to change what she wants."

"Maybe. But that's not a good thing to want her to change because of me."

"It's called compromise. It's what you do when you're in love." He grins ruefully. "At least that's what I did with Evelyn."

"But it's better with Flora?"

"It's like nothing else matters. It's like Evelyn wasn't real, and I can't see how I was so upset about it."

"I'm glad. She's a great girl."

"You don't even know the half of it."

"When you came in, you said you had stuff going on. What's up? I sort of took over here."

"You had a good reason. But yeah, things with Flora happened, which you can probably guess."

"I'd have to be blind not to," I say wryly.

"Yeah, well, some other stuff, too. I called my old coach," he says slowly.

For a minute I don't understand. I think he's talking about Mikey, who he works with at the Baseball Zone. Or Imad, who is the unofficial manager of our team. And then it hits me. "The Jays?"

"Buffalo. Triple-A," he admits. "I didn't know if he'd even take my call, but he's always been a good guy. He helped me a lot or at least he tried to before I turned into a dick. Anyway," he continues before I can respond. "We talked and he told me to come down and talk to him in Buffalo. That I could hit for him, and see what's going on."

"Pitch?"

Dean shakes his head. "I think my pitching days are past, but he thinks there might be a place for me at first base. And if my hitting is the same—"

"Which it is. Deano, that's great! When's this happening?" I surface out of my misery, reaching for his happiness like a lifesaver.

"This weekend. I'm dropping Flora off with her family because she's got stuff going on, too."

But I don't get to ask about Flora's stuff before I hear the sound of a knock at the door. "Do you hear—?"

Dean is up and out of the chair before I can finish, returning after a minute with M.K. "Look who's here!" he says in a loud voice.

"I knocked," she says softly.

"You came back," I say dumbly, rising to my feet.

"Where do you want me to put this little guy," Dean says, shuffling Theo in his arms.

"I better get back to Flora's. Just wanted to pick up something."

"Hey," I say to M.K., ignoring everything Dean said.

"Hi."

Dean thrusts the baby back into my arms. "You need to tell her everything you told me," he says. "Especially about the peanut butter."

## *Chapter Eighteen*

♥

# M.K.

IT TOOK ME SEVEN minutes after Flora's words sunk in to decide to go back to Clay's.

I don't know what I want to do about his baby, but I do know I want Clay. I want him in my life, beside me, more than I've wanted anything.

The door shut behind Dean, leaving me alone with Clay.

And a baby.

Clay stands before me, a smiling, blond-haired little person in his arms. I study the baby first. Even I, who knows nothing about babies, can see the similarities. His blond hair is lighter but falls over his forehead the same way. The jawline is identical.

And the smile. Even with chubby cheeks and lack of visible teeth, the baby has Clay's smile.

"You came back," Clay repeats, finally breaking the silence.

"I had to." For once I haven't prepared what I wanted to say. I have no plan about this; I'll say this and Clay will say that and we'll get our happily ever after.

I have to admit, in that version, the baby magically disappears. I don't think I'll admit that to anyone else.

"Why did you have to?" Clay asks.

Flora told me to be honest and speak from the heart. That's easy enough for Flora who speaks anything that comes into her head. But I've always been careful what I say, measure the words I use as methodically as if I'm baking.

"I didn't want that to be the last time I saw you," I say.

Clay's face falls. "Is this goodbye?"

"No. I don't know. Only if you want it."

"I don't. I really don't." He takes a step forward then another so the baby is close enough for me to touch.

I don't touch him even though he smiles and reaches his arms out to me.

"M.K., I'm sorry. I did this all wrong. I've been a mess since Abby told me, in a complete whirlwind since she dropped him off."

"You don't have to apologize. It must have been a terrible shock."

"It's been a shock, but I don't think it's been terrible."

Wrong word. And that's why I don't speak from the heart. As I consider my next words, Clay keeps talking.

"I have a son now. I didn't know he existed, but I'm glad I do now. And as difficult as this is going to be, I'm glad Abby had him. He's like you—I had no idea I wanted him, but now I wouldn't give him up for the world. Like you." He smiles and I relax a bit. "I know this wasn't in your plan, but now that things have changed, I hope you might want to try flying by the seat of your pants for a bit."

"I've never done that before," I confess. Everything in my life has been laid out and organized. Carefully plotted and executed. I am not a laid-back person. I don't fly by the seat of my pants.

"Do you think you could try?" Clay pleads. "For us."

"For you and the baby?"

"For you and me. Theo isn't going away. He's here to stay, and I have to figure out what to do about that. But it's you I'm concerned with. You, I need by my side."

"You want a family?" I hold my breath, not sure how he'll respond. Not sure how I want him to respond.

"I want my girlfriend to accept Theo in my life. And I want you to help me figure out a future for us. For you." He gestures to me. "And me. That's all I'm asking right now. That's all I can ask."

Flora told me to speak from the heart, but she didn't say I had to be quick about it. So I take my time to consider what Clay said, what he's asking. He wants me to take on the role of mother figure to his son. He wants me to uproot my life because he got a woman pregnant, and she didn't want him—didn't want them.

The thought of Clay with another woman sends a spear of angst through my heart. I've never been a jealous person. Even knowing Ben cheated on me, there wasn't jealousy, only confusion about why. Why did he pick another woman? What was he missing from me?

There's no confusion about knowing Clay was with another woman. I know it was about sex, because that's all they had together.

Does it make me lose a little respect for him? I don't know.

I'm going to have to get past all that if this is going to work.

And that leads me to the question of the day, the one I was quick to answer with Flora, but when the catalyst is right in front of me...

Do I want this to work with Clay?

"Okay," I say softly. "I'll try."

Clay's smile is like a beam of sunshine. I've never seen him look so happy. "Do you want to hold him?"

A glance at the baby in his arms shows a happy, contented, little guy. I don't want that to change. "Maybe later."

# Clay

MY HEART IS FULL. I've got Theo in my arms and M.K. by my side.

The rest of the night passes in a blur. We talk, I feed Theo and settle him for the night. M.K. and I watch an episode of *The Big Bang Theory* and all I can think about is going to bed.

And not just because having a baby is exhausting.

Finally, M.K.'s head starts bobbing as she fights to stay awake on the couch, and I suggest we retire to the bedroom.

Theo is sleeping in the playpen in the corner of the room, lying on his back with his arms thrown over his head. "He doesn't have a crib?" M.K. asks after a quick glance.

"Abby only brought over the playpen. I guess I should get a crib for him. Might be more comfortable. He slept in the bed with me last night."

Her eyes widen with alarm. "Is he going to sleep there tonight?"

I wind an arm around her waist and pull her close. "No, *you're* going to sleep there tonight. He's good over there."

She nods and after a quick hug, escapes to the washroom.

"I'm really glad you came back," I call to her as I pull off my clothes. The sound of running water answers me.

I'm leaning over the playpen when she finishes. "I like watching him sleep," I admit, straightening with a guilty smile.

"He's very cute," she agrees as she climbs into bed. "Is Dean coming back tonight?"

I chuckle as I climb in beside her. "I don't think Dean is coming back anytime soon. Sounds like things are working out for those two."

M.K. gives an unladylike snort. "It's about time."

"I'll say. They've wasted a lot of time."

M.K. rests her hand against my chest, her head on my shoulder. "That's what I thought, too, but listening to her tonight, I really think it was for the best. They both needed that time."

"Deano was pretty messed up about Evelyn." I tighten my arms around her and give a sigh of contentment.

"Flora...wasn't." M.K. laughs. "I'm glad. I think she was over Thomas a long time ago but didn't do anything about it."

"That's what I've always worried about in a relationship," I confess, the words coming easier in the dark. "Becoming complacent. Content, but not happy."

"Bored?" M.K. offers.

"I don't want to get bored."

"I'll try not to bore you."

I smooth her hair, tucking my hand under her chin to lift her head. I drop a kiss on her lips, and another. "I don't think you need to worry about that."

"I missed you last night," she whispers. "And the night before."

I smile and settle her back against my shoulder. "I never slept with women before. Not sleep, sleep," I add as M.K. barks a laugh. "But I always left. Sometimes right after, sometimes when they were asleep. But I never stayed the night with a woman."

"Me neither. With a man, I mean. Not that there's been many since Ben. But I didn't want that intimacy with another man. It felt like a betrayal." I feel the vibration of her rueful chuckle. "Which is so ironic since he cheated on me."

"You've never told me what happened. He cheated; he died. You always leave it like that."

I sense her hesitation. "I've never told anyone."

"You don't have to tell me. Maybe someday, but I won't pry."

M.K. is quiet, and I think the conversation is over. I'm about to run my hand along her back for the beginning of foreplay, when she speaks.

"Flora knows that another woman was found in Ben's car. She didn't die in the accident—Ben did, but she hung on. But she had no ID with her—no purse, no wallet. Not even a phone. The police thought it was me, because it was my car. We both used it, but it was registered in my name. So the police thought it was me and called my mother. She and my sisters raced all the way from Niagara-on-the-Lake thinking I was dying. But it wasn't me."

"Oh no." I've not yet met M.K.'s family but I can picture the fear and horror as they made the drive to the city, hoping against hope that their daughter would still be alive when they got there. My chest tightens thinking of M.K. hurt, lying in a hospital, and even though I know it wasn't her, it chills me.

She swallows audibly. "It was bad. I don't exactly know what happened at the hospital, but once my mother saw that it wasn't me, she came straight to the apartment. She woke me up screaming about how Ben was cheating on me and how could I have let that happen. It took her twenty minutes to tell me he was dead. She kept going on and on about all my bad choices—moving to the city, being friends with Flora, the patisserie. She thought Ben was the worst of it because he had ruined any chance of me getting married. She told me I'd failed our family, that she wouldn't stand for having a fallen woman in the family. That it was my fault that I couldn't be happy. After all that, she told me he was dead. And a good riddance to him."

I glance down. M.K. has pulled away as she was speaking, her fingers carefully folding the sheet. "Oh, M.K."

"My mother is a difficult woman," she says stiffly. "Since my father left, she's put all of her hopes and dreams and disappointments on me and my sisters. Marrying us off has been her life's work. Because I'm the only one without a husband, most of the disappointment falls on me."

"That's not fair."

"No, it's not. But that's the way it is in my family."

"But can't you talk to your mother? Tell her what she's doing to you."

"My mother is a bit like a steamroller. You don't tell her anything. You go along with it or you get out of the way. I got out of the way. I know I made things worse moving here and starting my own life, but I had to."

"I'm glad. I can't imagine..." My family was far from perfect but it was nothing like M.K.'s. I hug her tightly.

"Flora knows some of it. She knows my mother, but I never told her about that night. I couldn't. It was..." She shivers. "Some of the things she said. I can't repeat them."

"I don't want you to think about it," I tell her. "It wasn't your fault. He was an idiot for cheating on you."

"Was he, though?" she whispers. "I wonder sometimes if it was my fault. If I could have done something."

"M.K., no. Stop." I hold her arms and make her meet my gaze. "I don't know what your relationship with this Ben was like, but if he made the decision to be with another woman, that's on him, not you. You can't make someone betray you like that, not unless you told him to go out and find someone else. And I don't think you did that."

"No, but...maybe things weren't as good as they seemed. It's so hard to remember sometimes. It's like my mother ruined every good memory I had of him."

I hug her tightly. I want to vent on her mother but I can't do that. I've never met the woman and already I dislike her. It's not a good start for our relationship. "I'm not defending your mother, but it must have been so upsetting to think you were hurt and then to find out it wasn't you. It would have been a relief, and some people deal with that in strange ways."

She makes a sound against my chest that might have been a laugh. "It was definitely a strange way of dealing with it."

"What happened to the other woman?" I ask gently.

"She died. It took them three days to find out who she was."

I want to ask, but M.K. doesn't offer any details. "Did you ever find out why?" I smooth her hair, running my hand down her back. She shakes her head.

That surprises me. M.K. is so curious, always needing to know the reason why. For her to have gone two years without knowing why this Ben was with another woman... "Maybe you should." I suggest.

"There's no point."

You could prove your mother wrong. But I don't say it. I also don't mention that maybe it was innocent, that there had been a reason she had been in the car, but I don't. She's shared enough tonight. M.K. hasn't had a problem talking to me and being open with her feelings, but I've sensed there's always been things she's holding back.

This is a big one.

I hold her against me for a long time, stroking her hair, her back, until slowly I feel her begin to relax again. I close my eyes, willing her to fall asleep, but her soft voice rouses me. "Clay?"

"M.K."

"Is the baby always going to sleep in here?"

"I hadn't really thought about it. I want him close, in case he needs me."

"What if I need you?"

"You've got me." I pause for a moment, listening to M.K.'s breathing. "Do you need me now? Because...great!"

## *Chapter Nineteen*

♥

# M.K.

OF COURSE THE BABY started crying just when things were getting good. Clay tried to soothe him with words thrown over his shoulder, but the wailing kept increasing.

Let's say it was awkward and leave it at that.

Eventually he settles, Clay gets back into bed and falls asleep right away.

It takes me a while since I'm so conscious of the baby breathing—deep even breathing with the odd little snore that might have been adorable if it didn't keep me awake.

Clay has a baby, therefore I'm sleeping in a room with a baby. I haven't planned for this.

In fact, this is exactly what I planned against. I didn't want a baby; I *don't* want one.

What do I do now?

I fall asleep, deep and dreamless, unconsciously moving away from Clay while I sleep.

Usually my internal clock works well in the morning, and I use the alarm to make sure it does. But this morning, the internal clock doesn't have a chance to do it's thing.

At first I think the cry is from one of the cats, and I bolt upright with dread. Scarlett once got locked in the linen cupboard, and her crying woke me up in the middle of the night. But when I realize it's Theo, I pause.

What am I supposed to do?

Clay is still fast asleep, his soft snores not even pausing at the sound. Shouldn't he be waking up? Should I wake him up? But just as I'm about to shake him awake, Theo's cries stop.

He stopped crying and I didn't even have to do anything. This is a good baby.

But then there's a sound like he's grunting, which pulls me out of bed. I hover beside the playpen and Theo looks up at me, green eyes alert.

"Hi," I whisper cautiously.

His face scrunches and I brace for wailing that will bring Clay running, wondering what I've done to his child. Instead, he grunts again. Added to that, there's the unmistakable sound of something hitting the diaper and a few toots.

"You're pooing, aren't you?" Theo's face relaxes, and he gives me a toothless grin despite the sudden odour. "What am I supposed to do about that?"

"M.K?" Clay sits up in bed, his hair mussed from where I ran my fingers through it earlier. "You okay?"

"He cried," I report. "And then he pooped."

Clay leaps out of bed, clad only in a pair of boxer-briefs. I don't have a chance to admire the view before he's beside me and lifting Theo from the playpen.

In all the weeks I've been sharing his bed, I've never seen him wake up so quickly.

"Good," he says, grabbing a baby blanket from the pile on the dresser and laying it on the bed with one hand. "Can you get me a diaper from the bag? He didn't poop at all yesterday and I was beginning to worry that he's constipated."

I grab a Pampers and hand it to him, in awe of the ease in which Clay interacts with the baby. Theo squirms on the blanket, thinking it's time to play, no doubt, while Clay keeps a hand firmly on his stomach as he reaches for the container of baby wipes. Then he unbuttons the yellow sleeper.

"I talked to Liv, and she told me only to use sleepers with a zipper," Clay says as he undoes the diaper and grimaces. "I guess this means he's not constipated. She says the ones with buttons are more trouble than they're worth."

"You talked to Liv about him?" I've heard all about Clay's sister-in-law Liv, how she's one of his best friends even after the monstrous crush he used to have on her.

He's never admitted he still had feelings for her, and I've never asked. I didn't have to. But I did believe him when he promised I'd never have to worry about her.

"After Abby dropped him off, I needed Liv to talk me down," he admits.

He told Liv before me. He needed Liv. The realization shouldn't hurt, but the sting is there and it's sharp.

"She gave me a bunch of good advice," he continues, not realizing my thoughts. "Including always cover up the pee-pee." Once he's cleaned off the mess, he whips a cloth off the dresser and drapes if over Theo's little penis. "They can pee straight up, no warning whatsoever."

"Great. Did you just call it a pee-pee?"

"You don't like it. I'll come up with a better name. Penis sounds wrong."

"But that's what it is."

"It's too manlike," he argues. "Especially with someone—" His voice drops into a sing-song playful tone. "—with such a little pee-pee. Don't you worry, little buddy. It'll grow."

My eyes widen with horror. Am I dreaming? Pooping and pee-pees. Does Clay even remember what he did with his penis last night?

"Well, you look like you're handling this," I say carefully. "I'll get ready for work."

"I'm sorry he woke you up."

"You don't have to apologize," I say, not liking my tone. "He's a baby. They wake people up."

"I know, but—" He smiles ruefully at me. "This wasn't the night I had planned."

"You were going to make me dinner," I say lightly. "We were going to talk about...things."

"And we will. Tonight," he promises. "I'll make dinner, and all you have to do is look cute and drink wine. And maybe hold Theo for me." He finishes buttoning up and lifts the baby into his arms. "I know I don't have to hold him all the time, but I like it. He fits, you know?"

"You're making up for lost time," I say softly.

"That's exactly it." He smiles. "I don't know how I'd do this without you."

"I'm not exactly doing anything to help."

"But you're here. You're with me. And you love me?"

I still. It's the first time that word has come up. I know Clay has been hesitant to say those three words, and I—I don't know what was holding me back.

A lot of things had held me back.

"I'm doing that wrong, too," Clay admits with a grimace. "I need to start with saying, I love you. I love you more than you know."

I take a deep breath. "I love you, too." I reach up to kiss him, my shoulder brushing against Theo, who thinks this is play and grabs a hunk of my hair in his fist. "Ow."

"Ow?" Clay asks, his lips against mine.

"He's got me."

"He wants a kiss, too," Clay says as he unfurls the tiny fingers. "But they're all mine. Hang on." He steps away to settle Theo back in the playpen. His gurgle of discontent follows Clay as he comes back to me standing beside the bed with the baby blanket and dirty diaper.

Thankfully he puts down the diaper before wrapping his arms around me. "I love you, M.K. Moira."

"M.K.," I correct firmly. "My mother thinks your name is Clayton."

"Technically, it is, but she shouldn't expect me to answer if she calls me that."

"That's what I told her." I run a hand across his bare chest. "Everything will work out." I'll come up with a plan, I decide. A schedule—some way to organize this new life. Some way of helping me deal with this. Because I need to deal. I love Clay, and I don't want to lose him.

"I know it will," Clay says. As he kisses me, Theo's gurgle becomes a cry.

# Clay

I BUY A CRIB for Theo the next day and set it up in the living room. I also get Pearl to pick me up the best baby monitor she can find.

It takes me two weeks to finally make M.K. the meal I promised her, and another week before we go out again on our own.

My parents fell in love with Theo as quickly as I did, and even though they still haven't met M.K., they agreed to an overnight visit so we could go out one night without him. That was last weekend, and a good time was had by all.

I had fun with M.K., but I miss Theo when he's not around.

I like to think that despite the never-ending exhaustion, I'm a pretty good dad. I quickly become an expert in all things Theo, able to predict when his first tooth is about to arrive, taking him to his doctor's appointment without a major mishap, and starting solid foods right when the books tell me to.

There's still a spot of baby cereal on the kitchen ceiling that I can't reach, but every family has something like that, don't they? Like a badge of honour.

I also know way too much about baby poop. I know if M.K. spent more time with Theo, she'd have his bowel movements set out on some kind of graph, but I don't go that far.

Liv did suggest I make a note of what foods cause a more-violent reaction and avoid them. We only started cereal last week. I'm a little scared of the little jars of baby food. Liv told me I need to start making my own, but I think I'll go with the tried and true Gerber brand.

M.K. kisses my cheek as she sits on the couch beside me. "You're stubbly," she says with a frown.

I rub my chin, the two-day stubble prickly against my hand. "You don't like it? I was thinking of growing it out." I had given it a moment's thought this morning when I was in too much of a rush to shave, but no more.

She raises her eyebrow. "You want to be like Dean?"

"You don't like it? I thought all women liked the bearded look."

"I like you being you." This time her kiss hits my lips, and I slide my hand around her neck to make it last longer. "If I wanted someone who looked like Dean, I would have gone for Dean."

I laugh loud enough for Theo, playing happily in his ExoSaucer, to glance at me with curiosity. "I'm not sure how well that would have gone over with Flora."

M.K. smiles. "I like Dean, but he's not my type."

"What is your type?"

She stretches her legs out on the coffee table beside mine, her feet resting against my calves. I forget she's so short until I compare her to me—when she's standing up close to me or lying beside me. "He's a little tall for me. But I think Flora likes his bigness.

Thomas was..." She makes a face. "He wasn't much of a man. Too fussy for me."

"Dean is definitely not fussy."

"Definitely not."

"Am I man enough for you?" I ask with a sideways glance.

She kisses me in response. For once Theo isn't sitting on my lap, and I take full advantage of having both hands free.

Until Theo gurgles loudly and distracts me.

"Look at him, sitting up like that," I say happily as Theo gnaws on the colourful plastic. "I really think he's advanced for his age."

"How many four-month-old babies do you know?" M.K. asks, pulling away to watch him.

"He's five months now," I correct. Theo and I had celebrated with cupcakes. I had made chocolate ones and Theo had destroyed two before I took them away from him. "We should have a party or do something for his six-month birthday."

"Why don't you just wait for a year?"

I shrug. "It's so long to wait. Besides, Liv does the six-month party with her kids. Apparently everyone does it in England."

M.K. curls her legs under her, my side noticeably cooler now that she's not leaning against me. "How is Liv?" she asks politely.

"She's good," I say, shifting the pile of baby books on the table so I can stretch my legs out in front of me. Dean moved out as quickly and as quietly as he came, but Theo's things have more than taken over any space Dean had taken up. Toys and carefully folded clothes are piled against the wall until I can buy a toy box and a dresser for him. Bouncy seats, the Bumbo, the play mat are stacked in the corner.

It's a far cry from the spartan space I used to live in. Dean had been worried about taking up too much space in the one-bedroom condo. Theo has had no qualms about that.

I haven't brought up the living arrangements with M.K. since the day I asked her to move in. There hasn't been the right time, or I forget, or she's too tired. I make a mental note to talk to her tomorrow right after work. M.K. starts to fade too close to bedtime. I know I'm going to lose her soon.

"I should introduce you to Liv." I glance over at her with an expectant smile on my face. "She'll love you."

"I'm not sure I can manage a trip to London," M.K. says carefully.

"I meant with FaceTime. That's how we talk. I haven't seen her in over two years. I think she's coming back with Rance for Christmas, though. I want you to meet her before then."

"Christmas seems so far away."

"It's only six weeks. It'll be fun, won't it? Playing Santa for Theo."

She smiles. "You're going to totally spoil him, aren't you?"

"The best thing about it is that he won't know any different," I say happily. "It's not like we have more kids. We'll have to be careful when that happens that everything is fair."

M.K. coughs, and reaches for her glass of water. "More kids?" she asks.

"I thought two more. Girls would be nice, don't you think?"

"Not if you're talking about my sisters," she says in a choked voice.

"Our kids won't be like your sisters. Or my brothers. They'll be like you and me—perfect."

"I'm far from perfect," M.K. says ruefully.

"You're perfect for me. And our kids will be beautiful like you."

"Only if they have your smile."

"I want you to teach them to bake," I say. "Beautiful bakers."

"I can open another patisserie and name it that." She laughs.

"Only if you have enough to still bake for me," I warn, pushing her back against the arm of the couch. Lying down, I rest my head against her stomach. "Do you know how much weight I've gained since I met you? It wasn't bad when I could still go to the gym, but with Theo, it's been too long."

"I think you're okay." M.K. smoothes a hand down my back, and I arch with pleasure.

I'd never had this easy affection with the other women I'd been involved with. Touch meant sex, and sex meant leaving at the end of the night. There had been no cuddles, or snuggling, or spooning, and although M.K. isn't as affectionate as I would like, it's still better than the alternative. I'm happy with everything I get.

I'm happy with her.

It's been weeks, barely three months since we met, and it feels like I've known M.K. forever. Contentment swells and surges within me, and I bury my nose into her shirt, the buttons rubbing my forehead, her scent the sweet smell of butter and chocolate.

We talked babies. Our babies. We talked about children before even finalizing the living arrangements. Maybe now is a good time to talk—

Theo screeches suddenly, and my head whips up. "Is he okay?"

"Seems fine," M.K. says. "Happy."

"He's jealous that I get to cuddle with you." I make a move to lie back down, but M.K. puts her hands on my shoulders. I groan.

"You're going now, aren't you?"

"I have to. I hate waking you up in the morning. It's so early, and if you've just gotten back to sleep after Theo, it's not fair," she finishes.

"It's not fair for you to leave me either," I grumble, only half seriously.

"I'll stay Saturday night," she promises. "Reuben's going to open on Sunday, and we've got Flora and Dean's that night. Maybe I'll even get to sleep in."

## *Chapter Twenty*

♥

# M.K.

I'M WIDE AWAKE WHEN I get home, despite what I told Clay. He's always worried that my early hours at the patisserie are too much for me. Every time he mentions it, I think of what my mother would say—that I spend too much time there and Clay will grow to resent it. I've always been able to function on little sleep, but lately I've used my tiredness as an excuse to be away from Theo.

He's cute and sweet, but it's a little much watching Clay with him sometimes.

"What have you guys been doing tonight?" I ask Gulliver as he follows me into the kitchen. Scarlett answers for him, a loud meow that I agree with, even though I still can't understand cat talk.

Standing in the middle of my kitchen, immaculate as ever, I find myself at a loss. I should go to bed because four thirty is early, but I'm too twitchy to sleep. I could read, watch TV, but neither interest me right now.

I can bake, but there's no recipe drifting in my mind, demanding that I make it.

I can call Flora, but she'll be with Dean, and I don't want to intrude. Especially since I have no idea what's making me twitchy and distracted.

I feel alone, and that's unusual for me.

So I do what makes me feel better at times like this. I organize my cupboards.

With a KISS playlist at an acceptable volume as to not wake up the neighbour's baby and the cats looking on with their usual expressions of boredom, I tackle my kitchen.

An hour and a half later, my spices are arranged in alphabetical order, my baking cupboard with the dry ingredients has been swept out and tidied and my colourful silicone spatulas and slotted spoons look happy in their now-neat drawer.

It doesn't help.

"What's wrong with me?" I ask Gulliver, who jumps off the chair and pads over to me to comfort or looking for affection; I'm not sure which.

I take the comfort and settle on the floor with him, which brings Scarlett over. "Clay is amazing. Things are great with him," I assure them, petting both equally. "Why am I in this funk?"

I'm not in a funk. I'm just...bored. I'm never bored.

"I should just go to bed," I say to Scarlett. But Gulliver has crawled into my lap, purring, and his weight makes it difficult to move.

When I finally get to bed, I have a hard time falling asleep. The bed feels empty without Clay, but lately it's even more difficult to fall asleep when I'm with him.

He talked about babies tonight. *Our* babies.

I roll over onto my back and stare at the darkened ceiling. Pennywise is perched on the pillow beside me, his breathing deep and even.

Now I can finally get into what's bothering me.

I've never wanted to have a baby.

I never played with dolls growing up, never had tea parties where I was the mother to a stuffed bear and a Rub-a-Dub Dolly. If there was a tea party then my sisters were hosting and I was in the kitchen gathering freshly baked cookies. When my sisters thrust their newborns at me, I smiled politely and let someone else hold them.

I've never felt maternal. Watching my mother take on both parenting roles, I quickly realized that I didn't want that. Swearing off marriage should have taken care of my non-maternal feelings, but meeting Clay has forced me to rethink things.

We've talked about the future—if you count talking about babies and a quick will you move in query. There's been no mention of the living arrangements since then, and I'm scared to bring it up because I'm sure it's going to open a box of *I don't want to talk about it.*

How do I tell him I don't want children, especially when he's so madly in love with Theo? Unless I love Theo as much as Clay does, I'm always going to come in second with him. How can I tell him marriage isn't in the cards for me?

With Ben it was different. We got engaged because it was the practical thing to do. It would save on rent, better organize our evenings, and it was easier cooking for two. Even his proposal lacked romance, but I wasn't looking for romance. I wanted a partner, someone I could push towards my mother with a *See? I found someone myself.*

Clay is different.

I'm not pushing him towards my mother, but holding him close, afraid of what she'll say about him. Afraid of her taking the idea of Clay and running with it, which will undoubtedly result in a wedding not of my choosing.

I could elope like Flora tried to...

I shake my head. Why am I even thinking about marriage? Clay's so caught up with Theo he can't even remember to finish the conversation about us moving in together. And we've only been together a few months.

I want to be with Clay, and yet I don't want to think about the future. It doesn't make sense.

I turn back on my side, willing my mind to stop with the internal monologue, and for a little while, it listens to me.

# Clay

FLORA IS HAVING A party on Saturday night which means Flora and *Dean* are having a party, because they are now living together.

Theo's arrival coincided perfectly with Dean finally getting together with Flora because as easygoing as he is, I'm not sure he would have enjoyed sleeping in the same room as a five-month-old baby.

I love parties. I'm in my element at big get-togethers, being social and talking to friends and meeting new people...new women.

I'm not going to meet any new women at this party because M.K. is going with me. And I'm glad she'll be with me. It's the first time we've gone to a party as a couple and I'm excited.

I'm a little nervous about bringing Theo, though.

Flora told me to bring him; in fact, she seems excited about it.

M.K., however, doesn't seem overly excited to see Theo tucked into his car seat when I pick her up. "No babysitter?" she asks as she sets a canvas bag of wine and a huge plastic container on the floor of the back seat.

"No go." I asked my parents to watch him, but they have a surprisingly active social life with bridge games, theatre tickets, and monthly murder mystery parties. Tonight coincides with one such party and while I was on the phone with my mother, she told me all about the cowgirl costume she's come up with. "Flora says it's okay to bring him."

"Of course it is." She wiggles Theo's foot and smiles at him. He gurgles in response.

"He really likes you," I say, watching them in the rearview mirror.

"I think he likes everyone who pays attention to him. He's a bit of a flirt," she says as she climbs into the front seat of my new sedan. I had to do away with the Audi R8 because it really wasn't baby friendly.

I still miss it. I miss how it felt to drive around in such a cool car and how other drivers looked at me; some with envy, some with admiration.

People look at me when I'm with Theo, but it's different.

"What's in the box in the back?" M.K. asks as I pull away.

"I made cupcakes this afternoon," I tell her proudly. "Theo and I hung out in the kitchen and made them for the party."

"That's fun."

"I let him taste the batter. I don't think that's a good thing, but it didn't do anything to him. He seems to prefer chocolate over lemon."

"As everyone should," she says.

"I thought you liked my lemon cupcakes?"

"I do, but chocolate is chocolate. I didn't name the patisserie Pain au Lemon, did I?"

It's a short drive to Flora's but impossible to park. We end up three blocks away and I take the car seat with Theo's diaper bag and bouncy seat loped around my arm and chest like some weird bandolier. M.K. carefully balances my box of cupcakes on her container, and I tell her I'll come back for the wine.

"Dean said Flora's niece is coming tonight," I say as we pick our way along the icy sidewalk. It feels more Christmassy with the fresh dump of snow, but nothing is good with the ice. "Maybe she'll want to babysit Theo."

M.K. laughs. "Flora's niece is twenty-five. You met her in Las Vegas—the tall blonde?"

"That was Flora's niece? The scary blonde?"

"She can be a little scary," M.K agrees.

"The first time I saw her we practically had to pull her off the guy." I laugh at the memory of how we first met.

"It wouldn't have been the first time we've had to pull her out of a fight," M.K. says. "Patrick will be there as well. You remember he's Flora's nephew? Different brother than Ruthie's dad."

"So Ruthie and Patrick are cousins. And Flora is an aunt, but they're only a few years younger?"

"Her brothers are even older than yours. Flora has an interesting family tree."

"I can't imagine hanging out with one of my nephews like this." I shake my head. "Like having to behave and everything."

"Neither Ruthie or Patrick do much behaving, so Flora doesn't see the need to." M.K. stares at Flora's door. Her containers reflect the season—pine boughs and pomegranates with a tiny decorated

Christmas tree in the centre. Neither of us have a free hand to ring the bell, but Dean must have been watching for us, because the door opens immediately. "Hey, let me take that," he offers, reaching for M.K.'s load. "Or that," he says, switching his gaze to Theo.

"I'll put him down and go get the wine. M.K., can you get him, make the introductions?"

"I've got this if Dean can take the baby," M.K. suggests, pulling the box back from Dean's grasp.

"Gimme the little dude," Dean says happily.

I hover by the door as Dean disappears with the baby, unable to stop the worried expression on my face.

"He's fine," M.K. says.

"I'll be back in a sec," I promise and with a last look for Theo, head back to the car.

When I return with the wine, I'm greeted at the door by a woman a few inches taller than me with an interesting shade of rose-gold hair. "You're much more attractive when you're holding many bottles of wine," she drawls, her gaze flicking up and down.

I flash her a smile. "I think I remember you…"

"Of course you remember me."

"Ruthie," we say in unison.

"Should we hug?" she asks, taking the bag from me. "I feel we're on the hug level."

"Hug away." Her arms encircle my shoulders with a surprisingly strong grip. "Good to see you again."

"Has M.K. forgiven me for her getting arrested that night?" Ruthie asks as she pulls away.

"You'll have to ask her, but I'm going to have to say no," I say with a laugh as I follow her into the living room. Flora's house is bigger than both mine and M.K.'s, but so packed with people it's difficult to see the extra space. "But it would have been a lot worse if we hadn't gotten together."

"I knew you'd find your way to each other," she tosses over her shoulder. "Just like Flora and Dean. Some people are fated to be together."

"I like the sound of that." I frown as Ruthie stops in front of a makeshift bar in the corner of the room. "None for me. I'm the DD."

"You sound perfect for M.K." Ruthie sighs.

"Does she often need a DD?"

"No, *she's* always the responsible one. It's always been that way. She's a bit tightly wound, don't you think?" Ruthie helps herself to the bottle of open red on the bar, pouring herself a healthy glass.

"I happen to like the way she's wound. But I'm doing my best to help her to relax."

Ruthie studies me, her mouth twisted in neither a smile nor a frown. "Maybe you are going to be good for her. Better than that dud, Ben."

"What was he like?" I ask despite myself.

"Just that—a dud. She could have done so much better, but at least he got her mother off her back for a while. I don't know what surprised me more, that they got engaged or that they found him with another woman." She sipped her wine, keeping her gaze on me over the rim of the glass, no doubt to monitor my reaction.

"She doesn't say too much about it."

Ruthie snorts. "She doesn't say much about anything that bothers her, so good luck with that. My friend is a bit closemouthed."

"And you call her a friend?"

Her face softens. "M.K.'s like a sister to me, always has been. I know we have our disagreements, and she really doesn't understand me, but I love her to death. Don't tell her that," she hisses before she disappears into the crowd.

"So you met the niece," a voice behind me says. I turn to see Trev, Imad, and a few of the ball team. "She's something." Trev scowls after Ruthie.

"Certainly something," I agree, watching the rose-gold hair move through the crowd. "What'd she do to you?"

"Wouldn't give out her number?" Imad asks with a laugh.

"I didn't even ask," Trev protests. "She's not my type."

I meet Imad's gaze. "I thought every woman was your type," I say with a grin.

"No, that's *you*, bro," Trev says.

"Not anymore," Imad corrects him. "Not since M.K. Rashida says you're like a new man."

I smile widely. "She's great. But I also think it's because of Theo. Have you met the little guy yet? Best kid ever!"

I scan the crowd for Dean and Theo, not noticing M.K. slip away behind me.

## *Chapter Twenty-One*

♥

# M.K.

BY THE TIME I get into the kitchen with the baked goods, Dean has Theo out of the car seat, holding him up to the others crammed in the living room like Rafiki lifting Baby Simba to the masses.

Flora is the only one who turns away from Dean and Theo, following me into the kitchen. "What'd you bring, other than the most cutest baby ever?"

I blink with shock. I've never heard her baby-talk voice and it's one I'd rather not hear again.

"Pastries, and Clay made cupcakes. He's gone to get the wine." Flora's kitchen is a good size, but the counters are so cluttered with plates and bottles, and bags of chips that I feel my insides clench. "Go see Theo. You know you want to."

As Flora darts away, I take advantage of the quiet to do a quick tidy; sorting the wine into red and white, and putting a selection of white in the fridge, finding bowls to fill for two different kinds of chips and putting away the dishes drying in the rack.

Satisfied, I finally take off my coat and join the others in the living room.

"You were cleaning my kitchen, weren't you?" Flora asks with a rueful grin.

I shrug. "Had to be done." I turn as Ruthie, all six feet of her, moves to engulf me in a hug. I return it even though all is not entirely forgiven for the night I spent in jail in Las Vegas. If it hadn't been for that, Clay and I wouldn't have missed those first weeks together. When I think of how we might not have found each other...

"You dyed your hair again." Gone are the blonde, braided extensions, and the cherry-red curls. Now her hair is a rose-gold colour, falling down her back is messy waves.

"I like variety." Ruthie raises her glass of wine to me. "You, apparently, like babies. That's new."

"Who doesn't like babies?" I ask, glancing around for Clay.

"You, or so I always thought."

I've known Ruthie since she was three days old. Flora had dragged me to her brother's house after school to show off her new niece. Since then, she's wormed her way into Flora's life, and therefore mine. "Things change," I say shortly.

"Do they?"

Thankfully Patrick interrupts and lifts me up in a burly hug. "Hello, Boss Lady," Adam chirps from behind him. "I'm not calling you Boss Lady tonight. Tonight, you are M.K.," he adds in an ominous voice.

"That's fine."

"Tomorrow you're back to being the boss lady, but I'll remember everything you do tonight and report back to Reuben."

"That goes for me too."

"I love Reuben," Flora announces, overhearing our conversation. "He's so big and hairy that I always want to give him a hug when I see him. But I don't because I can't tell if he's a huggy person. Is he?"

"I've never been tempted to give him a hug, so I can't help you there."

"I know exactly what you mean." Adam gushes. "He's like a big, hairy teddy bear. Kind of like your guy there." He gestures to Dean, towering over Clay and the baby.

"You're welcome to give Dean a hug, Adam." Flora grins. "I know you want to."

"Only if Patrick would approve." He links hands with Patrick. "Now that we're really, officially, together."

"What's so official about it? Just that you're dating now?"

"I like him. He likes me. We've said the words." Adam sighs and Patrick squirms with embarrassment.

I smile at them. "I'm happy for you."

"Be happy for me, too," Ruthie interrupts. "I'm engaged."

"You're what?" Flora cries. "When? Who?"

"Four days ago." Ruthie waves her hand and I make out a band on her third finger that looks suspiciously like the plastic ring from a Ring-Pop. "I would have told you sooner but we only came up for air last night."

"TMI, dear cousin," Patrick groans.

"Not for me." Adam grabs her hand. "Do tell *everything*!"

"Before this turns into the Ruthie show, we need the champagne. Dean and I have something to tell you. And then I want to hear all the G-rated details."

"You can tell me the R-rated ones later," Adam whispers to Ruthie.

"Let me just grab the wine from Clay," I say. "I don't think he's made it to the kitchen yet."

Of course I make it over to Clay's group just in time to hear Clay give Theo credit for making him a changed man.

I slip back into the kitchen before he notices me.

"Can you believe Ruthie?" Flora hisses as I hover in the doorway, a queasy feeling I don't recognize growing in my belly. As Flora plucks the bottles of sparkling wine out of the snow by the back door, I push forward resolutely to arrange the plastic wine flutes on the counter.

Clay loves his son, and Theo has changed him. It doesn't matter who gets credit or who comes first.

It's always going to be Theo, I realize. But that's how it should be.

"I should get proper glasses," Flora admits, oblivious to my thoughts. "But I'm not much of a champagne person."

"Sparkling wine," I correct after a quick glance at the label of the bottle. "Champagne can only be called champagne if it was made in the Champagne region of France. Anywhere else, it's sparkling wine. Except for Italy, where it's known as prosecco, and Spain, where it's cava. This is cava," I add, expertly easing out the cork. "It's nice."

"Spoken like a winemaker's daughter." Flora sighs, holding up two cups for me to fill.

"So why the bubbles tonight?" I ask, trying to hide my anxiety. "Is there something you might want to tell me in here?" If Flora and Dean were going to announce their engagement, she would tell me first. She tells me everything first.

At least she used to. Before Dean.

"You'd be the first to know if it was anything that earth-shattering," Flora promises, knowing exactly what I'm talking about. "And I think you'd have something to tell me first."

"There'll be nothing to tell," I say shortly.

"But with Theo—haven't you thought…" Flora trails off as I open a second bottle.

"No. Why would I? I have no desire to get married." I keep my gaze on the bottle, not meeting her eyes.

"But there's a baby to think about," she presses.

"It's not my baby. What happens if she comes back and wants Clay, as well as Theo?"

Flora's eyes widen. "Do you think that's going to happen?"

"I don't know anything that's going to happen," I admit. "Clay is so caught up with Theo that we barely have a moment together. I sound jealous," I say after a moment, giving my head a shake. "I feel jealous, too. That's what's wrong with me."

It's like the proverbial light bulb goes on, but it does nothing to illuminate me. "How can I be jealous of a baby?" I demand.

"Because you can be jealous of a baby," Flora says matter-of-factly. "Archie once told me that he was furious when Ruthie was born because he felt like he lost his wife. He got over it pretty quick, but he said it was a bad couple of days."

"I'm not jealous of Theo. He's a baby. But he's not my baby."

"Yes, you've said that," Flora says patiently. "Do you want him to be your baby? Would that make it better?"

"I don't want my own baby. I never have."

"But things change." Flora widens her arms, sending wine sloshing over the edge of the glass. "Look at me."

"What's changed?"

"Let's take these in and I'll tell you. But we're not finished with this conversation," she warns, catching the stems of glasses in her hand and heading back into the living room.

After the glasses have been handed out, we toast Dean's announcement that he made the roster of the Double-A farm team for the Toronto Blue Jays, the first step of his progress back to playing in the major leagues. He reports to Dunedin, Florida for spring training in February.

"As first base," he adds, his flush of being the centre of attention blending in with his red beard. "We'll see how the pitching arm can handle it when I'm there."

"I'm so happy for you." After I give Dean a hug of congratulations, I turn to Flora. "But what about you? You can't go with him. What about the store?"

"You're right, but it's not because of the store." She glances at Ruthie and Patrick, both with expectant smiles on their faces. "I'll be opening the Toronto branch of Shaunessy's Nurseries in the spring."

I can't help the pang at Flora's news. Although she's kept me informed about her rapprochement with her brothers and how they want her back in the family business now that Thomas is fully out of the picture, hearing her news and seeing the flush of happiness on her face is bittersweet.

Of course I'm happy for my best friend. She and Dean are both getting what they've always wanted, and they're doing it together. But it means things will change.

I don't like change.

# Clay

"EVERYONE HAD NEWS TO share tonight," I say as M.K. gets ready for bed. I love watching her come out of the bathroom, wearing one of my T-shirts. I know she doesn't get much sleep with Theo, and since she's up so early with the patisserie, sleep is important to her, but I miss having her here.

I sleep better when she's next to me.

"I'm so happy for Dean." M.K. sits on the edge of the bed, rubbing cream onto her arms. "I can't wait to see him play at the Rogers Centre. I hope he can pitch again." She laughs suddenly. "Flora was so excited when we first saw him play, and that was before she even met him. I don't think I'd be able to hold her back this time."

"I don't think Deano needs saving from her. He's pretty smitten with her."

"And she's pretty smitten with him."

"What about you?" I ask as M.K. slips under the covers. "Are you just as smitten?"

She raises an eyebrow, somehow making the gesture sexy and inviting. "What do you think?"

"I think you're a smitten kitten," I say, pulling back the covers to display her long, bare legs. "At least I hope you are."

"A smitten kitten. That's me." She cuddles close to me, my hand stroking her back.

"What did you think of Ruthie being engaged?" I ask. "I don't know her well enough, but that was a surprise, wasn't it?"

"Nothing with Ruthie surprises me."

M.K. stiffens slightly, and I don't know if it's talk of Ruthie or engagements. I don't want to have this talk now, but it seems like a good opportunity. It's not like I want *that* talk, but lately, I've been wanting to feel M.K. out about her thoughts on the future.

If she has thoughts about a future with me.

I've never wanted to talk to any woman about it, but M.K. is different. I'm different with her. I'm a better person. I didn't once have the urge to flirt with Ruthie tonight or talk business with Rashida. I looked after my boy and talked to my friends about their lives and had a great time.

"I can't imagine any engagement lasting very long," M.K. continues in a voice laced with condescension. "Ruthie isn't the type."

"What type is she?"

"Fun. Ruthie is all about fun and excitement. I'm sure being engaged is fun, but married life won't be, and that's where she'll draw the line and move on to the next victim. She's got a trail of broken hearts across the country."

"I guess it's good that Trev didn't fall under her spell tonight." Part of me hoped my friend and Ruthie might hit it off, but there were no sparks, only annoyance from both sides.

M.K. sighs and I feel her relax. "Ruthie is amazing in her own way, but she's very selfish. I don't think that will ever change."

"I think she's cool. Or I would think that if I stopped being scared of her."

"You can't be scared of Ruthie," she chides. "She's harmless."

"I don't think she is. But it's cool. She's scary cool."

M.K. laughs softly, the sound cutting off as Theo's cry breaks into the room. "I thought he might have problems falling asleep," she says. "I think he was overstimulated tonight."

"What's that?" I throw off the covers, but M.K. is already up.

"I read about it. Too much noise and excitement for babies. It makes it difficult to settle down."

I watch in amazement as M.K. heads to Theo's crib. This is the first time she's gone to settle him in the night.

"Hello, little man." I hear her soft voice over the baby monitor. "Can't sleep? Come talk to us."

Not only is she holding him, almost cuddling him against my Lacoste T-shirt, but she brings him back into the room. "I know you're not supposed to bring babies into bed—"

"Who says that?" I reach for him. "I think it's a great idea. For a while," I add, with a glance at M.K. "I don't want him in here all night. That might be bad parenting."

"I think it might disrupt his sleep patterns, but there's been no long-term effects…" She trails off as she notices how I'm looking at her. "Oh. Well, that wouldn't be good for him either."

"I kind of want you all to myself for a bit."

"I'd like that too," she says softly. She lies down carefully, giving Theo the spot still warm from her body.

The three of us lie there for long minutes, Theo quickly falling back asleep, and M.K. watching him.

I watch M.K. I can't read the expression on her face.

"I know this hasn't been easy for you," I begin in a quiet voice.

"It's fine," she says shortly, and I stifle my sigh of frustration. She shut down, just like she does when I want to talk about Theo or the future. "He seems fine now. Why don't you take him back to his crib?"

She's open about everything in her life except what she wants from me. And lately, I really want to find out what she thinks about that.

## Chapter Twenty-Two

♥

# M.K.

I SLEEP AT HOME Sunday night.

I tell Clay it's because Monday will be busy, and I need a few extra hours of sleep. I still have problems knowing Theo is in the next room. The baby monitor picks up his every movement, every cry in his sleep. I woke up with a start two nights ago after a bout of bad gas was broadcast into the bedroom.

Clay knows all this. He knows I miss him when I'm not curled up beside him, but he respects me enough not to argue or complain.

What Clay doesn't know is how I felt holding Theo last night.

I've been good. While I've been slowly deconstructing the walls around my heart for Clay, I've reinforced the ones for Theo.

It's too soon to fall in love with a baby.

Even though we had planned to talk about the future, the discussion never happened. He loves me; I love him but I refuse to let myself love Theo.

What if we don't work out after all, and I'm heartbroken with the loss of him and his son? Or worse, what if the mother comes back? What if she decides she wants Theo back or doesn't want another woman in her son's life?

Some nights I lie awake wondering if it came to a choice, would Clay pick me or Theo.

So I haven't let myself fall in love with Theo.

It's been harder than I imagined it would be. He's so cute and loves to cuddle. He smells amazing.

All the things I love about Clay.

But last night while he was crying, I needed to be with him. And as I was holding him, comforting him, there was a distinct tug at my heartstrings. It was strong and it was insistent.

*Let me in,* a voice seemed to say.

After he quieted, after both he and Clay fell asleep, I locked myself in the bathroom for half an hour until the temptation to pull Theo back into bed with us passed.

It's like I'm watching an avalanche of snow fall off a mountain. From a distance it seems like slow motion, a dangerous but beautiful display of the power of nature, but anyone in its path is well aware of how destructive and deadly it can be.

Letting myself fall for that baby is not a good idea for me.

・♥・♥・♥・♥・♥・

"You look like you've had a rough night," Adam says sympathetically midway through the morning rush. "Hard night? I guess not," he says with an impish grin. "Baby keep you up?"

"I was at my place last night."

He rolls his eyes lasciviously. "That's why you didn't sleep."

"Should you really be talking to your boss like that?"

"You're not my boss—you're my friend," he says in a singsong voice. "I was invited to the same party as you."

"Because you're finally, officially dating Flora's cousin," I say meanly. "I didn't invite you."

"You love me, and you know it."

"I love it when you refill the milk containers before I have to ask you," I shoot back. Adam chortles as he heads off to refill the containers.

"Your phone's abuzzin'," Reuben calls. He's working at the cash register where I left my bag and phone. I hurry to check it with a smile, thinking it's Clay.

It's my mother. The dutiful daughter persona is so ingrained that I answer it without a moment's thought.

"You need to bring Clayton for dinner on Thursday," she greets me. "It's Wanda's six-month birthday and everyone will be there." Wanda is my sister Millie's latest child. She's already talking about getting pregnant again, no doubt trying to compete with Molly.

My mother doesn't give me a chance to respond. "Your sister has decided that since society doesn't reflect the importance of milestones, from now on they will be celebrating half-year birthdays."

Anyone not thinking society celebrates milestones should check out the greeting card selection in the nearest drugstore. But of course I don't say anything about this to my mother. "I've heard it's a thing. But unfortunately, I can't make it."

"But it's a party!" My mother's voice swells like a balloon. She hates it when anyone says no to her.

"One I'll have to miss, I'm afraid."

"I hope you have a very good reason. Your sister will never forgive you for this."

"Millie never responded to my message after Wanda was even born, so I doubt she'll even miss me."

"It's because you left a message. There was no personal touch. You should have made the time to come down. You should have been at the hospital. You could have come into the delivery room!"

"No, I really couldn't. I'm sure I should do a lot of things, like massages and manicures like they do, but I don't because I opened the patisserie. Which is kind of like my baby, but none of you realize that."

"You'll be spending less time there when you and Clayton get married," my mother says in a knowing voice.

"I doubt that."

"Don't argue with me about this. You saw how your father and I drifted apart when I went to work in the winery."

I furrow my forehead with confusion. Is she really blaming her working for my father leaving? That's a new one.

"That won't happen," I say, not wanting to argue. "We're fine."

"Just fine? Not good? Not great? Not fantastic? What kind of relationship are you in?"

"A good relationship between two busy people, one of which has a son."

As soon as I say the words, I want to suck them back, like pulling a bubble back into the wad of chewing gum.

I hear my mother's gasp over the line, and for a moment I think of the scene in Harry Potter where the aunt swells like a balloon.

"A son!"

"It's nothing," I say quickly, hoping to dam the hole before the flood. I leap to my feet, needing to face this standing, not like a child bowing to authority.

"It is not *nothing*. He has a child? Why did you never tell me?"

"Because it's none of your business."

"How can you say that?" I've wounded her, and a wounded animal is more dangerous than anything. I literally brace my feet for the attack. "After everything I've done for you."

"Mom, look, I should have told you, but we just found out—"

Another mistake. "What do you mean, you just found out? How old is this child? Has he cheated on you already?"

"No, he's nothing like Ben."

"How can you say that? You had no idea Ben was even involved with anyone else. You were completely oblivious to the fact, a fact that is sorely disappointing to this family. Women should know these things. They should be able to sense them, like I did. Like I knew about what your father was doing with that...that...hussy!"

Again, she's distorting the facts, but this isn't the time to correct. "Clay is nothing like Ben or Dad. He just found out that an ex-girlfriend had his baby. Theo is five months old. I haven't even known Clay for that long."

"He has a baby!" Her voice turns sugar sweet and my head begins to ache from being whipped around during this conversation. "Oh, Moira Margaret, how wonderful! You've got the family you've always wanted. You can marry Clayton and adopt this child and I can have another grandchild! A grandson! I don't have one yet, and until you get over this childish fear of having a baby—"

"It's not a fear, and it's not childish. Despite what you want me to do, I don't want a baby. I don't even want to get married. And it's not my family. Theo is Clay's baby. He's not my baby, and he will never be my baby." A surge of rage builds up like my own flood, and for once I don't check it. "This is not a ready-made family, as much as you pretend it is. I don't want a ready-made family, because I don't want a family. I don't want to get married. I won't be having children, and I won't raise one that doesn't belong to me just to make you happy. Can you please respect my decision?"

Silence on the phone. But not from the doorway of my office.

I whirl around to see Clay and Theo.

# Clay

EVEN THOUGH M.K. IS at her place, I still wake up early. I miss her beside me. I miss the feel of her in my arms, the smell of her skin, the way she curls into me after she turns off her alarm, like she's desperate for a few more minutes of sleep.

Theo takes on her role of wake-up call.

"Good morning, little guy." His answering smile touches my heart in a way I never thought I'd experience. It jolts me every time I see him—this is mine. He's mine. But even after these couple of weeks, it's like I've always had him.

This has gone better than I ever could have imagined. Not that I ever imagined a woman from my past handing over my child. For a guy who shied from commitment, that's the last thing I'd ever thought of.

But now I have a baby. And I have M.K. Life is pretty perfect right about now.

Because it's so early, I bundle Theo into his car seat and take him into work. I can't drop him off at the babysitter's until eight o'clock, and if I want to be honest, I've been looking for a reason to bring him in and show him off.

Only Rashida and Pearl know much about him, mainly because I tend to keep my personal life personal at work. It's bad enough that they know my family's business, but they don't need to know mine.

But Theo is different. However he came into my life, I'm proud to call him my son.

As I lug his car seat, bulging diaper bag, and bouncy chair into my office, I realize this is why mothers are so strong. Baby stuff weighs a ton. But it's worth is as I set Theo up in the seat beside my desk. He's out of sight for anyone walking by, but as soon as Pearl comes in with my morning coffee, she'll see him.

Not that I ask Pearl to get my coffee—she does it on her own accord. "If I'm getting one for myself, it's not much trouble to pick up one for you, too," she always says. So every week I add to her Starbucks card. It's not M.K.'s coffee but it'll do.

Thinking of M.K.'s coffee at the patisserie makes me think of her. I miss her when she doesn't stay the night. I make a mental note to stop in for a kiss and a coffee when I leave to take Theo to the babysitters.

Two hours later, Pearl finds me. I've demolished my inbox, and Theo has grown bored with the colourful danglies hanging from the arch over his chair and has let himself be lulled to sleep by the vibrations.

"Good morning," Pearl trills, taking in my rolled-up sleeves and mussed hair. "You look like you've been here for a while." As she sets my to-go cup on my desk, her gaze falls on Theo. "Oh! Baby!"

Her voice is more excited than loud but still does the trick to wake him up. His face contorts with a cry but as Pearl drops to the floor beside him, his eyes blink open and he falls under the soothing spell of Pearl. It's like she's the man-whisperer, always able to calm me down.

"He's so precious," she coos, tickling his foot.

"He'll want to be picked up," I warn.

"And then that's exactly what I'll do." She has him unbuckled from the seat and up into her arms in record time. "He's just so sweet." She bounces, she coos, she tickles. And Theo loves it.

"I wondered when you'd break down and bring him in," Rashida says from the doorway.

"He was awake; I was awake. I had a pile of work to do that I hadn't brought home. I'll take off in a half hour to drop him off at the sitter's."

"Then we have time to play with him." Rashida holds out her arms to Pearl. "Give him here."

"I am not sharing," Pearl all but growls.

"I get to have a turn," Rashida whines.

"No," Pearl says, stalking out of the office with Theo.

I laugh at Rashida's expression. "He'll poop soon, and she'll give him back," I say.

Rashida cocks her head. "Did you seriously mention baby poop?"

"It's a thing."

"It's a thing that all new parents talk endlessly about. I never thought you'd ever fall into that category."

I rub the back of my neck. "Neither did I."

She perches at the edge of my desk, and I rescue my coffee in the nick of time. "So how's the Daddy stuff going?"

I shrug carelessly. "I don't see what all the fuss is about," I say, knowing Rashida has two boys, and my words will undoubtedly provoke a reaction.

"Then you're clearly doing something wrong," she retorts in an icy tone.

I chuckle. "No, it's intense. But good. I don't know other babies, but he's so *good*. Easy."

"You'll pay for it later," Rashida says knowingly.

"If he's anything like me, I'll be tearing my hair out by the time he's a teenager."

"You won't have any hair left by then. Or it'll have gone gray."

"Fatherhood does not automatically mean losing my hair."

"Just wait. How is M.K. with the changes? Does she love it? Instant motherhood without any of the pregnancy hassles."

I'm not sure how to answer that. The best I can say is that M.K. tolerates the baby. She seems uncomfortable with him and won't touch him unless absolutely necessary. I chalk it up to her inexperience with babies and keep the hope that she'll loosen up.

Saturday night proved it's possible. I need to give her more time.

"She's good," I say. "It's different and not usually what you expect when you've started a relationship, but she's good."

"I'm glad. I like her a lot."

"So do I."

• ♥ • ♥ • ♥ • ♥ • ♥ •

After prying an ecstatic Theo out of Pearl's arms long enough to allow Rashida a brief cuddle, I pack him back into his car seat and set out to drop him off at the babysitter's. M.K.'s patisserie isn't exactly on the way, but I make the detour. Rashida's words have stuck in my head. I need to give her time. She needs to spend more time with Theo. We have to figure out the living arrangements because I want her with me all the time.

And even the cats. Theo would love to play with Gulliver and Scarlett.

Maybe not Pennywise.

She'll want me to stop in with Theo, I tell myself as I park in front of the patisserie. She'll want to see him.

"Man and baby," Adam sings as he catches sight of me. "Come see me! Or," he says, his voice dropping with mock disappointment. "Go see your girl. She's in the back office."

"I'll come see you later," I promise, hefting the car seat to avoid a group of customers.

"I'm much more exciting than M.K.," he taunts.

"I've no doubt you are."

M.K. is rarely in her office during the morning rush, so I knock quietly when I reach the door. When she doesn't answer, I push the door open.

"He's not my baby and he will never be my baby," M.K. says angrily. She's on her phone, and her back is to me. Even though I know I should back away, I can't. I stand frozen in her office as she destroys me without a moment's breath.

"This is not a ready-made family, as much as you pretend it is. I don't want a ready-made family, because I don't want a family. I've been telling you this for years. I'm not getting married. I won't be having children, and I won't raise one that doesn't belong to me just to make you happy. Can you please respect my decision?"

Oblivious to her words, Theo gurgles with delight to see M.K. She turns, her face falling as she sees me. "Clay."

She lowers the phone as I take in her sweet face, the scar stark white as her cheeks turn red. Her blue eyes are dark with anger or guilt.

I can't read her expression.

"Clay," she says again. "I need to—"

I turn and walk out of her office, Theo's seat bumping against my leg.

## Chapter Twenty-Three

♥

# M.K.

"I HAVE TO GO," I snap at my mother. "I hope you know that now you've completely ruined my life." Her protests ring in my ears as I hang up, but my only thought is of Clay.

"Clay, wait!" The patisserie customers gape after me as I rush through, still in my immaculate blue apron. I catch up as he's at the door. "Clay, please."

The coldness of his gaze sends shivers through me. He says nothing as he leaves, Theo kicking his stocking feet with delight from the sights and smells of the patisserie. I follow them to Clay's car.

His brand-new, four-door Audi sedan that he picked up last week, trading in his precious sports car because of Theo.

Everything changed because of the baby.

"Please, let me explain," I plead.

"I don't know what you need to explain," Clay says, his voice unrecognizable. The doors unlock with a beep beep. "You sounded fairly clear on the phone. You don't want a family. You don't want Theo. End of story."

"I was talking to my mother."

"Is that supposed to make a difference? Are you lying to her now?"

"I didn't lie to you."

"You told me you wanted to make this work with me." He hefts Theo into the car, snapping his seat in place. "Actually, no. You never came right out and told me that you wanted Theo. Or to be part of our family."

Our family. Like I've already been cut out, like a nasty plantar wart I had on my heel once.

"I want you," I say miserably. "I want you the way things were."

Clay straightens. For once he isn't smiling, his blinding white smile that blinded me and led me to love him. "Well, I'm sorry, M.K., but things have changed. And I know you're not good with change, but I thought you'd make an effort for me. I should have realized you were—I don't know what you were doing with me."

"I love you."

He stares down at me, his eyes icy. Everything we shared, everything that's happened between us seems to vanish in a puff of smoke.

I want to grab, it but it slips through my fingers.

"If you love me, you love my son," Clay says, his words cutting through me. "That's the way it has to be. From what I heard, there's no chance of that with you."

He picks his son. I always knew he would, but I had no idea it would hurt so much, like the searing pain I felt when my arm brushed the oven door. Only worse.

Much worse.

"Clay..." I whimper.

A quick, vicious shake of his head. "I can't let you hurt him. I can't make you do this. I can't make you do anything you feel so strongly about. I love you, but I love him, too."

The tears drip down my cheeks as he gets in the car.

"Clay," I whisper as he drives away with his son.

# Clay

I DON'T KNOW HOW to do it without her.
As I drive away without a glance at M.K. standing in the parking lot, I realize how much I was relying on her to get me through this. Theo is my son, but I needed M.K.

I'm not sure what I needed her for. Reassurance? Help? Help would be nice. The next few years stretch before me, exhausting and lonely, a single father with his son.

Theo is still crying, small, snuffling cries without much behind them. I know he's upset, but so am I. "There's nothing I can do, little buddy," I say to him with a glance over my shoulder. I only see the top of his blond head over his car seat. "She's gone."

How could M.K. not tell me she didn't want this?

Why didn't I ask?

The realization hits me with a punch. I never once asked what M.K. wanted, what she was okay with. Did she even want children? I implied that we'd get married and have more without even acknowledging her.

I didn't listen.

I didn't listen when she tried to explain either.

I try to turn around to go back, but the traffic is too heavy. It's ten minutes before I can make a left turn to head back to Pain.

When I pull into the parking lot, M.K. is gone.

Did I really think she'd still be standing outside? And if she was, what was I supposed to say to her? That it's fine that she hates my kid; I can love him enough for the both of us.

Would I say that?

I pull out of the parking lot without stopping. I don't know what I'd say to her, so it's better not to say anything.

• ♥ • ♥ • ♥ • ♥ • ♥ •

After I drop Theo off, I don't go back to the office. Driving aimlessly through the city for a bit, I end up at the Baseball Zone, the training facility where I first met Dean. I don't expect to see him there, but the thought of destroying a few baseballs in the batting cage sounds perfect for my mood.

It's been a while since I've been there, and I don't recognize anyone as I grab a helmet and a bat and head into one of the cages.

Twenty minutes later, I'm still pounding the balls with my shirt sleeves rolled up and the hem hanging loose over my dress pants. I've taken my shoes off because the soles have me slipping over the fake turf.

I had been a serious ballplayer until I went to university. The sport had come easy to me as a teen—I had been a star second baseman with a .340 average, but my interest faded at school, with those continuing to play more determined and focused than I was.

Plus—girls. There were no girls on the baseball team, and there were so many everywhere else.

I need to focus on something other than women for once in my life. Which is ironic, since I've met the one woman who makes me forget about everything else.

"I heard you come in," says a voice behind me, making me swing wildly and miss the pitch. I glance over my shoulder to see Dean standing behind the mesh net.

"How'd you hear that?" I miss another pitch and swear under my breath.

"You're trying too hard," Dean says.

"Story of my life," I mutter.

"Really? I'd say the opposite."

I turn, and a seventy-mile fastball just misses my shoulder. "What's that supposed to mean?"

"You just let her go?"

"She talked to Flora," I mutter, the bat back in position. The next ball goes careening off the right-hand net.

"Would have been a foul," Dean says.

"I know it would have been a foul." I grit my teeth, ready for another pitch, but the machine blinks red, signaling the end. With a huff, I turn back to Dean who stares at me sympathetically. I glare at him through the net until finally my shoulders slump with resignation. "What did she say?"

"She was upset."

"I figured that because of the tears," I snap, slamming the tip of the bat on the ground.

"You left her crying?" Dean asks, his expression a mix of surprise and disgust.

"What else was I supposed to do?" I demand, throwing up my arms. "She tells me she hates my son."

"Did she actually say that she hates him?"

"No, but—"

"And did she say it to you?"

"No. I heard her on the phone."

"And who was she talking to?" he asks patiently.

"I don't know," I mutter.

"Flora said it was her mother. And I don't know M.K. like you and Flora do, but even I know that she's got a messed-up relationship with her mother."

I push open the door to the cage with more aggression than I need to, and it flies back into the net. "I know that."

"Have you talked to her about it?"

"What am I supposed to say?"

"How she feels? Women love to talk about their feelings."

I flip off the helmet and put the bat back into the rack before running my hand through my hair. No, I don't know that women like to talk about their feelings because I do everything I can to avoid the topic. Anyone tries to tell me she's happy-scared-upset, and I'm out of there. At least that's how I was with my other girlfriends.

But since M.K., I realize I can't call them girlfriends. Even Abby, the mother of my child, was only a woman I dated. Briefly dated.

We never once talked about our feelings about anything.

Suddenly I feel very inexperienced.

"What do I do now?" I ask, not enjoying feeling so vulnerable.

"Tell her you're wrong, or sorry, or something. Fight for her," Dean says. "If M.K.'s what you want. If you want it to work, it's not supposed to be easy."

I nod, gnawing on my lower lip. "Do you really think I have it easy?" I ask.

Dean shrugs. "Look at your life. Seems pretty sweet. Not that it's a bad thing, just how it is."

I nod again as Dean steps into the batting cage.

## *Chapter Twenty-Four*

♥

# M.K.

AFTER CLAY DRIVES AWAY, I duck into Fleur, hoping Flora is having a quiet morning. Just as I push open the door, I remember Flora hired Heather, an ex of Clay's, and say a quick prayer that she isn't there.

Of course she is.

Not only are Heather and Flora standing behind the counter, but Ruthie slouches against it, the three of them in the midst of an animated conversation that stops when the bell tinkles to announce me.

"Imogene's having the baby," Flora cries, her face lit up with happiness. And then her face falls. "What happened to you?"

"That's great about Imogene," I croak, wishing I could go a day without hearing about babies. An hour. Five minutes.

"Yeah, but—M.K., what's wrong?" Flora looks imploringly at me. "You've been crying."

I swipe at the wetness still coating my cheeks and shake my head. "I'm fine."

"Is it Clay?" Is it my imagination, or does Heather sound excited at the thought?

I refuse to look at her. "He heard me on the phone with my mother," I say to Flora in a low voice.

"Not pleasant, but not the end of the world."

"It was about how I didn't want kids. Didn't want Theo. I said a bunch of stuff." I glance at Heather, who quickly replaces the expression of delight with pity.

Flora nods, her face unreadable. "Ah. I wondered about that."

"About what?"

"About what your mother would say," Ruthie answers for her. "I'm sure that was a treat." Being from Niagara-on-the-Lake and the niece of Flora, Ruthie is well aware of the intricacies of the relationship I have with my family.

But I still don't like the tone in her voice. "She was just being my mother."

"Let's go in the back room," Flora suggests, pushing away from the counter. "In case anyone comes in. Heather, you okay out here for a bit?"

"Sure."

I don't imagine the resentment in her tone now.

The back room off Flora's shop is her workroom, filled with pots of baby flowers and bags of dirt. There's a musky smell that doesn't smell very flowerlike. I stand awkwardly in the middle of the room, careful not to touch anything. Ruthie shuts the door behind us.

I love that Flora is so passionate about her business, but I've never shared her love of gardening. It's so, well...dirty.

"Why is your new girl so interested in this?" Ruthie asks Flora, fingering the leaf of a potted plant.

Flora slaps her hand. "Don't touch anything."

"She dated Clay," I explain. The heaviness weighing down my shoulders has nothing to do with Clay's past relationship with Heather this time.

Ruthie snorts. "That's...awkward."

"I know and I'm sorry, but I really need someone with Imogene gone, and she's a good worker," Flora says defensively.

"I can't tell you how to run your business. I wouldn't even come in here with this, but I don't know what to do."

Flora has always been able to point me in the right direction. She may not have a daily planner or a monthly schedule, but she knows what to say so I can manage my life. "What happened?" She gives a heavy sigh. "Tell me everything."

I tell her about the conversation with my mother, about how I turned around to see Clay in the doorway. "I don't even know how much he overheard," I finish, feeling my chin begin to tremble, signaling the onset of more tears.

I can't cry here, not if I have to walk out in front of Heather.

"We should have finished the conversation I started the other night," Flora says. "At my place."

"I didn't know we needed to finish it. It sounded finished to me."

"Oh, but I think we do."

"And what part of the conversation did you feel the need to continue?" I ask.

Flora stares at me across her work table. "Where did you see this going with Clay? Before all this?"

I have no idea where Flora is going with this. "He asked me to move in with him, but then Theo showed up, so that was off the table."

"How do you know? Did you ask him? Bring it up? I bet he's been pretty distracted with Theo."

"I haven't said anything about it." I hear the stiffness in my voice, can feel my shoulders hunch forward, like I'm physically closing myself off.

"What about what you have planned?"

"I have nothing planned."

Flora laughs so loud that even I smile at the absurdity of my comment. "I haven't planned anything because I don't know what Clay wants. All he wants is Theo right now, and I want to give him time with his son."

"But raising him—wouldn't that be easier with you helping?"

"I'm not a mother substitute."

"Do you want to be?"

"I've never wanted kids." My voice is louder than it needs to be, filling the tiny room.

Flora pulls at her hair. "Kind of ironic that you've always said you don't want kids only to end up with a guy with a baby."

"He didn't have a baby when I met him."

"Would that have changed things?"

I don't reply, because I don't know the answer to that. "What do I do?" I ask Flora, who smiles sympathetically.

Flora meets my anguished gaze. "I don't know if there's much you can do. You don't want kids. Clay has a son. How do you feel about him?"

"I love him. Clay," I correct. "I love Clay."

"And Theo?" she prompts.

"I don't know," I admit.

She winces. "That can't be good. It's hard enough being a parent; it's impossible to be one if you don't love the child."

"But he didn't ask me to be a parent." The realization floods me, and I'm not sure if I'm angry or relieved about it. "He said he wants to be with me. That he doesn't know how to do it without me, which is silly because I don't do anything with the baby."

"How can you not love a baby?" Ruthie demands. "I'm in love with Imogene's belly, and I can't wait to get my hands on the little lump inside."

"Well, you'll just make the perfect mother, won't you?" I snap. "I won't."

"You keep saying that, but you don't know for sure," Flora says soothingly.

"Is this about your mother?" Ruthie asks.

"Ben didn't want kids either," I protest, hearing how feeble it sounds even in my own head.

"This isn't anything like Ben," Flora says gently.

"It is. I spent years with him not wanting kids, and I can't just change my mind overnight."

"Why not?" Ruthie asks.

"Because..." Because I have to adjust my life plan. I have to change the way I think about things; look at how it's going to affect the rest of my life. Weigh the pros and cons. "Because I can't."

"You could." Ruthie nods.

"It's not that simple," I argue. "You can go off and traipse around the world at the drop of a hat, meet strangers on buses and fall in love, but I can't."

"You fell in love with a stranger in Las Vegas," Flora points out. "That was very unlike you."

"But that was Clay."

"And this is Clay's baby."

That silences me, my chest heaving with words I want to say but can't. So I try another tactic. "How could I possibly be a good mother with the example I have?"

"That's not the only example you have," Flora says quickly. "You have your sisters—Meaghan, anyway. You have Imogene. You have my—you have Archie's wife. You're not your mother."

"How do you know that? I find myself sounding more and more like her these days."

"You can stop that anytime." Flora touches my arm. "Look, I know you're scared. Having a baby is a scary thing, and you don't have nine months to prepare. Clay was just given this—" She pauses, searching for the right word. "This gift, and he's trying to make the best out of it. Is he worth losing because you're scared of making a mistake?"

"I'm not scared of that!"

"No, she's not scared," Ruthie says, sounding decisive for once. "She'll make a great mother, or stepmother, or whatever she's going to be because M.K. wins at everything. You can't fail because you don't fail."

"Thanks?" I say with confusion. To my knowledge, Ruthie has never complimented me once in my life.

"But you are letting your mother win with this," she continues. "She wants you to get married to a nice son of a winery owner and have babies that can take on the family business, just like your sisters. And you dig in your heels and say no way. I've always admired that about you, your stubbornness."

"Thank you?" I'm not sure where Ruthie is going with this, but I don't like the sound of it.

"She's absolutely right," Flora cries.

"I'm always right."

"You've got tunnel vision." The words tumble out of Flora's mouth in her haste. "Your mother wants *This*, and you say no. Because of what she tries to make you do, you can't let yourself see that anything close to it might not be a bad idea."

"I don't understand. Are you saying I don't want Theo in my life because my mother *does?*"

Flora and Ruthie glance at each other. "Pretty much," Flora says.

"That's about right," Ruthie adds.

Could it be that easy?

Could I be self-sabotaging this because of my mother? In a strange way, it makes sense and some of the heaviness on my shoulders lightens a little. Theo is an innocent, tiny child, and part of Clay. Could I let myself love him?

Because that would solve everything.

"She wants you to get married and settle down, with someone *she* picks," Flora continues. "Someone *she* thinks is right for you. But she doesn't know you, so how can she possible decide that?"

"She can't," Ruthie insists. "I'd never be able to pick for you, and I know you like the back of my hand. I'd never have picked Clay for you."

"Forget about what your mother wants—what do *you* want?" Flora demands.

The answer is easy. "I want Clay." My voice is firm and strong.

Ruthie throws up her hands. "Then go get him. Or that little shopgirl out there is going to."

Flora reaches for my arm. "It's not just Clay now," she warns. "You love him, and that's great, but you have to love the baby, too. Can you do that?"

The pause runs long and drawn out before I can answer.

# Clay

I DRAG MYSELF INTO the condo that night, feeling every pound of Theo's car seat weighing on my shoulders. The babysitter told me he had been fussy all day, and I can't help but wonder if he somehow picked up on my feelings. Can he pick up my disappointment? Did he understand when M.K. said she didn't want a family?

She doesn't want Theo. Or me with Theo.

I never imagined rejection would hurt so much. When Launa Robins broke my heart in sixth grade, I was inconsolable for lunch recess and then I moved on. I can't imagine moving on with anyone who isn't M.K.

How can I trust another woman?

Theo's eyes flicker open as I lift him from his seat, and I brace for the bout of crying. Instead, he slaps his fat little hand against my cheek, rubbing it against the end-of-day stubble.

"Do you miss her, too?"

How can she not love him? I thought she could love me enough. I love her enough to give her time, not to put expectations on her. We never discussed it, but to be with me was signing up to co-parent. I never asked her what she thought, what she wanted.

I just loved her and hoped that was enough.

Theo and I have a quiet evening. I find myself thinking of things that I want to tell M.K.: about how Pearl stalked around the office with the baby in her arms like he was the crown prince, how Rashida moped when I came back without him. About how I finished the graphics for the new line.

I don't remember the last time I spent time alone, without any plans to see a woman.

After I finish my dinner of pasta, and give Theo another try at his cereal, getting more on his face than in his mouth, we settle in the living room with another recap of the Jays post-season on Sportsnet.

"Your Uncle Deano is going to play for these guys again," I say to Theo who ignores the screen, instead fixated on the danglies on the arch over his play mat. "You better pay attention and learn all you can. He'll teach you to play ball because he's a lot better than me."

Theo coos in response.

"And Aunt Flora will teach you the right flowers to give to a girl," I continue. I stop myself. Can Flora still be Aunt Flora if M.K. is no longer in my life? How will this work? Will it be like a divorce—our friends have to pick sides?

I can't expect Flora to give up M.K., and I couldn't dream of asking her. Does this mean I'll lose Dean, too?

The lump in my chest grows as I glance down at the papers spread around me. I pick at the sheet I'd been doodling on during a conference call yesterday. It's a logo I'd been playing around with for M.K.—Pain Au Chocolat in a flowing script, with a perfect bun on a white plate at the end.

Simple, classic. Elegant, like M.K.

Hard, unyielding, uncompromising.

I crumple up the sheet and throw it across the room.

It only makes it to the end of Theo's play mat and I watch as he wiggles, and shakes, and finally rolls over onto his belly, reaching out a hand for the paper.

"Hey," I say as what he did sinks in. "You haven't done that before. You rolled."

Theo gurgles and stretches out his hand. "You can't have that," I tell him. I stand and give him a rubber block instead. "You can have this."

He crams the block in his mouth and I smile. I may not have M.K. as the love of my life, but I have this. This could be enough for now.

My cell interrupts my musings, and I grab it like a lifeline. But my heart sinks when I don't recognize the number. "Hello?"

"Clay, it's Abby."

My heart reaches the bottom of my stomach with a thud. "What's up?"

"How's everything with the baby?"

"Did you call just to ask?"

"Of course, but..." There's a long pause. "I talked to my mother. She said she can take him."

"Take him where."

"Take him to live with her."

"No." The response is instinctive, definite. Absolutely not.

"This is a lot to take on," Abby argues. "I gave you a couple of weeks because that's how long it took me to figure out it's impossible to raise a child alone."

"It's not impossible. You need to plan things."

"I never thought you were much of a planner. So I talked to my mother, and she can take him."

"I said no. I'm keeping him. If you can't, then I will."

"Are you sure about this?"

"As sure as I've ever been about anything. I'm not letting Theo out of my life." Like you did. The unspoken implication hangs in the air. "And I want some sort of agreement between us about this. Something saying that he's mine, and I have guardianship of him. That he's mine."

"You think I'm going to take him back from you?"

"You didn't tell me about him for four months. I'm not taking any chances that you'll change your mind again."

Abby sighs. "You don't think much of me, do you?"

"Not at all. I think you made the right decision for Theo. Not every woman is made to be a mother. You realized that and did what's best for our son."

"You think it's best he's with you? Not my mother, who's raised two kids?"

And one of them turned out like you, is what I don't say. "I don't know your mother, but I'm sure she's a lovely woman. But I am the best thing for Theo. For him to be raised by his father."

"And whatever girlfriend is around for the weekend?" she says snidely.

"There's no girlfriend around for the weekend or the week. I'll be doing this on my own." My voice is firm even though my heart aches for M.K.

"I thought you were dating someone."

"She's no longer in the picture. I'm going to focus on Theo for the time being."

"Wow. That's new."

"Being a father will change anyone."

"She broke up with you, didn't she? You didn't give her time to adjust," Abby says slowly. "This is a big thing for a new relationship."

"And some people can't handle big changes."

I shouldn't be angry with M.K. but I can't help it. I thought she cared more to try.

"Tell her I'm sorry," Abby says sadly. "And I'll sign anything you want me to."

## Chapter Twenty-Five

♥

# M.K.

THE NEXT DAY, I have a rare afternoon off for a doctor's appointment. Because it's at the hospital where Imogene gave birth, I decide to stop at Gap Kids before I go to get a present for the new baby.

I drift through Gap Kids on my way to the baby section. Brightly coloured shirts lead into a more pastel environment, with more greens and yellows than purples and oranges.

I quickly find a pretty, pink dress for Imogene's latest. Even though I know it's impractical, I've never seen anything so sweet.

"Do you need help with a size?" A saleswoman appears at my side.

"She's a newborn, so small, I guess?" I've never bought baby clothes before. I've only ever given my sisters gift cards for my nieces and nephews, always resentful of my mother's demands to get gifts to take the time to select something meaningful.

It's not that bad in here. I should have taken the time.

The saleswoman laughs. She looks a few years older than me, with a wide, sincere smile. "Depends on how big she is. Do you know the birth weight?"

"I have no idea." I shrug helplessly, not liking the sensation. "I have no idea about any of this."

"Then I'm here to help you. Is it a first baby?"

"No, her third. All girls."

"Then there will be lots of clothes to pass down, so she'll have the essentials. That dress would be perfect because it'll be something for her own. I'd get a size six months because it's a winter dress."

"That makes sense."

"Let me show you these tights that would be perfect with it. It'd be a nice outfit for Christmas."

Christmas is a month away. How will Clay handle his first Christmas with Theo? A pang of regret pierces me, so sharp that I wince.

"Are you okay?" the saleswoman asks with concern.

"Fine. Yes, the tights." I blindly accept everything she hands me. Every time I look at the boys section, I see Theo. Theo wearing the red sweater, crawling across the floor in the corduroy overalls. Lifting his arms up for a hug in the striped pajamas. Suddenly all these feelings swell in my chest, making my eyes water, and my throat tighten.

I blink wildly as relief spreads over me. I love him. I love the little guy.

I can love him.

I turn back to the saleswoman, swiping a quick finger under my eye. "Can we look at some clothes for boys as well?"

# Clay

I LET MYSELF INTO the condo, my feet heavy as I carry Theo inside. I'm so tired, more than I should be even with taking care of a baby.

I know it's because of M.K.

As disappointed as I am, I miss her even more.

I don't take in the smell at first, thinking it a remnant of the cupcakes I made last night to take to Pearl. Or the scented candle I've started burning when Theo has a really explosive diaper. The sweetness of chocolate drifts down the hall, as well as the sound of the oven door opening.

The sound of music. Music that I don't listen to.

Still carrying Theo in his seat, I slip off my shoes and pad down the hall.

M.K. is in my kitchen. Before I let my heart overflow with happiness at finding her here, I stop myself. "What are you doing here?"

She jumps with alarm. "I didn't hear you come in. I called Dean and he let me in because I don't have a key. I'm sorry if this is presumptuous," she adds quickly, her gaze imploring. "I didn't know—I thought maybe…" Her gaze falls on Theo, and her face breaks into a soft smile. "Hi, Theo. You've grown."

"It's only been a few days."

"He can grow in a few days. And he might need a haircut soon. You've got lots of hair," she coos, reaching out for his foot now kicking with delight. "I saw Imogene's baby today and she's totally bald."

"Is that why you're here? Did Imogene make you come?"

"No one made me come. I wanted to because I missed you. I missed him," she adds. "I was very surprised about that."

"So am I," I say in a quiet voice.

M.K. takes a deep breath. "I'm not going to apologize because it was you who walked into the conversation."

I frown. "I don't think that's the best way to begin."

"There's no good way to begin, but I hope the ending will make up for it. I've learned a few things in the last couple of days, and it started because of what I said to my mother."

"That you didn't want a family," I prompt. "That you weren't raising Theo. That you didn't want a baby and definitely didn't want to raise someone else's."

"I did say all of that. Would you like to know why? Or what I figured out?"

"What did you need to figure out?" My arm is beginning to ache, and I set the car seat on the table. Theo wriggles with anticipation of getting free from his restraints, but I don't let him out yet.

"That I've been going against everything my mother wants for me. I haven't even let myself think of the options because I'm so busy arguing against it. I've been rebelling, as Ruthie puts it. Can you imagine me rebelling?"

"No," I say sharply, relenting as her face falls. "Yes. You stood up to your mother when you moved here and started the patisserie. I'm not surprised if you did it again."

"I have been. It just took a while for me to realize it. All my decisions not to have children are because that's exactly what she wants me to do."

"I don't understand—you want kids now?"

"I don't know. I've never contemplated it. Until now. Until I can't stop thinking of him—and you. I really can't stop thinking about you."

"Me neither," I say in a gruff voice.

She sweeps a hand towards the counter. "I don't know how to make this up to you so I bake. It's what I do."

"I know."

"I also have trouble with change."

"I know that, too. Sounds like you've done some soul searching."

"I have good friends." She drifts closer. "And an even better boyfriend."

I hold my ground, my heart beginning to race. "Is that what I am?"

"I'd like you to be again," she whispers. "I'd like you to be more someday. I'd like to consider all of my options with you. If I have any left."

It's the hopeful tone in her voice that breaks me. "M.K." I reach for her, my fingers skimming her waist as she pulls away.

"Wait." She darts to the stove and pulls out a tray of cupcakes. "Honey vanilla," she says. "I used some of your honey. I have the same kind."

"From the market."

She nods. "I think I saw you there once."

I laugh, my voice tinged with relief. "I think I saw you walking home."

I itch to hold her, to find out if this is real or some fantasy I've concocted. But while I hold out my arms, M.K. goes first to Theo in his car seat still on the table.

"I think we need to get to know each other a little better," she says, sure fingers unbuckling him. I hold my breath as she lifts him out, little legs kicking with joy. "I'm M.K.," she says, tucking him under her arm, Theo reaching for her hair. "I'm not your mommy." She glances at me and I see the tears in her eyes. "You have a mother and I won't take that away from you. But I'll be..." She takes a deep breath. "I'll be whatever you need. Whatever you both need." Her dark gaze turns to me. "If you want me."

I wrap my arms around both of them, feeling M.K.'s chin against my shoulder.

"I bought him some clothes," she says in a muffled voice. "His pants are getting a little short already."

I laugh and tighten my arms around them.

The End

Is it time for Ruthie to find love?<br/>
Pleasantly Popped

And keep reading for a sneak peak of
I Saw Him Standing There
the first book in the
Oceanic Dreams series

# Acknowledgements

♥

Beautifully Baked is for all the readers of Perfectly Played who asked for more.

I had never planned on continuing the story. Perfectly Played was the first straight love story that I've written—one with no squabbling sisters, saving the world, or dark twist at the end (Absinthe Doesn't Make the Heart Grow Fonder, for those of you who haven't had the pleasure!) I had the story of Flora and Dean in my head for a long time, and once it was written, I thought that was it. I loved my secondary characters (especially Ruthie and Adam), but that was it.

But you wanted M.K. and you wanted Clay, and I want to make you happy.

Thanks to all the ARC readers, and bloggers who love my books. Thanks to the readers who keep reading, as well as telling me what they want me to write.

Thanks for all the lovely ladies of the Oceanic Dreams group, both authors and readers. Being a part of that series was so much fun!

Thanks to my kids who support me and for your little comments that let me know that you think your mom being an author is still cool.

Because it is.

*I Saw Him Standing There*

♥

## Chapter One

*DAY ONE—MIAMI*

I had one leg out the window by the time the banging started at the door.

I knew Eduardo was coming today but I thought I'd have more time. When I first met him, Eduardo used to be known as Fast Eddie. This con, the one he was coming to collect for, was supposed to be the one to bring us to the big leagues.

The problem was, I didn't want to go to the big leagues. And I had no idea how to tell him I hadn't been able to go through with his latest confidence scam. There was nothing for him to collect and a whole lot to clean up after.

I sat on my bedroom window ledge, the cement scratching the backs of my legs, and contemplated my options.

It was only a short swing from the ledge over to the balcony next door, only a short four-story drop if I fell.

The banging inside was getting louder. "Siggy! I know you're in there!"

I winced, tightening my grip on the window frame. Eduardo does not sound happy. He was expecting me to meet him at the door with smiles and a stack of bearer bonds I was supposed to have acquired.

No smiles. No bonds.

Our carefully laid plan had gone horribly, terribly wrong, all because I had been struck by an attack of conscience.

"Siggy! Open the door!"

With a deep breath, I turned on my belly and hung from the ledge by my fingers. Swinging my legs to get enough momentum, I flew across to the other ledge, landing awkwardly with the heavy backpack and my camera bag slung across my chest.

I could lose the backpack, but the camera went everywhere with me.

The jump down onto the neighbouring garage was relatively easy compared to the first part, as was the next drop. Eduardo stuck his head out my bedroom window as I landed easily on the cracked sidewalk.

"I want my money, Siggy!"

"I don't have it," I called up to him.

"You better be on your way to get it."

With a last glance, I took off down the street, Eduardo's bellow of rage following me.

Andy's car was parked around the corner from my apartment. With a quick glance behind me, I popped the lock with the handy bent coat hanger I shoved in my bag for that very reason. With a silent promise to see the car back to Andy, I climbed in and twined the right wires together under the dash. The car roared to life.

I was out of the neighbourhood before Eduardo could huff his way down the street, leaving Surfside behind me with barely a hint of remorse except a sinking feeling in my stomach.

Beaches and palm trees flew by as I drove. I didn't stop until I passed the Lincoln Mall in South Beach.

Once I passed the mall, I deemed it safe to stop and called Andy. "I took your car," I confessed as soon he answered. "I'll get it back to you. I promise."

I heard noises in the background, Andy rummaging in his closet-sized apartment to find his keys. "I didn't take your keys." Another skill I'd learned from Eduardo. There had been talk of me becoming some kind of Baby Driver, like in the movie, but the arrest of one of Eduardo's friends after an easy liquor store heist had put an end to that.

Andy sighed. "What did he do to you?"

When I arrived in Miami four years ago, I was on my way from transforming myself from the empty-headed party girl who let a man get close enough to take advantage of me and my family, to a badass who wouldn't stand for it. I no longer wanted to be Seraphina Park-Smith; daughter, sister, wife. I said goodbye to my old life and became Siggy Smith, using the nickname my brother had given me as a child.

Eduardo had taught me ways to survive and thrive on my own. Quite a few of those skills skirted the lines of legality while some of them were just morally questionable. I went along with it because I'd been mad and looking for a way to get revenge.

Then the desire for revenge faded and I was left with only two things: the realization I'd become someone I didn't like very much; and Eduardo, who liked who I'd become a little too much.

"I thought last night was to be the big score," Andy said when I didn't answer.

"I couldn't do it." There was a tiny nugget of pride that I hadn't gone through with the plan. "There were kids involved. Eduardo's not going to understand."

"No, I daren't say he will. But I get it. You're not that person, my darling. You don't fit in with us, as much as you try."

"You could have told me sooner!"

"I thought you were happy."

Had I been happy learning the ropes to become a con artist? It had been fun at first, but then it started being serious. I found myself out of options when I snipped the family purse strings.

"I don't know where to go," I admitted.

"You could go back to your family," Andy said in a quiet voice. "You know they'll have forgiven you by now."

"I doubt it." The coolness in my voice covered the longing.

"Think about it. And be careful with my car. Send me a text where you end up and I'll come and fetch it."

"Thank you. I'm sorry."

"For what? Not pulling off the scam? I would have been sorrier if you had. Love you, darling. And I'm proud of you. Whatever happens."

Andy had become my family and had been since he found me shivering at the airport three and a half years ago, all my worldly possessions in my bag, dried tears streaking through my makeup. I had been a perfect mark but instead, he took me in and took care of me.

I was glad I hadn't let him down.

I said goodbye and tucked my phone into the cupholder, wondering what to do now. The backdoor of the car opened.

I glanced around in horror, expecting Eduardo, the cops, my father, anyone but a woman. Prada shades covered most of her face, and she held a glittery phone in her hand. With an exasperated huff, she swung a Louis Vuitton carry-on into the backseat. "A little help would be nice."

I could only stare at her. "I'm not a cab."

"You have an Uber sticker on your window."

Darn it. I forgot Andy sidelined as an Uber driver. "But I'm not —this isn't my car." What was I supposed to do, admit I stole the car? "I'm not on duty right now."

"Just drive me to the cruise terminal and you can call it a day." She plunked her handbag on her lap and my gaze lasered in on it. Kate Spade Maise Satchel in hot pink.

My heart hurt for a moment at the sight of the bag. "I like your bag."

"Of course you do. Put my suitcase in the trunk and then drive."

"I can't put it in the trunk. It's—ah—broken." Or unavailable because I had no key.

She lowered her glasses. "What do you mean, broken?" She glanced around Andy's ten-year-old Toyota with a disdainful expression. "What kind of Uber car is this?"

"I mean, not *un*broken. I can't get into it. So you should get another ride."

"Do you have a body in there or something?"

I lowered my own cheap plastic sunglasses and gave her a look. Her eyes widened and I thought she was really going to jump out of the car. Then I relented. "No body. Just broken. I'll put your suitcase in the back seat."

I didn't know why I agreed. Maybe because I didn't have a plan, and I needed one. I couldn't keep driving aimlessly.

"So where to, once you get to the port?" I pulled away from the curb. Miami Port wasn't too far, enough to give me enough time to make a plan. I could head to the bus terminal and—

"It's me."

I thought she was talking to me until I glanced in the mirror and saw her holding her phone to her ear.

"I have to go; it's all booked. No, I'm not looking forward to it. No, I'm sure it's going to be horrible. Seven days at sea with obnoxious strangers. It's going to be hell."

Hell was this drive with the obnoxious stranger in the backseat.

She paused in her conversation and from the scowl on her face, apparently didn't like the response she was getting.

"It's some sort of love cruise. You board, you fall in love, or you stay in love, or something silly like that. Like being on a boat is some sort of magic spell. *It's not.*"

"Turn down the music."

It took her asking—demanding, rather—twice more before I realized she was talking to me.

"Don't you love this song?" The music was a bit loud but that was how I liked to drive.

"No, I really don't and it's difficult enough to have this conversation without Kelly Clarkson blaring in my eardrums."

Some people were not nice. There are all sorts out there—nasty, rude and basically horrible people live in this world. I didn't know why they were like that, but they are and no matter how nice and considerate you are back to them, it really makes no difference.

This woman was like that. I didn't know who she was talking to on the phone but I wish they'd wise up and hang up on her and let me do my Good Samaritan deed in quiet. With Kelly Clarkson blaring in my eardrums.

But you know what they say about no good deed going unpunished.

I was punished from outside the car as well. Traffic was terrible, definitely not helpful when I was running for my life.

I thought about how Eduardo's face puffed up tomato red when he was angry. And I remembered when Jimmy had his knee problem that happened the same time the deal he was doing with Eduardo fell through.

Yep. It was definitely time to get out of Miami.

My mind was foggy with ominous thoughts as I drove towards the port of Miami, the one-sided conversation in the backseat fading into the background. But the chime of her cell got my attention, as did her excited gasp.

"Oh! Peter!"

She sounded so different that I glanced in the rearview mirror to see a woman transformed. She was smiling and when she pulled off her sunglasses, there were actual tears in her eyes. "I'm so glad you called." She *cooed* into the phone like she was talking to a baby.

Or a man.

"Okay. Okay. Okay, okay…yes…okay… Oh, yes!"

I snickered under my breath. Had she forgotten her words?

"Stop the car!"

"We're not at the terminal."

"I said, stop the car. Right now. Here. He'll pick me up."

"Who?" I couldn't help but ask. After all, if I was acting as an Uber driver, then I was responsible for her, wasn't I?

"Peter." She all but sighed.

"Who's Peter?"

"He's *Peter*. Here, stop here. He'll be here soon."

"Should I wait?" If I hadn't turned around, I would have missed the look she gave me. *Of course, you should wait, you moron.*

Even in love, she was still mean.

"Is he going on this cruise with you?" I asked as I pulled over.

"Of course not and now I don't have to go either." She clapped her hands suddenly. Whoever this Peter was certainly put her in a better mood. "I don't have to go!"

"Do you get your money back? I mean, if I'm taking you to the boat, doesn't that mean you're supposed to be getting on it? You can't just not show up for something like that. They may hold the ship for you."

She stared at me. "They won't do that."

"They might." I had no idea if a cruise ship would hold off sailing if a passenger didn't show up but it was fun to play with her.

"They might for me," she agreed. "Here." She rummaged in her Kate Spade and pulled out a slim black leather portfolio. Taking out a handful of papers, she thrust them between the seats. "Take my ticket."

"What? No!"

"I'm not going to use them. You might as well."

"They won't really hold the boat for you. I just made that up."

"You'd be surprised how many people wait for me."

"I can't use your tickets. I mean, really, I can't. They won't let me. Besides, they're in *your* name." A glance at the papers showed her name was Petra Van Brereton.

"Take my passport."

"Are you kidding me?"

She threw it into the front seat. "I'll get another one. You look enough like me that no one will notice. It's always a hassle boarding; you can slip right through. And you'd be doing me a favour. My parents are going to be furious when they find out about Peter. This way we can get married and they'll think I'm still on the cruise and won't even look for me."

I glanced at her picture. Other than both of us having brown hair, we really looked nothing alike.

I started to hand the documents back but then stopped. Eduardo would never find me in the middle of the ocean. And I'd be doing her a favour. I knew all about upsetting parents.

"My uncle is the captain. I'll call him and clear everything. Use my passport to get on, and then everything will be fine."

"I don't know..."

"Seriously, take it. I don't need them. It's a love cruise—"

"Like the *Love Boat*? You know, that television show from the seventies?" I asked. Her expression changed to annoyed confusion. "It must be on Netflix by now."

"I have no idea what you're talking about. Take the tickets. Take my bag. Go on the cruise. Have a nice life."

I took the tickets.

What else was I supposed to do? She wasn't going to use them, and it was better than wasting them.

Petra was too busy kissing the tall, handsome man to notice when I pulled away with her suitcase. The tickets for the cruise lay on the passenger seat.

I promised myself I'd return Petra's passport as soon as I got back.

When I pulled up to the terminal, I saw a big, beautiful boat docked at the pier with crowds of people on deck.

The *Oceanic Aphrodite*.

If this was really some sort of love cruise, at least it had a good name.

What did you think? Want More?

I Saw Him Standing There

Available now!

*Also By*

♥

**Don't**

Don't Tell Me You Love Me

Don't Want to Be Friends

Don't Stop Me Now

**Charlotte Dodd series**

The Secret Life of Charlotte Dodd

The Missing Files of Charlotte Dodd

The Best Worst First Date Ever

The Hidden Past of Pippa McGovern

The Last Stand of Charlotte Dodd

**Sisters in a Small Town**

Coming Home

Hanging On

Stepping Up

### Love and Alliteration

Perfectly Played

Beautifully Baked

Pleasantly Popped

### Oceanic Dreams

I Saw Him Standing There

Unexpecting

Unexpectingly Happily Ever After

Absinthe Doesn't Make the Heart Grow Fonder

### Kid Lit

The Dragon Under the Mountain

The Dragon Under the Dome

## About Author

♥

Holly Kerr is the author of eighteen novels; chick-lit, romantic comedy, and women's fiction novels, but don't ask her to explain the differences in the genres. She grew up a farm girl but now calls Toronto home, where she lives with her three very tall children, following their sports exploits like any dutiful mother.

She's a lover of Marvel movies, Star Wars movies...really, any movies, and has a surprising amount of worthless pop culture info stored in her head. She likes oceans over mountains, tea over coffee, and can mix a darn fine dirty martini, with extra olives, of course.

Visit her at www.facebook.com/HollyKerrAuthor and www.hollykerr.ca to sign up for her newsletter.

Made in the USA
Monee, IL
21 January 2022